CORYDON

& THE SIEGE OF TROY

CORYDON

& THE SIEGE OF TROY

TOBIAS DRUITT

Alfred A. Knopf   New York

Copyright © 2009 by Tobias Druitt

All rights reserved.
Published in the United States by Alfred A. Knopf, an imprint of Random House Children's Books, a division of Random House, Inc., New York.

Knopf, Borzoi Books, and the colophon are registered trademarks of Random House, Inc.

Visit us on the Web! www.randomhouse.com/kids

Educators and librarians, for a variety of teaching tools, visit us at www.randomhouse.com/teachers

Library of Congress Cataloging-in-Publication Data
Druitt, Tobias.
Corydon and the siege of Troy / Tobias Druitt. — 1st ed.
p. cm.
Summary: Having gone their separate ways since the disastrous fall of Atlantis, Corydon reunites with the two gorgons and the Minotaur to help his friend Sikandar, Prince of Troy, fight against the heroes who have besieged the city.
ISBN 978-0-375-83384-7 (trade) — ISBN 978-0-375-93384-4 (lib. bdg.)
1. Mythology, Greek—Juvenile fiction. 2. Trojan War—Juvenile fiction.
[1. Mythology, Greek—Fiction. 2. Trojan War—Fiction. 3. Minotaur (Greek mythology)—Fiction. 4. Monsters—Fiction. 5. Adventure and adventurers—Fiction.] I. Title.
PZ7.D8245Cos 2009
[Fic]—dc22
2008012373

The text of this book is set in 12-point Column Book.

Printed in the United States of America
March 2009
10 9 8 7 6 5 4 3 2 1
First Edition

To our own Lares and Penates: Ivan, Hermione,

Coco (aka the Snake-Girl's baby), Thelma, Lulu, and

our hens Sthenno, Euryale, and the rest.

ACKNOWLEDGMENTS

Corydon came to life because of many people, and we'd like to thank them all.

First, Nancy Siscoe and her colleagues at Knopf. Nancy improved all the books enormously and was endlessly patient, kind, and sympathetic with our unpracticed hands. Then we thank Catherine Clarke and everyone else at the agency, and Nancy Gallt in New York; they were crucial. Then, too, we're grateful to all the friends who read the book, especially Hugo, Jacopo, Elissa, Kate, Jessica, and above all Julie Hearn, without whom Corydon would never have seen the light of day. Above even her, those who have said they liked the first two books; that gave us the courage to go on.

CORYDON

& THE SIEGE OF TROY

ONE

On the side of a sand hill in the Arabian desert, a shepherd boy watched over his flock. He still thought of himself as a shepherd, though his flock was composed of lithe goats, and its glory was three milch camels.

Corydon was not alone. The flock belonged to his gang, who had assembled it by a series of lightning raids on the people who lived on the vast desert's margins.

There were three other boys in the gang, and all of them were outcasts. There was Azil, who had been exiled for stealing a camel to try to win a race. There was Bin Khamal, who understood wind and weather so well that people had said he was a djinn and sent him away out of fear. And, best of all, there was Sikandar, who had once lived somewhere greener, somewhere with sheep, but who now trod the lonely wastes.

Corydon didn't know why Sikandar couldn't go home. The gang didn't spend much time analyzing things. They talked, of course, to pass the long desert days and nights, but they said little of the past. All of them were trying to forget their former lives.

Corydon most of all. There were still nights when his dreams tossed him from the sight of ruined cities and metal monsters to the screams of dying warriors. And sometimes the wind seemed to sing to him of a place a goddess had named. *Troios . . . Troios . . . ,* it sang. When the ghibli blew across the dry desert, it seemed to whisper of a city of towers. . . . But Corydon tightened his blue headdress around his ears. Deaf and sullen, he would not hear what the ghibli wanted to tell him. Cities of towers . . . He was fatal to them. He, Corydon, had destroyed an entire city, the greatest in the world. . . . He had done the Olympians' will, though he had thought he was defying them. Clearly, if Troy needed saving, Corydon Panfoot should stay away.

He loved the desert because it did not know his name. It was utterly indifferent to him. It might kill him, but it would do so without malice, just by being itself. He loved being forgotten. Disappearing into its vastness.

Sikandar approached him shyly.

"Lord," he began, "I must ask when we move. The camels must find more grazing soon. The goats also. And the tracks we saw . . . perhaps someone we might raid?"

"Don't call me 'lord,'" said Corydon a little irritably. "I'm just a shepherd like you. And don't worry about the grazing. Winter is fast approaching, and with it the rains will come. Till then, we can hold out by using the oases. As for the tracks, we must follow them cautiously and attempt a raid when the moon is dark." *The dark of the moon* — memories surged over him. He let them run into the sand like water. "Are the animals all watered?" he asked.

They had stopped at a well. It had been called "The Sweet," but the water tasted as if liquid iron and seawater had gone into it. The taste was so bitter that only the camels drank it willingly. It tasted like the tears of giants. Again, Corydon tried to crush his memories. Sikandar's voice helped.

"Yes, lord," he said. "All have had water."

"DON'T CALL ME 'LORD'!" Corydon shouted. And then his heart filled with sadness. Sikandar looked forlorn, as if his last protector had struck him. "I'm sorry," Corydon said. "It's just—"

"I know," said Sikandar. "We are all in a desert of the heart, where the ghibli blows all day and fills our mouths with the sands of memory."

Corydon smiled. Sikandar had the poet's heart that showed the true shepherd.

As they packed up the tent and stowed everything on the camels, Corydon reflected on how difficult it was to escape from who you truly were. He was still Corydon, poet and shepherd, and because he was still Corydon, he couldn't escape for long from all he had done and suffered. But at least he felt sure he could do no harm here.

"Mount up!" he ordered. Each camel could carry two boys, though every time they came to dunes, all had to dismount. The third camel was a beast of burden, carrying their supplies. One boy had always to be with the goats, too, which meant one of the riding camels had an easier time. It was still early, and the desert was almost cool. Corydon had always heard that deserts were cold at night, but this one wasn't, only less scorching. They had to move now, before the heat of the day began. The sun was only just below the horizon, and the stars had paled. He had already scanned the camel tracks they were following. He moved his swift black camel into the lead. Corydon knew that a trot would be best for the early morning. A gallop would tire the camels, and when the sun appeared, the camels would collapse, especially if they had to cross any dunes. The other boys followed, keeping the goats between them.

It soon became clear that they were gaining on the other caravan. The tracks were fresher, and they saw a pile of camel dung. Azil examined it for a moment, then said, "One hour. Maybe two. And they have at least four pack camels. It may be a silk or spice caravan from far away. The camels are laden with more than men."

A caravan, laden with spices! All four boys felt eager. With their bags full of spices, they could trade in a nearby town and increase the herd. More milch camels and goats would reduce the hungry times, when all they had to eat was rock-hard sand-baked bread or a few dry dates.

"Careful," Azil warned. "They are many. We must not come too close to them until darkness can cloak us. Then we may steal in and . . . liberate some camels—"

"And some saddlebags," put in Bin Khamal. "Their saddlebags must be groaning in oppression. Only we can set them free!"

All the boys laughed. Spirits were high. Guided by Azil, they stayed carefully upwind of the caravan, and about an hour distant, until the hammering heat of day began to fade into the gentler heat of night.

Speaking low, Corydon took the initiative. "I'll go ahead," he said, "and scout their camp. Make camp here yourselves, but be careful. Don't make a fire, and we'll all have to do without water for a while. Wait until the moon rises—luckily, she's almost at full dark—and then follow my tracks. You know what to do when we get there." They nodded, though inwardly all felt scared of robbing so great a caravan.

Corydon made his way cautiously. Though not a great tracker like Azil, he could follow a clearly marked trail. After an hour of walking over hot sand, he could see the red star of the caravan's campfire. It helped to orient him in the vastness of the desert. There was no wind at all now, and the hot air was motionless. He felt as if he were walking through stagnant water. He was also beginning to be very thirsty. He took a small sip from his waterskin; it would be hours before they could replenish their water supply because the caravan was occupying the oasis.

Now he was approaching the first date palms of the oasis. He slowed and dropped to his belly. There might be guards posted if the caravan contained something truly precious. But he could see nothing to worry him, only the merchants sitting around an immense campfire, drinking coffee in tiny cups and listening to a minstrel tell a tale of a djinn. Under cover of the minstrel's song, he crept close enough to see that the camels were pastured on the opposite side of the oasis. Curses! Cautiously he crept around to them, remembering to stay low. It was a big oasis, and he had to crawl on his belly for almost an hour before he saw the first picket rope of camels before him.

Camels were irritable, but they were not stupid. Some camels would refuse to be ridden by anyone other than their owner. If others tried to mount them, the camels would fight them off with teeth and hooves. This was exactly the kind of disturbance he couldn't afford. He could see which camels were the best and fastest—that big black milch camel there, with her rangy legs, and the small white. But he couldn't tell if they were one-owner camels. Still, he might at least make himself smell more familiar: he wrapped himself in a saddle blanket that had been left lying on the ground and rubbed himself against one of the saddles. It might make a difference.

Beside the camels lay the heavy loads the men of the caravan had been carrying. The caravanners had unloaded them to make sure the camels were well rested for the morning ride but had not wished to transport the heavy saddlebags far.

Corydon crept over to the bags that the big black had been carrying and slipped his hand inside the first bag. Soft, sandlike substances, seeds and other things, were sifting between his fingers. He withdrew his hand and caught a whiff of spices.

The second bag contained soft, many-colored silks. But the third bag contained a surprise. A hard stone. Then another. Jewels! Nearly a hundred rubies, sapphires, emeralds, and diamonds. A gift fit for a king . . .

A flash of steel in moonlight caught Corydon's eye. Some weapons, perhaps? He wasn't certain, but he crawled forward, not sure of what he'd find. Just then something tapped his shoulder. Corydon spun around and with infinite relief saw that it was only Sikandar. He put his finger to his lips hastily and motioned to the boy to get down. Sikandar dropped obediently onto the sand. Behind him were the others.

Corydon motioned to the black camel's saddlebags. Understanding, the boys took one each as Corydon crept forward to where the camels were tied. He hoped the scent of the blanket would fool them for long enough to allow him to lead two—or, with luck, three—away. But, from his kleptis days, he knew he must not be greedy. One was all they really needed, to carry their share of the booty away. He approached the tall black. She snorted imperiously as he undid her picket rope, but she did not resist as he put his hand on her bridle to lead her away. She followed him with that graceful camel walk that looked as a tree might if it became mobile. He gave the picket rope to Sikandar, who began soothing the camel's agitation as Corydon crept back to untie the small white.

But this camel was not fooled. As soon as she smelled his hand, she knew he smelled wrong. She gave a roaring gasp of fury and aimed a bite at his hand. The other camels, disturbed by the sound, had gotten his scent and began to bellow. Now the animal noise was joined by the angry shouts of men, alert to the camels' raucous cries.

"Go!" called Corydon to his friends. He pulled up the picket ropes of all the camels and sent them loping into the desert. Then he sprang to the unruly white camel's back. As he'd expected, she was furious and immediately tried to dislodge him, but using all his monster-strength on the bridle, he managed to force her to turn and follow the black they'd already stolen. She set off at a fast trot, her feet thudding on the sand, and ahead he could see the other boys, insecurely mounted on the black, with the saddlebags slung across her neck. Corydon urged his mount on until they were riding level. Behind him he could hear the men of the caravan trying to catch and calm their camels. But they had stolen the fastest camels, and once they were out of sight, their trail would be difficult to follow in the darkness. As they crested a rearing sand dune, and then another, Corydon began to breathe more easily.

"We must stop—your camel will founder!" he shouted. They

nodded. Their makeshift camp was over a few more low rises, but Corydon was becoming less sure of the exact direction. They had the black camel lie down in the lee of a dune and transferred the heaviest saddlebags to the white camel to distribute the loads. Azil began scouting for pointers to direction. At last he found one, a line of pebbles kicked by one of them on their outward journey. Feeling his shoulder blades prickle with awareness of pursuit, Corydon urged everyone to remount, to press on. The first faint light of dawn began to break, and still there was no sign of their camp.

Then they found where it *had* been. But the camels and goats had scattered, and it might take hours to round them up. Corydon wondered why they had gone. Had something alarmed them? They had never strayed before.

It had been a long time since any of the boys had had water or food, too, and their overburdened beasts could not go on in that fashion for much longer. Bin Khamal slipped from his camel and cursed bitterly.

"Corydon," he said, "there's a sandstorm coming from the east."

The news was as bad as could be. A sandstorm would cover their tracks—though that was the only good thing to be said for it, for it would also cover their missing goats' tracks. And they needed water and pasturage, which would be impossible to find in a howling cloud of sand.

"How fast is this storm coming up?" questioned Corydon.

"Very fast. In about thirty minutes its center will be here. You can see it as a smudge on the horizon," said Bin Khamal.

There was a thick blot to the east. It grew larger by the second, slowly moving back and forth, back and forth, like a snake trying to fascinate its prey.

Bin Khamal turned to Corydon and the others.

"I think I know what to do," he said. "But I must be alone."

What? Corydon couldn't quite bring himself to trust Bin Khamal to this extent. If his plan failed or if he were somehow planning to make off with the booty, they would be finished.

"I will stay with you," he said firmly. "Sikandar, Azil, you must travel due west, away from the storm. With luck you may reach the Bar El Kabir caves. There's an underground river deep within them, or so a trader once told me. Look out for a rock shaped like a man's finger; it marks the entrance."

"No!" Sikandar exclaimed. "Lord, I do not want to leave you."

"You must." Corydon was curt. "Sikandar, I have seen many things worse than a desert storm." Corydon glanced at the sky. Already half of it was shielded by the graying, blinding storm. "Now go! You have no time to waste." The first hard rumbles of thunder rang out as the two boys galloped away on the black camel.

"You should not have stayed," said Bin Khamal.

"I had to," said Corydon.

"So be it, then," said Bin Khamal.

His face began to alter. At first, it was a subtle rippling, a widening, as if Bin Khamal had had an unusually good meal. But there was a textural change, too: smooth flesh began to dissolve, or to crystallize into a mass of moving sand so thick and so blown that it was like a solid dune rearing out of the desert. What had been Bin Khamal was now a dune seventy feet high, a dune made of sand thrumming violently with sound. . . .

Singing.

Corydon had heard the sands sing before but never at such close range. The cries were fierce, savage, a low keening that was more like the roar of mighty ocean waves than a sound made on land. He knew that the Arabs thought singing sands were the home of the djinn, but he had never realized that the sands *themselves* were djinn. It was clear that Bin Khamal's weather knowledge was djinnish.

And he was singing to the storm. Enchanting it.

Already the storm had begun to sing back to him. The thunder crooned in rhythm with his song. The leading edge of the storm had stopped short of where they were, and flashes of lightning served only to punctuate Bin Khamal's deep, rich chanting.

Suddenly Corydon realized that a face had begun to materialize in the sky, where the sand clouds of the storm were thickest. Two blue bolts of lightning shot from the eyes into Bin Khamal's eyes. Corydon reared back in horror, but the glowing light did no harm; instead, it seemed to radiate warmly from the djinn's face, from both faces. Then the storm's leading edge rolled up, and it began to move away, leaving only a small scatter of whirling dust devils in its wake. Bin Khamal gradually melted back into boyhood again.

"You *are* a djinn," said Corydon bluntly.

Bin Khamal blushed. "I didn't want anyone to know," he said shyly. "I thought you would not wish me to stay if you knew."

"Well, I won't tell anyone," Corydon promised. "But now you have told me your secret, I will show you mine." He lifted the corner of his pant leg so Bin Khamal could glimpse his goatleg and foot.

Bin Khamal was silent. "Are you a djinn, too?" he asked, after a long moment of thought.

"No," said Corydon. "I'm a monster and the son of a god. The god Pan." Bin Khamal looked blank. "He is a god of shepherds," Corydon explained. "But we are not in his lands. Was the storm a djinn, too?"

"That was *my* father," Bin Khamal admitted. "But my mother is mortal, and human."

They both took a long drink of milk from the small white camel, which had waited disdainfully, caring nothing for sandstorms or djinns. "Let's go and find the others," said Corydon. They mounted and pointed her head west for the caves.

T W O

THE OTHER BOYS WERE WAITING FOR THEM. AS THE storm had not chased them, they'd taken time to round up their camels and goats and set up a camp of sorts in the cave. They had made a small fire and had killed a goat, which was roasting on a spit.

There was a river in the cave. Corydon and Bin Khamal were so hot and thirsty that they plunged straight into it.

"Why do you get thirsty when you are really part of the desert?" Corydon asked quietly. "Does it come from your mother?"

Bin Khamal said solemnly, "Sand drinks water, Corydon. When it rains—and it does sometimes rain, even in the Sands—the water is drunk very quickly. Sand is thirstier than any boy. It can drink a whole river. It could drink you." He laughed and dunked Corydon.

When they emerged, cool and free of chafing grit for the first time in days, the smell of roast goat made them all feel their hunger. Sikandar had rubbed it with a paste made of some of the seeds and nuts from their stolen booty, and it smelled like paradise. They shared it and shared, too, the remaining bread and dates.

They ran their hands unbelievingly through their treasures: jewels glinted in the soft firelight, spices poured out in scented streams. Emeralds and rubies, turquoises and moony pearls, purple shimmers of amethyst; amber, cardamom, cassia, spikenard, and balm. Silks waved their vivid sheen in the light. Corydon picked up something scented, coiled like a papyrus scroll. He tried to unroll it, but it crumbled in his clumsy fingers. There were resins, too, frankincense and myrrh fit for a pharaoh's tomb.

They packed it all up again. They were rich beyond imagining.

They said nothing of their tender dreams and hopes. They did not want to break the spell. Each felt certain that such wealth would vanish somehow. It would be missed, certainly. And they needed to get to market quickly.

They lay down to sleep. The firelight flickered on the walls. Just as Corydon's eyes were beginning to close, one log fell into the fire with a hiss, and the flames blazed brightly as its bark caught. Corydon caught a sudden glimpse of the cave ceiling.

It was painted with hundreds of small figures, black and red and ochre. Corydon could see a strange beast with spots and a neck longer than a camel's and long, long legs. It was running from men who were chasing it. Then there was another picture: men were standing triumphantly over the beast and were plunging sticks—no, spears—into it. The painting reminded him painfully of Euryale's hunting sketches. He missed his old friend from the Island of Monsters. He missed all of the monsters and the simpler days before the gods had taken such an interest in him. Looking up again, Corydon also saw dozens of figures—yes, swimming, just as he and Bin Khamal had done. But most interesting of all was the depiction of a huge lion, mouth open, pouring out flame.

"The Nemean lion!" breathed Corydon. Now that he looked more closely, he could see that the lion was flanked by a lioness and several cubs, all with tiny tongues of flame emerging from their lolling mouths. Not *the* Nemean lion, then. Nemean lions. A whole pride of them. Corydon wondered if there were any left in the vicinity. But when he sat up eagerly, he saw that the others were already asleep. He decided not to wake them.

The cave was so enclosed that there was no way of knowing when it was dawn without going outside to see. But sleeping on rock made for a restless night. Corydon woke and went outside in what turned out to be deep night; the stars showed there were at least four hours till dawn.

The next time, it was Sikandar who woke and who crept out to see golden desert sleeping under the tender blue of a morning sky. Full of sleep, water, goat, Sikandar felt fine and enthusiastic; he swung his arms and sang half a song as he looked out, pretending to be an emperor of vast domains, conscious of the king's ransom stored in the cave behind him and conscious of the life he had fled. He felt a little lonely, and he decided it was time to waken the others.

He had just turned to go back into the cave's watery coolness when he saw a group of riders cross a rise far ahead. He shaded his eyes with his hand to see them better. They were all tall, superbly mounted on fine, fast camels whose long legs swallowed yards of desert with every stride. All were wearing white headdresses, and the gold braid on the headdresses' borders caught the light.

Another rich caravan, perhaps.

No. Too well armed. Sikandar's eyes were good. In the clear air, he could discern that each man carried a heavy sword, spears, and a bow.

Then . . . what?

Behind Sikandar, Corydon and Azil emerged from the cave, rubbing their eyes as the strong light hit. Sikandar pointed to the advancing line of figures. They were heading straight for the cave.

Bin Khamal came out. After one rapid glance, he said, "Whatever goods they are trading, I do not think we wish to buy from them. We must go swiftly."

All the boys rushed back into the cave, packed up frantically, brought out camels and goats. The line of heavily armed men was much nearer by the time they emerged.

"Mount up!" said Corydon. He flung himself onto the large black camel's back, hardly caring about the jarring shock. He urged the camel forward just as the nearest rider hurled his spear. It landed less than a foot away, striking the sand with a dull thud.

"They mean to kill us!" Bin Khamal breathed. "Go! Go!" The goats and camels hurtled forward at a rough, bone-jarring trot. Another spear whistled through the air, striking a white nanny, who gave a bleat of surprise to find herself pouring out her lifeblood onto the sand. Corydon swerved as another spear thudded down.

"No! We'll never make it! Bin Khamal!" he cried. "Your other self! Can you push them back while we retreat to the caves?!"

Bin Khamal nodded. As he dismounted, Corydon caught the bridle of his camel and led it away as the boy began to dissolve into a thick, buzzing column of sand. Then he spread himself over the face of the desert, howling, blocking out tracks, filling the air with grit. The pursuers checked. They tried to ride around the storm—they could see its edges—but the wild storm that had been Bin Khamal placed itself over and over again between the kleptis gang and its pursuers. Corydon and the others managed to gather some of their flock and get back to the cave while Bin Khamal howled. Gradually, the small storm came closer to the boys, then dwindled into a boy again. Bin Khamal flung himself down in the sand.

"I did not know you were a djinn," said Sikandar with awe. "It was very useful for us."

"I cannot do it again today, Corydon," said Bin Khamal apologetically. "If I take that form often, or stay in it too long, it will become my true form."

"It is your true form," said Azil stonily. "You are a monster."

Bin Khamal was silent.

Corydon spoke sharply. "Perhaps you would prefer the spears of those who pursue us! He has saved us all. And," he added, "he is not the only monster among us. A monster leads you." He displayed his goatleg. "And I say we should follow these caves deeper. If there is a river in here, perhaps there is an outlet, and we can slip away from our pursuers. They won't be sand-blind for long."

He brought a small oil lamp out of his pack and lit its wick with his tinderbox. Soft golden flame sprang up from its olive oil. He handed the lamp to Azil and then headed into the cave, hoping he would follow. And, after a moment, he did.

Bin Khamal caught up to Corydon. "You speak as if you were proud of it, being a monster. I have always been so ashamed. . . ."

"I am proud of it," said Corydon flatly. "It means I am not like the Olympians."

There was a silence.

"Who are the Olympians?" asked Bin Khamal.

Corydon paused. "Once upon a time, the earth was inhabited by kindly gods. Simple gods of earth, like my father, Pan. They were not perfect, any more than men are perfect; they sometimes quarreled or misused their powers. But they had no will to rule men. They asked for nothing more than respect and friendship. But among their children rose up gods who wanted everyone to be like them and who rejected all who were not like them. They imprisoned or murdered the kind old gods. Then they raised up a race of heroes to rid the earth of all who were strange or odd or lame or monstrous. And ever since then, they have tried to teach monsters to be ashamed. But we should not be ashamed that we are as we are."

The boys were quiet then.

They walked for hours in near darkness. Corydon was certain that they were utterly lost in a vast underground maze of caverns that opened off each other like dreams. Most were the same red rock, big, small—some contained water so the boys didn't go thirsty—and all were not warm, not cool. Corydon remembered seeing flutes of high rock soaring to the ceiling, bridges of rock as thin as silk. He remembered beaches of mud, and his shoes and clothes were soon coated in a kind of carapace of it.

But at last, when all of them were very weary and wishing earnestly that they had brought food instead of the treasure from the camels, they came to a cave that was different from the others.

It was long and narrow, the shape of a man's throat, as if it were swallowing them. And it was striated with ribs sticking out from the crimson rock, ribs that were white . . . like shelves.

And that was when Corydon saw them.

Row upon row of bottles in every jewel color, opal and peridot and chrysoprase, agate and emerald and jade, amethyst and ruby, garnet and turquoise. They were inlaid with gold and silver and other precious metals. Some were triangular, like tiny pyramids; others were square as dice. There were ovals and spheres and every curving, lovely shape. Entranced, Corydon moved closer. With each bottle was a stopper made of gold or silver and shaped like a teardrop. Some bottles had their stoppers in them, as if something precious were already stored inside. The other boys gasped. It looked like their long and weary flight had led them to more unimaginable treasure.

Bin Khamal's gasp had not been a gasp of pleasure, however. It had been a gasp of horror. And as he looked at them more closely, he gave a scream, a dreadful sound that rang from roof and wall.

Azil turned to him. "Why do you scream? These are riches enough to buy a whole city."

Bin Khamal was speaking in the tongue of his own people, of which Corydon had learned only a few words; he caught the word for djinn, which he did know. "Bin Khamal!" he shouted. "Speak Arabic! Or Hellene! What is the danger?"

"Soul-traps," Bin Khamal almost sobbed. "Corydon, they are soul-traps. . . ."

Suddenly, to Corydon's astonishment, Bin Khamal rose into the air. He hovered there, as if lying on a comfortable bed. Then, with terrifying speed, he shot toward one of the walls. Corydon could see that his friend wasn't doing this himself; his mouth was open in a scream of terror. Also, as he flew, he was *shrinking,* and now already he was the size of a baby.

Corydon dived for the cave wall. Using all his goatish climb-ing skills, he managed to scale the shelf-laden walls. His hasty feet sent bottles crashing to the cave floor, but he didn't have time to pause. He managed to fling himself at the now-tiny Bin Khamal as he hurtled toward the wall. But the boy was going faster than an arrow, and Corydon couldn't stop him from flying into the mouth of an open bottle.

The stopper leapt into the mouth of the bottle, and Bin Khamal was gone. Corydon seized the bottle in one hand, holding desperately on to a shelf with the other. Climbing like a monkey, he reached the floor of the cave in seconds and began trying to pull the stopper out.

It wouldn't budge.

Frustrated, he looked around.

Azil was crouched in the corner, plainly afraid. Sikandar was gaping at the floor.

And Corydon saw the smashed bottles from his hasty climb. He was about to hurl the bottle containing his friend to the ground also when he saw— But what he saw made him freeze. From each broken bottle, a thick mist was rising, condensing. . . . There were ten or twelve of them.

Corydon began backing up as soundlessly as he could until he stood against the wall.

The thin mists were casting their own glow. Now they were coalescing into a variety of forms.

They were djinns.

Corydon saw an elongated blue giant as tall as a mountain rush past, his form strung out to such a length that he took five minutes to rattle by, faster than the fastest camel, a blur of movement. A troupe of stout pink djinns forced themselves through the entrance with a resonant squelch. A djinn flung himself into a whirlwind and would plainly have been a sandstorm if there had been any sand to storm. Others simply made a harsh sucking noise, like a wave on sand, and flung themselves aloft.

"Wait!" shouted Azil suddenly, recovering his nerve. "Aren't you supposed to grant us wishes?" But the djinns took no notice at all. Their one thought was escape.

Corydon remembered Bin Khamal because the bottle was agitating itself very slightly in his hand.

He flung it to the cave floor, hoping Bin Khamal wouldn't just vanish into the cave as the others had. But although Bin Khamal raced twice around the cave in whirlwind form after his soul-trap smashed, he flung himself to the ground again. "Run!" he cried.

Corydon realized another bottle would trap his friend if they lingered, so the boys all rushed out of the cave and back the way they had come.

"Why don't they give wishes anymore?" Corydon asked, on Azil's behalf.

"Djinns give wishes only to lure people into releasing them. They are hard work; to make them come true, we have to put some of ourselves into each thing wished for, and that permanently ties us to earth and to humans. So we do it only when there is no other way. And you, Azil, should not be sorry. People began making traps like that one to try to force us to give them wishes, to harness our powers so that they might have bigger houses than their neighbors or more wealth or prettier wives or longer hair. Humans were willing to cage living things to be richer. Why should we of the Sands have any respect for that? And, besides, human wishes always,

always come to grief. The girl who wishes to be prettier than anyone else loses all her friends; the man who wishes for riches cannot sleep for fear that someone will rob him. More does not mean more joy."

Finally, after what seemed like long, hungry hours, Azil saw a faint light, and when they pursued it, they found it was the last light of day. They all desperately wished to be gone from these caves, but it was too late to find new shelter. With resignation, they laid themselves down for the night.

By midday they had managed to gather most of their flock and set forth again to market. They were all a bit jumpy still, and Corydon's monster sense prickled so that he was constantly looking back over his shoulder. He was just beginning to feel foolish about it when a gleam of light caught his eye.

It came from the point of a spear.

"They've found our trail!" gasped Azil.

"Ride!" shouted Corydon. All the camels shot forward. And the goats raced to keep up.

They rode all through the dreadful heat, but the heavy footfalls behind them never slowed. They went on riding even after the sun went down, but the strong, relentless pursuers kept after them, out of spear range but not losing any ground.

They kept on riding, on camels stumbling with tiredness. They paused at a well to allow the camels a snatched drink. It was almost dawn. This small respite lost them much of their lead. They mounted only just in time to avoid being speared.

"Who are they?" gasped Corydon. He looked back. The men's headdresses still looked immaculate. Their camels ran on tirelessly.

Bin Khamal spoke in the hard voice of one whose mouth has been dry all day.

"Corydon," he said, "we have a great treasure here. I think someone wants it back."

Sikandar spoke. "We could give it to them," he said, "if it saved our lives."

"I doubt that it would," said Corydon, noticing their long, bright swords glinting palely in the blue dawn light. "And I am not ready to surrender yet. I have seen a bigger army of heroes than this and lived to tell the tale." As he spoke, though, he noticed that one of the riders was much taller than the others. He thought to himself that perhaps the heroes he had met so far weren't the very best heroes. This tall man might be better than anyone he had ever faced.

Aloud, he said, "We need to make a plan. We cannot simply blunder on like this."

"We must trick them somehow," said Bin Khamal. "The weather will be of no help. And as long as they can see us, we cannot mislead them through tracking tricks."

Corydon thought. Then, without warning, he veered off to the left and galloped away, leaving the others to follow.

"Where are we going?" said Sikandar.

"To a cliff I know of," said Corydon simply.

The boys slowed the camels to a trot after a while, not wishing to tire their mounts under the ache and dazzle of the brutal sun. The heroes kept relentlessly on. Their camels were slowing, but they were not yet near the stumbling tiredness of the kleptis gang camels. The heat seemed to increase. Sweat poured down the boys' faces.

Corydon turned to see the tall hero taking a spear from his saddlebag. His face was twisted into a grimace of rage as he hurled it. A whistle of air. The boys stayed upright, knowing the spear could not reach them from that distance.

But a foot in *front* of Corydon's camel, a spear hit a little kid, trotting along, looking desperately for its mother. It bleated a sad, surprised note, then fell down dead. Corydon saw its glazed eyes as he steered his camel around the spear stuck in the ground. He looked in shock behind him.

At last, when he was almost so thirsty that he could not bear it, he saw a shadowy shape ahead. He could only hope that it was the dune he remembered.

Corydon told the others his plan.

"We must jump over the cliff."

"What?" the other boys all exclaimed sharply.

Then Bin Khamal asked, "Why should *we* go over the cliff? Why not lure them over?"

"That was what I thought of first," Corydon called. "But it wouldn't work. They are too clever, especially the tall one. No, our only chance is for them to think us dead."

"But—won't the fall kill us?"

"It might," said Corydon. "But the sea is below, and just there it is very deep. I once saw a whale, a leviathan, go by, blowing water. It is not the Middle Sea; it is some larger water."

Azil spoke. "This is the suggestion of a coward and a monster," he said disdainfully. "I would rather die with honor. I want to fight them."

Corydon sighed. "Azil, there are three times as many of them, each one is twice our size, and they are well armed. How can we

23

possibly fight them?" As well, he thought, *I am tired of fighting and battles. I never want to see or to be in another.*

"We need a miracle," said Sikandar.

Unbidden, Corydon remembered the other times he had been saved by miracles, such as the time Pegasos had come to his rescue in the Underworld. If only the winged horse could be here now . . .

"I can't give you a miracle," he said bluntly. "And we must do it now or throw ourselves on their mercy."

"I would rather die," said Bin Khamal with a faint smile.

"I think we can oblige you," said Sikandar.

"Faster!!" Corydon shouted. "When you reach the cliff edge, do not wait for a signal! Slide off your camel—why condemn them to our choices?—and jump with the wind in your hair. Ride!" The camels leapt forward in a loping gallop, ungainly but amazingly swift. And yet their pursuers drew closer, till Corydon could almost feel the breath of the foremost rider on the back of his neck.

They were sliding, almost falling down the immense dune. Corydon could see the cliff edge, much too close now. He tightened his grip on his treasure bag. Then he slid over the side of his camel. He hit the ground with a bruising thud, rolled as best he could, then . . .

He stood up for one instant, shook a defiant fist at the enormous hero looming up behind him. The hero's camel was keeping its footing effortlessly in the slithery sand. The white banner of his headdress streamed behind him like the tail of a comet of ill omen. For a second, Corydon could see his eyes. He had thought Perseus's eyes cold. This man's eyes were not cold but hot, white-hot with the longing to kill. His mouth was open in a battle scream that transformed his face in a rictus. The hate cry seemed to pierce Corydon's ears as the man raised his spear to run Corydon through.

And it was then that Corydon's miracle arrived.

Up from below the cliff edge came a flight of Sphinxes. Sixteen of them, their enormous wings spread. They were so big that they cast a shade over the cliff edge.

None of them spoke. That was not the Sphinx way. But they placed themselves between the boys and the onrushing heroes. One huge Sphinx reared up in front of Corydon, her wings spread to protect him. He crouched gratefully.

But, to his surprise, the man's battle cry did not cease. Instead, Corydon heard the whiffle as he flung his spear straight at the Sphinx's face, aiming for the eye. She must have used her mind powers on him—he was still moving, still trying to attack, so his will must have been very strong, but he was moving as if thigh deep in sand, and Corydon saw the Sphinx settle down like a cat on a warm rock to play with him. He uttered groans that sounded like his war cries slowed down. He also began to look confusedly at the Sphinxes, as if wondering why he hadn't reached them yet. He was clearly a man used to being abnormally fast and now he was impossibly slow, but he didn't seem to realize it. Corydon could see that his painful progress *felt* like running to him.

"This one is the strongest," the Sphinx said. "Some say a fleet of ships is best," she added, "some say a marching army of men, but I say it is the one you love."

Corydon was used to Sphinxes, so he didn't ask himself what on earth she meant. He looked for the other pursuers. Each stood as stiffly as if he had been shrouded in linen. The camels, too, were utterly still.

"Don't look into the Sphinxes' eyes," he hissed to Sikandar and Azil. Bin Khamal had already draped his head scarf lower, so that he couldn't catch their eyes by looking up at the wrong moment. It was clear that he, too, had met Sphinxes before.

Corydon decided to risk one question. "Why?" he asked. "Why did you come?"

The Sphinx did not turn her head. "One of you must not die. Must not be lost. One of you"—she paused, and suddenly her claws shot out with a dull rasp on the sand—"one of you has a future."

Not more prophecies! Not more being the Chosen One! I don't want it! I just want to be a kleptis leader!

Corydon's thoughts ran on a familiar track through his mind. As usual, the Sphinx heard him as if he had spoken aloud.

"Why do you feel so sure that I meant you?" she asked softly, her eyes still fixed on the tall hero, who was moving so slowly now that it could barely be detected.

Corydon decided that he didn't want to know what she meant. He wanted to get his boys together and go to a city and trade and buy and increase their goat herd.

"Who is he? Will you kill him?" he asked, pointing at the tall hero. He would have liked to hear that the man was gone for good. Those silver, raging eyes would haunt his nightmares.

"I will not," she said. "He has a destiny as well, though not here and not now."

Corydon was torn; he didn't really want the man to die, but he didn't want to live in fear of him. But there was no arguing with a Sphinx.

The other boys were keeping their heads ducked. "Come on," he shouted. And they set off in pursuit of their scattered goats and camels once again. If Corydon had looked back, he would have seen that the hero with the silver eyes had turned his head, with an immense effort, to look after them as they went.

T H R E E

THE CITY AHEAD OF THEM WAS THE LARGEST IN THE
kingdom of Nabataea. It is possible that if Corydon had not seen
Atlantis, he might have felt overawed by Tashkurgan, a city of
white stone. It was as crisp and pristine as if it had been carved out
of ice; all its buildings had an edge of newness. And yet this fresh-
as-linen city was set in a ravine as red as the blood of sacrifice.
Azil and Bin Khamal looked awed, but Sikandar seemed as un-
impressed as Corydon. There was no time to wonder why. At the
head of the ravine were guards.

"We come to trade," said Corydon quietly and respectfully, in
the language of the Arabs.

The guard looked at him quizzically. "You are very young," he
said, "to be trading in Tashkurgan. Does your father know?"

For a fraction of a second, Corydon wondered if his father did
know. . . . But he had long since stopped doing the errands of any
god, even beloved ones. "I have no father," he said. "I am alone."

The guard looked sympathetic. "All right," he said. "Move along. But remember that you must make an offering at the Great Temple. All traders must do so." The boys began the slow, careful walk down a narrow cliff path into the deeps of the gorge, gentling the camels and goats along. Bin Khamal said, "It is the temple of the winged lions. But I am not sure what the offering is."

Azil said, "I have heard of it, too. More winged lions, like those who just befriended us, I imagine."

Corydon opened his mouth to explain that Sphinxes were not in fact winged lions but then closed it again; he could see Azil had much more to say.

"I do not like it. For us, such djinn are evils of the desert. We appease them, but we do not befriend them." He looked sidelong at Bin Khamal and Corydon. "I know you as friends," he said stiffly, "but you are enemies to my people. The winged lions will be likewise friends and enemies to me. Sometimes the offering we must make to such creatures is too large."

Sikandar took his hand. "Azil," he said, "you lack ambition. You must walk with the immortals and try not to feel fear. For if you die in their embrace, if they devour you, you will only be doing what you are born to do. Humans are *made* to seek out something too great for us to conquer."

Corydon found this idea interesting. He wondered if it was because he was not human that he had spent his life yearning for the small things that did not content humans themselves: a fireside, a mother, a group of true friends.

He shook his head. He supposed it was the contact with the Sphinxes that had made them all so thoughtful.

Now they were passing two huge gate-statues of lions, lions with thickly feathered wings furled across their backs. The heads bore sharp horns, like those of a desert oryx, and heavy manes. The boys looked up at them in awe.

It was midmorning, and a crowd was cramming itself into Tashkurgan: carts of vegetables, carts loaded with grain, elaborately veiled women holding baskets, black-swathed men of the desert leading strings of camels, blue-clad caravan men bringing in spices and silks on camel- and muleback. Food traders were setting out their stalls, and a scent of spices filled the hot air.

"Aeee! The winged serpents! The winged serpents!"

Corydon looked up to see a black bat-winged shape streak across the sky, faster than a swallow.

Everyone flung himself to the ground. Corydon's mouth was in the dust of the street. But he raised his head. So he saw two immense shapes rising from the temple roof. They were winged lions, and they began to close in on the serpents.

It was an interesting battle, because the serpents were much faster and more numerous, but the lions were stronger, though slow and heavy in the air. The lions' tactic was to drop on the serpents from high in the sky and crush them in their teeth, breaking their necks. Three serpents died that way; the crowd scattered as the broken bodies fell on the city. Corydon found it exciting, though he felt sorry for the serpents. He wondered what they wanted—why they were so persistent. Then he saw that one of the winged lions was in trouble.

His flight had become erratic. One of his wings seemed to be almost paralyzed; he could beat it only feebly. He was snarling in pain and fear. As Corydon watched in horror, he plunged from the sky, tumbling over and over. All around, people were whispering and pointing. "It's the serpent poison," said a blue-clad trader. "He's done for." As he spoke, the lion fell on his back onto a group of fine white houses, crushing them. Not knowing why, Corydon got up and ran to the spot. The lion lay broken, his body twisted, his eyes still open. Then the great red mouth opened, and the lion spoke.

"Corydon Panfoot," he said, "you cannot hide forever. You are needed. And my brothers will tell you what you must do. You must do it. You must. Must." His golden eyes rolled back in his head as he slumped into death. Then they sprang open again. "Where are your friends?" the deep voice asked. "Where are they?" A single tear slid down the lion's nose. Then his eyes closed once more.

Corydon was blank with horror. He didn't even want to be known, but now he was known and, worse, accused. Of betrayal. And in his heart, he knew the accusations were just. The battle still raged overhead, but Corydon sat utterly still, holding the dead lion's head in his hands. He felt he had deserted a post of danger and had been caught doing so by one who had given his life for others.

Suddenly he began to cry, and the tears poured out. Sthenno! Euryale! The Minotaur! He did not say the name of the Snake-Girl: she was lost to him; he had lost her. But the others! How could he have—no, not forgotten, but neglected them?

As he wept for himself, for his friends, for what he now thought he was, the noises of battle above him gradually ceased. With a slow beating of wings, the other lion came and landed beside his dead fellow. The great creature ignored Corydon entirely. With an anxious pink tongue, he licked the forehead of his fallen comrade. The dead lion did not move. The living lion settled down beside him, paws regally outstretched, and threw back his head in a roar of grief and defiance. The fleeing serpents answered with shrill screams of triumph.

Corydon sat still and wept. He seemed to have a fountain of tears in him. After a while, he noticed that the living winged lion was weeping, too.

Finally, Corydon's tears ran out into a desert of numbness. He wiped his face and looked at the lion.

"Can—can I help?" he asked uncertainly. He was pretty sure he couldn't, but something had to be said.

"Help?" The great beast looked down his nose. "We are in dire need of help. But we do not ask it from those who abandon their friends and their fates."

Corydon was silent. The lion looked down his nose again. Then he spoke.

"You always long for an ordinary human life, Panfoot. But you know that is not your fate, can never be your fate. You cannot run or hide from who you are. In trying to betray yourself, you have also betrayed everyone you love, everyone who loves you."

Corydon burst out, "But do you truly know who I am? I am become Death, the destroyer of worlds! It was by my hand that Atlantis fell. I felled a city, a civilization. I am more truly a monster than any. It is a pity my village did not kill me on the day when they made me their scapegoat."

The lion said indifferently, "That is not the tale the stars tell. We gaze at the stars from our tower—that is how we know you—and they do not call you a murderer. In any case, what you say does not matter. What matters is that you love your friends, and they are your soul. And now you have another group of ragtags following you about and expecting protection. How are you to help them if you truly are Death, the destroyer of worlds?"

Corydon was appalled. He saw that he'd betrayed the desert kleptis gang as well as the monsters.

"But—" He wondered how to begin. "I can't take action. Last time I made a wrong choice and lost a friend, lost a whole city. At least by living this simple life, I am not hurting anyone."

"Look around you," said the lion austerely. Corydon looked. The three kleptis boys were standing in a group, watching, listening, wary of approaching the great lion. Azil's eyes were narrow with suspicion.

The lion said, "Already one of your followers is powerful beyond your reckoning, and another carries his own strange and terrible fate. And already, too, you and they have made powerful enemies."

He stood up. A phalanx of winged lions was issuing slowly from the temple roof. They landed in the square and were plainly about to bear their dead comrade away. They unfolded a white and gold litter and gently lifted the dead lion onto it.

"When you know yourself," said the lion, "then you may be of help to us. But now I choose to ask help of another." Slowly, deliberately, he padded across to where the kleptis gang stood. It was plain the boys were terrified, but they stood straight and waited.

"Alekhandros of Troios!" said the lion in his deep voice. "Stand forth. Your secrets are known, and they are not shameful. A task awaits you. It is difficult, but it is not impossible. Come."

The three boys stood still, and a dreadful silence fell all around them.

Then Sikandar stepped forward. He lifted his chin proudly. "I am Alekhandros, prince of the Trojans," he said. "What is your will?" His whole bearing had changed.

Azil drew in his breath sharply. His eyes widened. "A prince!" he breathed. Bin Khamal, on the other hand, began quietly backing away. Corydon was astonished. Sikandar himself was almost in tears.

"I am sorry, lord," he said to Corydon. "I am sorry. I knew this day would come. Sooner or later. I could only hope for later." He smiled faintly. "But—" Corydon took his hand. Sikandar smiled again, then gently let Corydon's hand drop. It was a gesture that seemed to seal him off behind a wall. The kleptis time was over, at least for him. "It is my fate," he said, "to resolve a quarrel between the Olympians. I hid because I cannot succeed. I can only fail. And when I fail, I may take my people with me into darkness. Every day I was hidden was a day of reprieve for Troy. But now our time is done."

"Then—don't do it!" Corydon called urgently, and Bin Khamal, too, ran and stood in Sikandar's way. "Stop!"

"I cannot stop," said Sikandar. "Now I am discovered, I must judge. Must choose. If I do not, *all* the Olympians will unleash their wrath on Troy."

The great lion nodded. "And on Tashkurgan," he said. "Every day, the winged serpents grow stronger. This city, too, will go to dust and desert if the serpents rule it. The Olympians are not our gods, but they have promised us that they will drive out the winged serpents if we can find the heir of Troy and persuade him to make his choice."

"But you can't be stupid enough to believe them!" shouted Corydon. "Surely you must know the Olympians are liars and tyrants. They will see you as monsters, and they will destroy you so that they alone may rule the people of Tashkurgan."

"We have no choice," said the lion, his voice sad. "And we know that you, too, Panfoot, have betrayed and abandoned your friends. It is time for us all to face our futures." And with the lion's words, three female figures appeared with stunning suddenness in front of Sikandar.

One was Hera; Corydon's stomach gave a sick squirm as he saw her blond helmet hair. The second was Athene. Her gray gown was spotless, immaculately pressed, set in clean folds over her ample, solid bosom. Her hair was plaited very neatly. She had a scrubbed, very healthy pink and white face.

Corydon noticed that she wore a kind of elaborate shawl, or scarf, around her neck. On it was what was obviously meant as a portrait of Medusa's severed head. He almost retched.

"I must choose the fairest," said Sikandar. "I must decide what all men desire most, and then I am to present my choice with an apple."

To Corydon, neither Hera nor Athene was remotely beautiful.

The third goddess was a stranger to Corydon, but he could guess who she was. To his surprise, Corydon saw Sikandar smile feebly at this one.

"Have you chosen her?" he asked urgently.

"No, but I may," Sikandar said.

Corydon looked at her. "Why?" he asked bluntly.

"Because I know her, at least," said Sikandar desperately. "Aphrodite is sort of an aunt."

Aphrodite did not look like any aunt Corydon had ever seen or imagined. She was tiny. She looked dark and sulky, with full, ripe lips, full, ripe body, full, ripe hair. She preened a little. Corydon was reminded of his friend Fee, but Fee had been much prettier.

Aphrodite held a mirror, and in it Corydon could see the figure of another woman brushing long flaxen hair in front of another mirror. It made him dizzy. Too many mirrors.

"That's Helena," said Sikandar. "Aphrodite will give her to me if I choose her."

"But, Sikandar," said Corydon, "the others are far more powerful. And they'll be really angry if you choose her. I've seen the wrath of Hera. She sank Atlantis. And Athene transformed a friend of mine into a snaky-haired goddess." *And she chose to stay that way*, he thought suddenly. Which didn't justify Athene's action.

"Oh, I know, Corydon," sighed Sikandar. "The have each promised and threatened and tortured me until it was clear there was no choice I could make that wouldn't bring disaster. I am all too well aware of the possibilities."

"Sikandar," whispered Helena. The girl in the mirror was the only one to speak. "I am a pawn in this game, too. I do not know what the gods have in mind, but I will help you fight for Troy. We must try to save her."

Corydon saw that Helena was as caged by her fate as Sikandar was. As he himself was. He felt a warm rush of pity.

And Sikandar evidently felt it, too. "All right," he said. And with these words a golden apple appeared in Sikandar's hand. "All right. I've known that any choice would bring doom to my city. But perhaps I can help one person. I choose Aphrodite. And I shall take Helena back to Troy with me." He held out the apple to the goddess.

Aphrodite gave a smile of pure triumph. She stuck her tongue out rudely at the astonished Athene and Hera, snatched up the apple, and took a huge bite of it. It did not seem to worry her that it was made of gold. Her white teeth snapped gleefully.

And as she bit, the other two goddesses gave loud shrieks of fury that did not die away. Instead, they grew louder and louder and louder until they sounded like the howling of the wind.

Then Athene's voice grew steady, calm, a little reproachful. "It was not for this, lion, that we agreed to protect your city." Her voice rose again in a cry of fury.

"We did not scare away the snakes," said Hera, "so that this viper could be awarded the prize." Her voice, too, rose again in that thin scream. "We shall keep our promise. The snakes won't menace your city. Because there will be no city. We raise the djinns against you, and they shall engulf your city in sand in a storm that will last for ten years. You will be buried under all the sands of Arabia. And all men shall know the fate of Tashkurgan, the city destroyed, scrubbed clean by the sand of the high gods."

Already Corydon could hear the high whine of the approaching djinns. He motioned urgently to Bin Khamal, who stood with his face white.

"As for you"—now Athene turned to Sikandar—"as for you, princeling of Troy, Zeus has decreed your doom long ere this, but we shall be its messengers. Your tallest towers will fall, and flames shall engulf you." Her voice held an anger that was greater than the sounds of the gathering sandstorm.

"It is fitting," said Hera, her voice full of spiteful satisfaction, "that Atlantis perished in water, Troy will be ruined in fire, and Tashkurgan in air and earth."

"You who had faith in the little gods of place," said Athene, her words sharper than the sting of the sand, "shall die in their elements. Do you understand? It is we who command."

"Bin Khamal!" called Corydon desperately. His friend reached his side.

"Corydon," he said, raising his voice above the scream of wind and sand, "I can do nothing. These are not the djinn of my tribe but the afreets of the far south. I can do nothing—I do not even speak their tongue."

And it was true. The clouds that were encroaching on the city's walls were different from the other djinn Corydon had seen. And he was reminded suddenly of Vreckan, who had swallowed Atlantis. The afreets looked greedy, and their burning sand made earth and sky the same substance, as Vreckan had united sea and sky.

He knew no one would hear him well above the roar, but he spoke all the same. "Sikandar—Prince—you must warn them in Troy. Go!"

"I will help him," said a low voice that could be heard below the shrieking winds. The small, dark goddess was there, her eyes slumberous. "If Troy is to burn," she added, "it will burn with the flames of love." She took Sikandar's hand, put it in Helena's, who

38

had been freed from the mirror, and led them into the gathering sand. But before they vanished entirely, Aphrodite turned and gave Corydon a smoldering look. "And I'll be seeing you soon, little Panfoot."

Corydon shuddered but managed to turn to Azil. "Go," he said, as gently as the wind allowed. "Have the life for which you were born. Be a shepherd."

But Azil ignored him, perhaps did not even hear him. He had already put his bow to his shoulder, arrow on the string. Sobbing, he fired at the oncoming storm.

A hand made of cloud and sand came out of it and tore him from the ground, hurled him up into the air. Then the hand let him drop. Corydon saw the tiny black shape of his friend falling, falling. A cloud of sand obscured the terrible landing. Though he ran toward the place, the swirling clouds hid it from his eyes. The wind's roar now held a trace of laughter.

Azil was gone. Corydon turned away. He felt the weight of his uselessness. He could not even cry.

Bin Khamal swallowed a handful of dust. "Corydon," he said, "I must go. The afreets"—he had to raise his voice above the wind—"the afreets will know. They will know me."

"When shall we meet again?" Corydon remembered Medusa saying that. He couldn't decide whether it was a good omen or not.

Bin Khamal shrugged. Both glanced one last time at the place where Azil's small, broken body must lie. The gathering sand stung their eyes. It was not worth saying things like "There are only two of us now." Both knew the kleptis life was over. Neither could speak. Bin Khamal put his hand on Corydon's arm for half an embarrassed second, then turned and ran from the bruised-plum clouds. Their livid color reminded Corydon of Medusa's skin, and there was something stupidly comforting in the thought, as if she were with him.

FOUR

CORYDON DID NOT GO INTO THE DESERT. AS THE
storm swirled, he turned and walked deliberately into the heart of
Tashkurgan.

Slowly the air went solid with sand. Corydon groped his way
through the almost invisible streets; people jostled him, blinded,
and his eyes, his nose, his face were prickly with sand. He wan-
dered without purpose, his only thought that he could not watch
another city go to destruction while he was safe outside it.

Through the swirling sand-wind, he caught a glimpse of a
light. Hurling himself suddenly sideways toward it, he found himself in a tavern.

It was shelter, anyway, he thought, as the whirling sand filled
the streets. The tavern was crowded with others seeking refuge.
Squirming, Corydon managed to find a quiet corner. The talk
buzzed and swirled in six different tongues.

And then he heard a conversation that gave him a jagged
shock, as if a bolt from Zeus had run him through the ear.

". . . a girl who could make snakes come out of herself; half snake she was, too. I dunno why he wanted her so much, but he couldn't . . ."

Corydon listened desperately. But by now the two men had moved on, and he heard no more.

It couldn't be. The Snake-Girl was probably dead. She was gone. He thought of the bronzy scales of the eidolon who had taken her place and fooled him. And he had loved her. He had loved a trick, a false image, a lie. Now he didn't know what he felt. If there was a real Snake-Girl still, what would she think of him?

A man brought around a pitcher of a thick white drink. Corydon supposed it was camel's milk, but when he tasted it, he realized his mistake. It was sweet and rich and delicate all at once; he'd never had anything so good. It seemed to drive the sting of the sand out of his throat.

He looked up over the rim of his beaker, hoping for a refill.

But he couldn't see the servitor. What caught his eye instead was a tall figure swathed in a deep blue hood, the hood of the desert people. Through the blue stuff, he could see the glitter of eyes. The man was watching him, unwaveringly.

Corydon stared back. He knew the rule of the island villagers among whom he had grown up: never, ever be the first to look away. But it was hard to go on holding the gaze of a man whose face was hidden.

Then the man began, slowly, to unwind his headdress. He bared a fierce, hard mouth, a high-bridged nose like a hawk's beak. Last of all, he unwound the blue covering from the rest of his face.

It was the man with silver eyes.

Corydon knew he was in trouble. The storm raged ferociously

42

outside, but he began to think of its roar with pleasure in comparison with the silence that enveloped him in the tavern.

The man flung back his cloak. Corydon saw his sword's gleam. Then he spoke.

"I could have killed you minutes ago, if I had chosen," he said in a voice that rang through the tavern.

Behind Corydon, the bartender was hurriedly stowing any precious-looking pottery vessels out of harm's way. The other customers were backing away, too.

Corydon's dark eyes still held the man's silver eyes. "I cannot run any further," he said fiercely. "Do as you will. As you and your kind have always done. Butcher me if you must."

The man was silent for a whole minute, thinking. Then he spoke again. "Do you not know," he said slowly, "that Rashid al-Haoud has put a bounty on your head so large that every bounty hunter in Arabia is out searching for you? You and your kleptis gang stole from the dowry he sent with his daughter. Yes, you know well what I mean—the jewels, the cloth, the spices. You have put him to shame. His shame will not be undone until he sees you on a spike in the sun in front of his house." His silver eyes flashed fire.

Corydon shuddered inwardly at the terrible death that awaited him. But he spoke bravely. "At least my friends have eluded your wrath," he said. "And if I can buy their lives at the cost of my own, I consent to that." *After all,* he thought, *I'm tired. Tired of running from heroes.* A vision of Medusa's cottage came to him, very sweetly. *And perhaps,* he thought, *I deserve death.* He thought of the thousands of dead Atlanteans.

But the hero with the silver eyes was silent once more.

"Come," he said at last. "I will take you."

Corydon stood up. It was obvious that fighting was useless. He was weaponless. This was very clearly the greatest hero he had ever met.

As they moved toward the door, it seemed that someone didn't think so. A man in a black cloak turned from the bar and drew a dagger, pressing it sharply into the hero's throat. "Give me that boy," he said hoarsely. "I've been watching him. I need that bounty—"

That was as far as he got. In a single movement, the hero's sword rippled out of its sheath and found a new resting place in the man's belly. The man looked down at it with a gasp of surprise. Then his soul went crying to the Realm of the Many. The hero's face did not change. His eyes looked just the same. He wrapped his face and head again, to protect himself from the storm. Corydon did the same.

When they stood outside in the roaring wind, the hero spoke. "I am a fool," he said. "I cannot kill you. You are a thief, but you have acted honorably. You were willing to die for your friends. And there is something about you that is noble. Something I had almost forgotten. But if we ever meet again," he said, and those astonishing eyes lit from within, like marshfire, "if we ever meet again, you must die on my sword."

Corydon stood still. Then he said two words with sincerity for the first time. "My lord," he said.

"My name is Akhilleus," said the man with silver eyes. "Now go."

Corydon took a breath of stinging dust. Then he drew his cloak about him and ran into the deeps of the storm.

Its scouring sand led him but also hit him in the face like a horde of angry wasps. Despite its buffeting, all he wanted was to get as far as possible from those silver eyes.

He had never met a hero like this one. Perseus had been a hero, but he had also been an idiot, frightening because of his stupidity. Pirithoos, Lysias—only Kharmides had been of normal intelligence. But this man was very, very far from stupid. Very far from Perseus's nervous fumblings. He was ... Corydon groped for words, wishing it were possible to play his pipes in the driving wind; it helped him think. This man was as an Olympian god should be. ... It was as if everything evil and disappointing in them, everything twisted, had somehow been smoothed and straightened. And Corydon had also sensed a great loneliness and depth of solitude more profound even than the Minotaur's, only here it did not go with the Minotaur's soft-footed bumbling but with hardness and strength.

The thought stung him like the sand. It threatened his world. How could a hero be so like, so like ... well, so like a monster?

Hours of stinging pain went by. Corydon's eyes were almost swollen shut when he began to feel the wind lessen against his sore skin.

As the darkness began to lift, he stumbled against rock. Where was he? He scraped his forehead against more rock, then obeyed an instinct to crouch low, finding his way forward free. He crawled into a space that smelled oddly familiar, though he didn't try to put a name to the smell at first. It was enough that his nose and mouth and eyes were out of the tormenting flying sand. He collapsed onto the cave floor. His mind gave a few last bright flickers before he fell into sleep.

* * *

He woke thinking of the other monsters, thinking he was in Lady Nagaina's stronghold, thinking he heard Sthenno's voice. But it was only the cry of some large bird outside the shallow cave in which he had lodged. A pang of sadness struck him as he felt the full loss of that past.

It roused him, though, and he sat up. As he did so, he became aware of the thick sound of breathing all around him. Of the condensation in the cave. Of the rich, spicy smell of fur that had haunted him. He remembered in a sudden rush where he had smelled that particular odor before.

The Nemean lion . . . One night Corydon had slept next to his old friend in the stronghold, enjoying his scented warmth. In a flash, he recalled the images he had seen in that other cave. . . . As the memory flooded him, he saw them. The humped backs of a huge lioness and, near her, the softer outlines of three cubs.

Nemean lions hated killing, but they also had terrible tempers, and Corydon remembered how fiercely his old friend had loved and guarded his rock. What if the thing he had stumbled on in the dark was *their* rock? They might not welcome an intruder in their cave. . . .

Just as Corydon realized that he might be in danger, one of the cubs stirred. He rolled over onto his tummy, sat up, washed his face, and noticed Corydon.

"Hello," said the cub. "What are you?"

Corydon held out his hand for the cub to sniff. "I'm the mormoluke," he said. "And you are a Nemean lion cub."

The cub tumbled backward in surprise.

46

"How do you know that?" he asked.

"I have met one of your kind before," said Corydon.

That was quite enough information for the cub. "Oh," he said, satisfied, then butted his mother fiercely. She woke, too, in a swirling rush of gold and amber fur, and her vivid jeweled eyes caught Corydon's steady gaze.

"You, go," she said. There was no room for discussion in her firm voice.

Corydon got up obediently.

"I will go," he said carefully. "A Nemean lion is my friend. I honor your people. I am sorry to intrude."

She bared her teeth very slightly. "You, go," she said firmly. "Go now."

"I'm going," said Corydon hastily. He couldn't stop his heart from aching a little. He had hoped for the furry warmth he remembered so vividly. He realized it had been a very long time since anyone had hugged him or ruffled his hair or played games with him or teased him. Perhaps it was because of seeing the cubs, but somehow he felt like a cub himself. He chided himself: *How old are you, Corydon?* Then he realized he had no idea of the answer. As he ducked through the entrance, he began to cry. He felt hideously ashamed. But he longed for arms to hold him. The salt tears burned his raw face.

And he felt a heavy paw on his shoulder.

The mother lion had understood him somehow, and with simple wisdom she gathered him softly against her wide, furry body. Her cubs gamboled around him, patting him with their soft paws, too. He relaxed into the scented furry warmth. His tears dried. She tickled him a little, and he began to laugh instead.

Monster-warmth, monster-love. The love of his own kind. He sat up, and she did, too. She met his eyes, and he saw that hers were full of tears as well.

"We, too, cry," she said in her soft, rumbling purr.

Corydon realized that there was no father lion.

"Where is your mate?" he asked.

All the lions burst into an ululating howl. A long sound that rose and fell, as if the rocks themselves wept stone tears. Corydon remembered the Nemean lion crying like that after a battle, and it was partly grief for his friend that made him want to weep himself. He knew that somehow the father had been lost to them. How did not matter.

He began crying softly again. This time his tears were for them. The cubs pressed against him.

After an ageless time, they all felt entirely empty, white and clean like new snow. "Hungry," said the mother lion. She tore a piece of meat from the carcass she had been saving and brought it to Corydon. He thought of the old days with Euryale, when she would devour bleeding chunks of meat while he and Sthenno watched the heavens. . . . His heart thrummed again; a new song was being born in his mind. He knew he had to go to the Gorgons. He had to find them. However dirtied he was by what he had done in Atlantis, he had to face them. He had to trust their love as he had entrusted himself to the clemency of the lions. Even to the clemency of Akhilleus—a hero who was also a monster . . .

But how could he reach them?

Nemean lions generally knew only their own territory. They were not offended by his refusal of their food; they were eating hungrily, and he wondered if food might be scarce.

"Are there other monsters here?" he asked without much hope. The mother lion shook her head.

"Now you are here," she said. "We, too."

One of the cubs rolled over, and Corydon saw a flash of unexpected intelligence in his face. "Once," said the cub, "I saw a bird-lion. Flying. And once a snake. Flying."

"You're a fibber," said another cub, pouncing.

"He is not!" said the third. "Anyway, I saw a monster. I saw one. Just yesterday. Big, big, big. A girl. A girl who had a tail like a desert serpent."

Corydon's head whirled. The Snake-Girl? Perhaps the men in the tavern really had been talking about his Lamia. Careful not to alarm them, he asked slowly, "Where did you see her?"

The small lion was obviously trying to think. He scratched his ear. "I think," he said carefully, "it was at the oasis. I remember her lying on the sand. I think she was trying to get warm. Sometimes you see snakes doing that in the morning. But you mustn't touch them, because they can hurt you with one bite. So I didn't go close."

Corydon forced a warm smile. "Thank you," he said. "Which oasis might that be?"

The cub frowned. He looked up, his eyes full of worry. "I think it was the one where you go that way, then that way," he said, gesturing with a small golden paw.

After the quickest goodbye he could manage, Corydon began to run in the direction the lion had indicated.

The Snake-Girl . . . Could she really be here? Here in the desert . . . and only yesterday? He remembered her sweetness, her intense shyness, her hatred of anything that impinged on her delicate world. From her inexact copy, the eidolon, he had learned something of the misery that had made her the monster she was. He had also learned a little of love from that machine, though the memory made him wince that he had been so tricked.

He reached the oasis in a skid of sand, after running all day, wild-eyed, with the voices of the sand-winds singing in his ears.

Of course, there was no one there.

There were the hoofprints of many camels, many hundreds that had drunk the sweet waters and left refreshed. Discarded date seeds lay all around. But there was no way to know which, if any, were the tracks that might lead to the Snake-Girl.

He sat down to wait. And he waited. And waited. He ate dates. He grew thin. But no one came.

At last, his stubborn heart admitted it. If she was here, her party had just been passing though. And he only had a cub's word even for that.

But somehow he now felt he and the Snake-Girl would meet again. And even that faint hope was better than the hopelessness he'd known before.

FIVE

HE TRAVELED ALL NIGHT, HIS MIND FILLED WITH AN image of warm golden fur.

When he arrived in the lions' pridelands, rosy-fingered dawn was caressing the sky. He ran on, tireless in his strength. His hunger was a steady pain.

Then, abruptly, he skidded to a stop. There in front of him was a small, pathetic bundle of golden fur.

His mind refused what his eyes saw.

It was the head of one of the Nemean lion cubs.

The eyes were open, as if the baby had seen his death. The baby body, legs splayed, lay on top of a rock. Corydon noticed how big the paws were compared with the short, sturdy legs. The cub hadn't had time to grow into them. He hadn't had time.

Corydon looked around. A blood trail led across the sand. He followed it numbly, and it led him to the mother lion, foam on her jaws. She had died defending her other cubs. Their torn bodies nestled at her side, as if she could still feel them.

Who? How? Nemean lions were difficult to kill, almost impossible. Their skin was like bronze armor.

Corydon looked at the mother's body and noticed for the first time that a spear still pierced her side. It had broken off in her death agony, but he could see the red shaft. He could see it was a Greek battle javelin, the kind thrown rather than thrust at a foe. He pulled it from her, wincing as if she could still feel its barb.

Then he examined it. The barb was made from a lion claw.

So. Whoever had done this had killed Nemean lions before and knew much of them. A Nemean lion's skin could be pierced only by a Nemean lion claw. And the killer was a Greek.

He sat still, dry with grief. Dry as a desert heart. Who? Who? Who? And why?

He jumped when he heard the bored voice from behind him.

"It was Ares," said the wingfoot god. "Who can say why? He does many such deeds." The words were muttered sullenly. One of his sandals tried to untie itself and frisked angrily from side to side. Hermes glared blackly at it. Slowly it settled back to the ground again.

"I shall go now," said the god. "High Olympos awaits me." Awkwardly he shuffled his feet. Corydon saw that he was looking at the outstretched paws of the youngest lion cub. He stood still for a moment. Even the restless sandals were motionless. "I liked them," he said abruptly. Then he leapt into the sky.

Corydon stood, astonished. Then black fury took him, and he cursed at the retreating figure. What good was an Olympian's pity now? The lions lay in their blood.

He made a pyre for the lions, digging a deep pit, bringing what scrubby bushes he could find, kindling a fire. The bodies were consumed by the quick, hot tongues, and he remembered Medusa's burning and could still find no tear, no song, no words for the griefs of the world. His heart was as bare and black as ashes. He didn't even know what to wish for anymore; he knew only that he must find a way to end the Olympians' rule and all its cruelty or die in the attempt. For he could live no more in a world that left them free to destroy the innocent.

If I am to die, he thought, *I could be with Medusa,* and his heart lifted slightly. He was glad she was not here, though, glad she could not see the lions' deaths. It would have made her cry with rage.

A great shadow passed over him, and a white and gold and lapis-blue body alighted in front of him.

It was a Sphinx.

She lay down regally, paws spread forward, wings folded. Around her sprang up the white pillars of a temple. Grass rippled outward from her reclining body. A fountain leapt suddenly skyward. The air turned cool and fresh, and there was a scent of flowers. Soon she was surrounded by her own dream landscape.

She was bigger than he had remembered. Was it the same Sphinx, his own friend—no, not friend—from the Island of Monsters?

"Does it matter?" she asked, in a voice like sliding water, a cool ripple of a voice.

"I suppose not," he conceded. Then rebellion welled up in him. "Yes," he said. "It does matter. What happens to us matters. She knows me and I know her."

The Sphinx was silent. In the silence he could hear the plaintive splash of the fountain.

"To the Sphinx all knowledge is indivisible. All is one. There is no she and I. There is only the Sphinx."

"That's—" He realized he'd been about to say "monstrous." He stopped abruptly.

"I am here to give you some knowledge," she said. "Here it is. You have asked the right question to obtain it. The quest to be someone is the root of all evil," she went on, and he sensed something like irony in her look. "It is of the Olympians. Each one wishes to insist upon himself or herself."

"But they don't want anyone else to do it," said Corydon sharply. "And so our insistence that we *are* must be a way to anger them. To thwart them. I will thwart them, Sphinx."

"For this you were born, Corydon Panfoot," she said tranquilly.

"But all I have managed so far is to survive. To hang on. I redeemed the Underworld with the Staff of Hades, but what of this world, the world where mortal men begin and live and die? Can it not be redeemed?"

"You do not have another Staff," she said.

"No," he said. "Is there another way?"

"There is," she said. "But think, mormoluke. Think. If once I speak of it, you will not be able to forget it. It will haunt you, shadow your steps. You have spent a long time running from your fate, into the desert places of the world. A long time longing for nothing more than to be allowed to be, to be Corydon, a boy with a few friends and some goats."

"Still, I will hear," said Corydon.

"And I warn you, Panfoot. This life cannot be utterly redeemed. Men will still choose wrongly. You must think, too, whether redemption is truly what you seek. What would it mean for the world to be redeemed?"

"No Olympians," said Corydon through clenched teeth. He thought of the warm, dead bodies of the Nemean lions lying on the hard, unfeeling sand. The wide look of staring surprise in the eyes of the smallest cub.

"No Olympians," she repeated.

"No Zeus, then! He controls them all."

"Will that be enough?"

"No, it will not," Corydon agreed. "But it will at least be a start. It will be something."

"Very well," said the Sphinx. "You know what you must do." Her golden eyes began to close.

"No, I don't." Corydon spoke urgently. "I'd have done it by now if I knew. Please."

"You *are* the Staff now, Corydon Panfoot. You have it in your body to redeem this world, as you once had it in your hand to redeem the Realm of the Many. Your mission was once to plant a seed. . . . Now somehow you are yourself the seed. If you plant yourself in the land, if the land becomes you, becomes your monstrosity, then the Olympians will be unable to bind and twist and deform it. Men will see, and they will act.

"There is a riddle in the land. You must follow the thread. Understand the land and the gods who live in it. But I, too, do not know precisely what act can bring you to your goal."

Corydon remembered what to ask. "Then," he said, "if you do not know, who can tell me more?"

"I can tell you to go to the city of Troy. Your friends are there.

That, I know, is the beginning of your story. Our story. It is all spun on the distaff, and it shall be Corydon who makes it spin. But I do not know how."

He began to wonder if oracles were of any use at all.

"Yes, you are beyond us now," said the Sphinx. "You know yourself. You know that there can be nothing in excess."

She was smiling slyly. He felt he was being tricked again. "What I want to know," he said evenly, "is why no god or monster can answer a simple question with a simple answer."

"Because that is not the way meaning is made. Meaning is in you. And in me. And we must make it ourselves."

Corydon smiled, too. This time his smile was a sly echo of hers. Had he known it, he would have seen his father's face mirrored in his own.

"Then tell me," he said, with a small bow of freezing courtesy, "tell me how to get to Troy."

"There are many ways—" the Sphinx began, but this time he cut her off, his eyes fiery with tears.

"Yes," he said, "but tell me. Which one. Should. I. Take?" His words were spaced as exactly as tombstones.

A shudder ran over the Sphinx, like a cat's quiver in a cold breeze. Corydon barely noticed, but she was remembering other angry, impatient heroes.

The Sphinx opened her huge golden eyes. Her white body stretched out, like a lion's in the sun. "You are in time," she said, and he caught both the meanings. He was inside time.

A sudden thought struck him. "Are the Olympians in time?"

Her eyes narrowed. Somehow he knew that what he had

asked was tremendously important. "They are above it," she said, "as the dead are beneath it."

He was so surprised that she had offered him an answer that he hardly knew what to think. "Is that true?" he asked.

"It is," she said. "But what is truth? You must find the truth, as you did before. And much that is true will not come to pass." Then, before he could stop her, she had broken into verse, singing in a voice as delicate as a silk thread, "Call no man happy, for the turn of the wings of a dragonfly cannot outmatch the speed of fortune.... See, that man who sits next to you seems to me a god, for your eyes are on him.... The moon is on the clear waters of home, but I sit here on the mountainside, lonely, lonely." Her singing was still clear, but he lost the thread of it, and it felt lost in a labyrinth of feelings for which he had no time and no words.

She was almost asleep, her eyes nearly shut. In her singing voice, she whispered, "Follow the light. To the height. These courts of mystery." She blinked, then added some more half-murmured lines. "The ice gulfs that gird his secret throne, bursting through these dark mountains like the flame of lightning through the tempest." Corydon sighed. Her brief impulse to speak clearly had vanished. Her voice went higher, like a lark soaring. "And from the sky, serene and far / A voice fell, like a falling star, / Excelsior!" She said this last in a high, silly voice.

Corydon knew the oracle was over. He had a kind of answer. He must get to Troy, and he must look to the land, become the Staff, and he must go upward. That night, he lay down by the Sphinx's fountain as it faded. While he lay half sleeping, his eyes dazzled by the vivid desert stars, he drifted into a dream of a thickly ridged peak whose snowy top lightly touched the white clouds that hung low in a vivid blue sky. He seemed to be rushing toward it as if borne on a Gorgon's wings. As he came nearer, the clouds thickened, and heavy lightnings began to gather; the peak turned dark and menacing. The dark clouds swirled lower, and he felt himself caught in their whirl; now he was back in Tashkurgan, seeing the desert engulf him and many others, weighted by hatred and impotent rage. And the mound of sand that had once been Tashkurgan grew and grew, until it became a child's copy of that lonely, forbidding mountain.

Corydon awoke to the thought that the Olympians had made another image of themselves.

It was the chill hour before dawn. He set off to walk to the sea.

S I X

It took four days to reach the city. Corydon had given a boatman a ruby from his stolen booty and had had to promise more on arrival before the man would venture the journey north to Troy. Before they could see the walled city itself, Corydon saw a shoreline covered with the sparkling lights of what looked like fallen stars. They burned hot yellow and vehement orange, and as the boat drew near, the stars spread out, farther, farther, a wide net of flaming stars.

They were the Greek watch fires. There were thousands. As many as the stars. Corydon realized he'd been expecting an army on the scale of the force Perseus had used to attack the Island of Monsters. But he was now facing an army a hundred times larger. The watch fires were fierce and unblinking.

Corydon could see black ships looking like great cormorants that wait with folded wings for an unwary fish to jump. Men moved about their decks, their armor bright and their javelins brighter still. The watch fires lit up the many tents on shore; a tent city had grown on the flat shingle outside the walled city of Troy.

The boatman insisted they land a half mile from the edge of the camp, fearing that any closer would bring death to him and his passenger. However, when he saw the forbidding rows of guards around the edge of the camp, he became warier still. Corydon handed him a ruby and sprang over the side of the boat and splashed to shore. The man tacked hastily to get away as quickly as possible.

Now to get into Troy itself. But how? It was clear that the Greeks couldn't get in. Corydon slipped past watch fire after watch fire, noticing how dejected everyone seemed. He heard fragments of talk: "The landing was all very well and good, but now they've got us pinned down." "It's the generals. They don't seem to know what they're doing." "They know, all right. They take all the gold and all the girls and leave us with nothing but blood and scars to show for being here." At another fire, he caught at different words: "What's it about, anyway? Nothing to do with us." "They say there'll be a big push tomorrow. Some new leader and a new army. Called the antmen. Brought over here specially." The others laughed at that. "Antmen?" said one. "What use will ant-sized men be against that?" He gestured at the massive wall that circled Troy. "No, but they say the greatest of all heroes . . ."

Corydon heard no more. He slid along until he was out of range of the firelight. He could sense the men's anger and misery hanging in the air, and he knew enough of armies not to want to be caught by men so unhappy.

Now the city wall towered above him. Corydon crept cautiously along it, noticing the orange fires streaming out from cressets that lined its top. Even in Atlantis he had not seen a wall so high, so thick. The west wind blew torch smoke wildly before it, and his heart lifted. The Trojans were holding out, which meant his friends were still safe inside—or so the Sphinx had said. He hoped for Sthenno, for Euryale, for the Minotaur. The last monsters. And maybe even Gorgos?

And the real Snake-Girl . . . Just as he thought of her, his keen ear caught the soft slither of a snake belly on stones, captured a faint hiss. He looked down, and a slender red and gold snake slid into view in a sudden flare of torchlight. Corydon could remember the Snake-Girl making a snake exactly like this during the battle against Perseus.

The snake did not slither past, as he expected. Instead, to Corydon's amazement, it reared up abruptly, its eyes fathomlessly black. Its tongue flickered. Corydon could see it was trying to speak. There was a kind of striving in its face. Finally it gasped, "LLLlllaaaammmiiiiaaaa."

Lamia! Was she here? And not in the desert? Was this a mirage? The snake fell to the pebbly sand and started back from whence it came. It paused to look behind it, and Corydon, understanding, followed it as silently as he could. The snake slid straight toward a tent, silk-sided and more splendid than most, scarfed with the red pennants of a hero or leader. The snake slipped under the tent flap. Corydon took a deep breath, then very slowly lifted a corner of the flap. Bending double, he could see into the tent.

Lying on a pile of silken cushions was the Snake-Girl, her serpent body gloriously gold and peacock green, her glossy black hair shining bluish in the lamplight. Corydon was amazed, delighted, and strangely shy all at once. Then he realized why she was lying so still. She had been bound, was tied to the central tent pole. Her eyes widened when she saw him, and then she jerked her head to the other side of the tent. Corydon saw that she was not alone, and then he heard the snoring. A big black-bearded man was asleep, a wine jar beside him. He looked like a villager after a festival, but his clothes were rich, and Corydon could see that he was no peasant. His hand was on his sword hilt. Corydon crept forward silently and swiftly untied the ropes holding Lamia.

The Snake-Girl rubbed her chafed wrists and then very softly slithered over to the sleeping man. She spat gently into his eyes. Corydon saw his face begin to change: his mouth opened in a yell, he lifted his fists to his face like a furious baby; his eyes opened, but they were—clearly—blind. The man's cries were rousing the camp; servants came running. Corydon caught the Snake-Girl's hand; they ran silently into the friendly dark against the walls.

An unwise decision. The Trojans on watch had heard the yells, too, and thought an attack was in progress. With shouts of rage, they began hurling arrows and javelins into the darkness. Corydon and the Snake-Girl swung back toward the Greeks, but now they, too, were arming, and the air was rent by the clash of bronze weapons, the twang of bows. They wove their way around men brandishing swords, spears; one warrior cuffed Corydon sharply, ordering him out of the way. The Snake-Girl was breathless, and terrified that her shimmering scales would show up all too clearly in the firelight.

They plunged down the beach, felt cool water splash their bodies. Without a word, both sank deeper into its embrace. At least they were safe for the moment. . . .

Just as Corydon thought this, something told him to look behind him.

In the cold pink shell-light of morning, Corydon could see a boat, swift as a seabird, pure white, skimming the water as if drawn by dolphins. In the prow stood a tall man, his scarlet cloak whipping in the sea wind. He wore no helmet, and Corydon could see no armor, but something told him this was the hero the soldiers had spoken of, the leader of the antmen. . . . The boat drew ever nearer. And as the man scanned the water with a cold, sweeping gaze, calm and exultant, Corydon saw his face clearly.

It was Akhilleus. The man with the silver eyes.

Corydon ducked so that only his eyes were still above the waterline. A faint swirl of water told him that the Snake-Girl had followed suit.

But it was no use. Akhilleus had seen him.

His words flashed through Corydon's mind. "If we ever meet again . . ."

The boat swept toward them. With a crack like lightning, Akhilleus drew his sword. It glinted in the dawn light. His eyes never left Corydon's.

He raised the sword high for a killing stroke. Corydon dived desperately. As he did so, he felt the Snake-Girl's body slide around him, fling herself in front of him. He surfaced, caught her around the waist, tried to pull her out of the way. While they struggled, the boat reached them. The sword flashed down like a diving fish. Corydon pushed the Snake-Girl clumsily out of the way, but she was a dead weight, her eyes fixed, her head flung back, inviting death. The sword had caught her arm; bright blood flooded into the water. Akhilleus's boat sped on and ground to a halt on the shore with a terrific crash. He leapt out, his silver eyes searching the water.

In a last effort, Corydon flung himself under the surface again, dragging the Snake-Girl with him. Her serpent tail thrashed like a mermaid's, and they were engulfed in her blood, making them an obvious target. He knew he couldn't hold his breath for long; desperately he swam for the deeper water and came up hard against a rock he hadn't noticed because it was entirely submerged. Feeling in the gloom with his hand, Corydon realized there was a small sea cave that might afford shelter, if his breath held out.

He flung himself into it, dragging the Snake-Girl, her body heavy and reluctant. And then his tortured lungs were granted air. . . . The Snake-Girl, too, took a gasping breath, and both almost cried with relief. The cave was larger than its opening suggested. He swam on, in darkness, and came to a place where faint dawn light was visible. . . . There was a little beach. . . .

But now that they were beached, and his lungs were no longer sending black and red warnings to his brain, Corydon noticed again how badly hurt she was. He tore off his cloak and ripped it into strips, tying one tightly above the orange-purple wound from which blood still poured. She was white, whiter than snow, and her black hair was like the wing of a bird of death.

"Lamia," he said, using the true name, which for him had become poisoned by the touch of the eidolon.

"I want to die," she said, answering his question. "I want to . . . Corydon . . . that man holding me prisoner, Neoptolemos . . . I cannot go on living. After what he did . . . I cannot bear it. I am for the dark, Corydon. My bright day is done."

Corydon did not answer her. He flung his arms around her. Her body felt small and fragile, like the birds she doted on.

He wasn't sure what she was trying to tell him, and so he didn't know a good answer, but finally he said, slowly, "I love you." He knew the words were true, and he also knew he needed her to stay. One small monster, from the wrack . . . He couldn't lose her twice. . . .

Her bleeding had slowed. Now her body curled toward him. She began weeping softly, and her tears ran down his arm.

"Corydon," she said, "you cannot know. And I cannot say."

"I don't need to know," he said. "I know I love you. You are a monster, and you are my friend. I am here to defeat the Olympians."

She laughed shakily. "You haven't begun very well," she said. It was a tease, but her voice was growing fainter. Corydon knew he needed help, needed it desperately.

And as he thought this, the water at the edge of the sea began to heave unexpectedly. Out of it came the oddest head Corydon had ever seen, in a lifetime of meeting monsters. It was huge and brown, with scales, and with a full row of gills along the ridgy neck. One eye was blue, the other brown, and both were staring. Sharp teeth were visible around the tight frog mouth.

"Help us!" Corydon cried.

The creature's mouth opened, and the terrible head nodded. Then it disappeared in a splash and ripple. *That was useful,* Corydon thought. Blood seeped from the Snake-Girl's arm.

Then the sea began to boil again. The frog-mouthed creature was back. With him was a man so ancient that his skin hung in folds, long and dragging on the ground. His arms were deflated sacs of skin, his beard a bushel of seaweed.

He looked like Proteus, the ancient boatman, and so Corydon was uncertain. Proteus had not been enormously helpful the last time they had met in Atlantis.

"No," said the Old Man. "I am not Proteus. I am Oceanus, his full brother. The sea has its chthonic past, as the land does. I am the shepherd of the sea, as your father is of the land. I and my brother are the second and third oldest of the children of Gaia and Ouranos. In order there is Kronos, firstborn and killer of our father; then I; then Proteus; then Rhea, Kronos's wife; then . . ."

The Old Man continued to talk about his genealogy. The Snake-Girl's blood fell on Corydon's hand, and he wondered if Oceanus was going to go on talking while she died before his eyes. It might be fatal to interrupt him, though. The Old Man was a Titan, and the earth powers didn't like to be interrupted. . . . He chewed his lip in an agony of impatience. Finally the Old Man mumbled his way to silence.

Corydon burst out, "Please help her." A sob caught at his voice; he swallowed, ashamed. The Old Man looked at the Snake-Girl for the first time. Her eyes had closed and her breathing was ragged. Her lips were white.

"She wanders between the worlds," he said in his high old voice. "She is lost between. Driven there by Neoptolemos. This wound comes from his father's sword, but the deeper wound is within. . . ."

Corydon was taken aback. How could Akhilleus, the shimmering hero, be the father of Neoptolemos, the bearded snorer he had seen in the tent? Next moment he was regretting asking anything like a genealogical question, even in what was normally the privacy of his mind. It launched the Old Man on another long ramble.

"Begot him when he was barely out of diapers, with Deidamia, who was the daughter of the king of Skyros, Lykomedes. Now there was a great king. . . ." He rattled on.

Corydon finally pointed to the Snake-Girl. "Heal her," he said. "Please. Then I shall hear all your tales."

The Old Man held out a stick as wizened and shaky-looking as he was. He touched its end to the Snake-Girl's forehead.

Her eyes opened. Her wound did not close, but it ceased to bleed profusely.

"I cannot heal her mind and heart," said the Old Man sadly. The frog-mouthed creature clambered unexpectedly out of the water, touched Lamia with the tip of a webbed finger, and gave a croak of sad agreement.

Lamia sat still, silent. Two more tears trickled slowly from her wide eyes. Corydon took her hand. Then they settled back while the Old Man told them tales, bewildering tales of men called Lysias and Lykabettos and Lysimakhos and Lysandros. Tales in which human names and identities flowed into each other like the waves.

It was tiring and boring, but it was also a song, and Corydon could see it was a rich one; he imagined kings and heroes listening to it, listening for their own names. As he thought this, he heard *his* own, "Corydon Panfoot, son of Pan, son of the goddess . . ." The Old Man clapped a hand to his mouth. Without another word, he flung himself onto his frog-mouthed creature and leapt into the waves with him.

"What?" said Corydon. "Son of a *goddess* . . . ? What could he mean?"

"What does it matter?" said the Snake-Girl tiredly. "You are who you are. Whoever your mother is. And it's Medusa who is your true mother. Not in the way she is Gorgos's mother. But you and she belong together. In your heart, she is your mother."

She had changed, Corydon saw. The old Snake-Girl would have been too shy to say all that. And now an awkward silence fell. Corydon seemed to hear the words "I love you" ringing around the cave like a harsh bell.

"I love you, too," said the Snake-Girl. She curled a vinelike tendril of snake tail around his wrist. The touch felt light, like a plant's caress, and cool even to his goosefleshed skin. "But I am no use to anyone anymore. I have nothing left to give you, Corydon."

He bent hesitantly toward the caress of her tail. "Well," he said stoutly, trying to ignore his own crushing shyness, "you will always be my friend. And I think that's useful. What could be more useful than a friend?"

She gave a very soft hiss. Two sea snakes slid out from under her glossy black hair and cavorted in the small waves. He decided to take this as a good sign. "Come on," he said, taking refuge in sturdy common sense. "We have to find the others, warn them that Akhilleus is here."

SEVEN

Corydon and Lamia broke the surface of the water with gasps, in the lee of a big Greek pentekonter. Luckily, no one on the warship noticed them, and looking at the shore, Corydon could see why. A Trojan sortie was attacking the Greek camp. A contingent of Sphinxes had launched itself from the high walls of Troy, and the Greeks stood gazing at them, their eyes whirling with hypnotic Sphinx-gold. Corydon caught a flash of bronze wings and spotted Sthenno and Euryale harrying the fleeing Greeks from the air. His heart soared in pure relief. They lived? Then he saw the familiar dark shape of the Minotaur on the top of a wall, directing the Trojans as they hurled flaming shafts down into the rear of the Greek army. He felt as if his heart might explode with joy.

From Troy's open gates came a flood of chariots. Corydon saw their wheels were scythed to slice off the arms and legs of warriors who dared come close. As they drove into the fleeing Greek cavalry, there was a horrible scream from a horse, and Corydon saw blood spurt up like grain flying under the thresher's flail. Suddenly he felt sick.

He looked up at the sky again. As he watched, Sthenno changed direction toward him. He could hear the clash of her feathers. Her birdlike voice rose in a thin scream. And she shot down from the sky, dropping like a stooping falcon.

"Mormo!" Without a pause, she swept Corydon and the Snake-Girl up in her claws and shot up into the heavens.

From their zenith, the battlefield was no longer frightening. It was a child's toy world, its small, racing figures comically frenzied, neither sad nor important.

Perhaps, thought Corydon, this was how the world looked to the Olympians.

The thought hit him as hard as a blow. *Of course.*

His own father was an earth god; he saw the world from where men stood. But All-Father Zeus (mentally, Corydon spat the name out) was lifted above all fray. He looked *down* on men, and so he despised them.

Sthenno banked sharply toward a second flashing bronze figure. Euryale. But was it really her? She seemed thinner and, oddly, less warlike. He could see the artist in her sweeping flight rather than the huntress. But when she saw the two figures clutched in Sthenno's claws, she gave a harsh ringing-bronze cry of welcome, and Corydon knew it was her.

They were over Troy now, the massive thickness of the ribbed walls behind them. It was a towery city, like Atlantis had been, and it was branchy between its towers, textured with thick leaves and thrusting twigs. The roofs were all flat terra-cotta tiles, red and ridged. The houses were white, rambling. It was like a brighter, leafier Atlantis.

Looking down, Corydon could see green courtyards where fountains burbled in the sunlight; they flew above a children's playground, and the clear voices rose to his ears like birdsong. It was a dusty city, too, and in its wide marketplace men sold silks and figs still, despite the war, and carpets and pots and scented trifles.

He thought of Atlantis, and of Tashkurgan, and he wished he were an Olympian so that he need not give his heart to things he was powerless to save. Not again. For the air was still ringing with the clang of battle. Behind the thick walls, men were disemboweling each other. He was glad he could no longer see them.

They swooped down a narrow, twisting side street, dusty and hot-looking, and then they lurched under a low archway. Corydon landed hard, and Sthenno's talons caught him, set him right. Then he was enfolded in the prickle of her great wings. With a clatter, Euryale landed, too, and he felt her talons rake lovingly through his hair. She extended her other talon to the Snake-Girl, and as she did so, Corydon saw that it was dyed red.

He had expected questions, explanations. But perhaps his year in the desert was like a long evening to the Gorgons, for they spoke to him as if he had been gone only for that long. Euryale noticed him looking at her claw.

"Not blood," she said. "I was mixing paint when the muster horn called us to defend the city. Come inside, and I'll show you." She led the way into the house. Inside, it was cool, and the stone gave off a soft dampness that reminded Corydon of their cave on the Island of Monsters. Sthenno bustled about, scrabbling for food for them, and produced a dryish hunk of bread and a few figs. Corydon looked surprised, and the Snake-Girl politely refused all of it. More quickly than he himself, she had seen that the city was running short of provisions. But Euryale gave her a piece of the bread.

"Yes, we are on short rations," said Euryale. "When we can, Sthenno and I hunt on the hills, and so do the Sphinxes, though it doesn't come very naturally to them. But the slopes are near exhausted. The city has eaten its own land bare. And now the Greeks have stopped the trade ships—"

"But the Minotaur has a plan," said Sthenno. "He has invented a flying machine, and if it works, the Trojans may be able to range farther. Euryale and I cannot be spared from the battle for a long journey, you see." Her voice was falsely bright, and Corydon could tell that she didn't altogether believe her own words. It was obvious that no flying device could feed a city that had once been nourished by trade fleets from all over the Mediterranean.

He nibbled his fig quietly. Euryale drew him aside. She was golden-eyed with curiosity. "How?" she said, pointing to the Snake-Girl, who sat pushing a piece of bread from side to side. "Is she real this time?"

Corydon suddenly realized with a cool shock that he didn't know. This could be another eidolon. . . .

No. "I know she's flesh," he said. "She was wounded. Bled. And Oceanus healed her. He would have known if she were an eidolon."

"Where has she been?"

The Snake-Girl looked up. "Ask me," she said without heat. "I hear you. I hear as acutely as a snake. I was sold into slavery. From Hephaistos's island. I was first the slave of Dionysos himself. He fed me with apples and poems and pomegranates from the Lady's tree of death and dreams, until I was sick with his pretense of love, with his prison. I spat him up, and he hated me. So he sold me to a new master."

Her eyes flared wide, like the eyes of a hunting cobra. Her voice went low, its hiss hard as baked desert. "Neoptolemos. He consumed me and delighted in my pain. I had time only to blind him, but I would rejoice to see one of my pets sink its venomous fangs into his flesh. Perhaps it is worth living to see that day." For a second, her eyes closed. She smiled, drugged by the distillation of imagined revenge.

Corydon found his eyes full of tears. One precious monster . . . but no longer the person she had been . . . Where had her gentleness gone? More than the Nemean lions had been lost. More than Atlantis. Why should they survive if it was only to become as cruel as those who sought their ruin?

But he said nothing. Perhaps the others, looking at his gaunt, tanned face, his sun-blasted hair, his hard eyes, felt the same ash on their own tongues.

Perhaps he was a stranger as well. And looking at Sthenno and Euryale, he saw that they, too, were not the same. They were like great bronze statues; their gleam had a comforting timelessness. But Euryale was far thinner, and Sthenno had a worn quality, as if the metal that made her was wearing thin.

He had imagined that their metal could never change or be destroyed. That it was forever, like the rocks of the island.

But it was written on their faces that this was not so.

His heart suddenly accepted it all. They were still his friends, even if they were not the same. Even if he was different, too.

"How goes the war?" he asked.

Sthenno looked at him hard. "For now, mormo, we can say we still live," she said. "We have so many advantages." Her voice was drier than desert sands.

"We do have the walls," said Euryale eagerly. "Do you know how they were built?"

Corydon and the Snake-Girl looked polite. Sthenno clattered over to a small coffer and began rummaging for a parchment. Not everything had changed, clearly. "Not now," she said absently. "I shall not tell you now. It is a long, heavy tale. But, mormo, there are so many on our side. The Sphinxes. The Selene Amazons are here in force, led by their queen, Penthesilea. We have the Minotaur. And his many devices. And then there are the daimons. I have been using my magic. Some of the gods themselves fight on our side. And yet—we only suffice. Only barely. Every day we go weary from the field. The Greeks—it is as if an inner fire drives them forward. . . . Not desire of gold. Not ambition. Something stronger."

Corydon's heart felt like a heavy, cold lump. He looked at this new, tired Sthenno and fought to make his face smile into hers. He squared his shoulders and knew he must find out more to help save the city. "What are daimons?" he asked warily.

"The Airish Ones," said Euryale.

"The People of the Stars, the asterions," said Sthenno. "They have told me much I did not know about some of the darker stars. Such as yours," she said to Lamia.

"I have a star?" asked the Snake-Girl in confusion.

"Yes," said Sthenno. "All living beings have a star. It can tell their fate."

Corydon began to close his ears to the gloomy prophecy he could see was about to be flung at his head. "What use are they?"

"Daimons do not really have a use in war, but they can sometimes predict the future," said Sthenno. "The Trojans have a priest called Kalkhas, and his priestesses are visionary, too, and they say one has ensnared Apollo in love so that he fights for us. They all brew a mighty magic against the Greeks. . . ."

Hastily, almost at random, he said, "What plans are there to break the siege?"

"Break the siege? It is all we can do to keep them at bay," said Euryale.

"And Gorgos? Is he here as well?" Corydon couldn't imagine Medusa's son sitting patiently around, waiting for Sthenno to brew up a spell.

"He has left the city to seek Philoktetes." Euryale's voice was a mixture of eagerness and fear.

Corydon didn't understand either. He felt shy and stupid in the face of the deep wells of knowledge of the immortals.

"Philoktetes has the bow of Herakles himself," said Sthenno. Corydon could hear the complex shudder in her voice as she said the name of the monsters' greatest foe. "It bears arrows of"—her voice sank to a whisper—"Hydra venom. . . ." Everyone was silent for a moment, thinking of the death of their own Hydra friend Lady Nagaina.

"We do not do well to make use of a weapon so ill-gotten," said the Snake-Girl. Corydon noticed how much braver she sounded.

"But," said Sthenno, and her voice rose eagerly, "there is a prophecy—"

Corydon and the Snake-Girl both groaned. Euryale gave a metallic sigh. "Not another prophecy, Sister," said Euryale firmly. Sthenno's protests were interrupted by the blaring of the trumpet.

"The Greeks are trying another attack," said Sthenno. "They press closer and closer. Usually we can count on a few hours at least between attacks."

Akhilleus! Corydon had to warn them. It must be he who was behind this attack. He saw in memory those silver eyes. He felt certain Akhilleus was a match for Euryale and Sthenno as well, and his heart also knew that Akhilleus was clever enough to want to knock them out of the battle. . . .

"Beware," said the Snake-Girl abruptly. "The Greeks have been reinforced. Akhilleus is here." Her voice was colder than her snaky skin. Sthenno stopped in her tracks. She folded her wings, despite a second furious blast from the trumpet. She bent down and took the Snake-Girl's small face in her claws. "I can hear that you have been hurt," she said gently. "I do not know this Akhilleus. But there is a black night in your eyes."

"He is . . . a hero like a monster." Corydon spoke hesitantly. "Like Perseus wanted to be. Only he actually is. Real, I mean. As we are. Not a sham. See?" His tongue seemed to rebel, as if he didn't want to conjure Akhilleus up—or as if he didn't want to give the silver-eyed man away. Which was it? He shook his head.

Sthenno looked interested, but Corydon could see that he hadn't frightened her enough. Her attention was still focused on Lamia. Euryale was frowning at the Snake-Girl, too. "You seem different," she said. "And I don't mean what you just said about Neoptolemos. There is something else. What is it?"

The Snake-Girl didn't shrink or duck her head as she once

would have with so many eyes upon her. She stared back, her black eyes fathomless. The trumpet sounded a third time.

"Yes," she said evenly, with a faint hiss in her voice. "I am changed. I am with child. A child I do not want to bear. It is the child of Neoptolemos. I shall kill it when I can."

Corydon saw a small flare of madness in the deeps of her eyes. His heart turned over with horror and sadness for what she'd endured.

He flung his arms around her. "Lamia," he said. She seemed passive in his arms, and she didn't hug him back. She looked at him, and her face was like cool marble.

"Corydon," said Sthenno, "we must go."

"Yes, I shall come, too," said Corydon, awkwardly releasing the Snake-Girl and then fumbling for his slingshot. He did not welcome war. But he could not let Sthenno and Euryale face Akhilleus alone. And perhaps he might find the Minotaur on the walls.

EIGHT

THEY ALL RAN OUT INTO THE STREETS, JOSTLING WITH a kind of swarm of men and women shrugging on corselets, checking swords, grasping spears. Corydon squirmed between two immense fighters, following Sthenno and Euryale as they cleaved a path through the throng. Many stopped and saluted them; it was obvious that they had proved their value to the city in battle.

They approached an immense, blue-glazed building that had to be the king's palace. From its great cedar gate issued a troop of armed men, and behind them the captains rode in gilded chariots drawn by prancing horses. It was clear that they intended to send out a sortie, to risk opening a sally port in the walls to allow men onto the plain.

An ominous noise began to sound in the distance. It was the terrible, even drumbeat of spears on shields. Corydon had heard it before, but this thunder was far louder. There must be hundreds of them—perhaps thousands. The beat went on, inexorable. It said,

"We are trained men. We will not break in a charge. We will hold forever, at our lord's command."

The sound filled Corydon's heart with fear, but a grim young captain riding in a chariot galloped up to them. His hair and beard were black, his eyes were wilder than wolves, and his teeth split his face in a grin of joy. He was already half-mad with battle before the fighting had even begun. He wore a tall helmet crested with gold and blue feathers; Corydon could see he was a leader, brave and reckless. He waved an arm at the Gorgons.

"Fly! We prepare a sortie. I call on you to break their line. If you fly in their faces, they cannot hold. No man can!" He clapped Euryale on the shoulder, reaching up to do it even from his chariot platform.

Corydon knew it would be a waste of time to speak; this young warrior was in no mood for argument and was already moving off. He also knew that warfare was all about breaking the other's shieldline; once the overlapping fence of hard shields that cradled soft human flesh fell to pieces, the enemy could be picked off easily. But he listened to the ferocious regularity of the beat, and he felt sure the men making that sound would not be broken.

"Take me!" Corydon called to Sthenno. Too late. In a bronze flash, the Gorgons had sprung into the air. The press in the streets had lessened, but Corydon could not see the tall man anymore either. He decided to make for the top of the wall, where he could observe and also perhaps use his slingshot. He began to run toward the tall wall, sure he would find stairs to the top somewhere.

At last he saw the stairs, and leading a phalanx of archers up them was a figure whom Corydon knew well.

"Sikandar!" he called.

Sikandar turned around. "Who called me?" The crowd fell silent.

Corydon gulped. "It is I, old friend," he shouted. Then he added, carefully, "Corydon," since Sikandar was still looking bewildered.

Sikandar gasped, then shouldered his own troops aside and quickly embraced Corydon. "Old friend! Lord!" he exclaimed. "Why are you here?"

"I have had enough of the gods tormenting my friends. I am here and I will save Troy. I do not know how yet. But I will thwart the Olympians somehow." As he said it, he realized that he sounded as silly as Gorgos—boastful, wild. And yet he had come to these words through a desert of despair. That made them true.

There was a strange ringing silence, in which even the beat of the Greeks seemed muffled. Sikandar heard the iron in his friend's voice, and he felt it in his heart like a spear. "What has happened to you, old friend?" he asked softly.

"The last straw," said Corydon. "Only a family of dead lions. But it is the last unjust death the Olympians and their followers will cause without my opposition." Springing to the walls, he shouted to the sky, "All-Father Zeus! You and I are enemies, and I will destroy you and all you love if you destroy this city!" He heard a very faint, nearly inaudible rumble. Thunder? Then all the Trojans around him broke into cheers. The louder thunder of the Greek shieldmen grew, as if in response.

And Corydon looked down and saw the menace pitted against Troy.

There were uncountable numbers of them, arrayed with

precision: each upright, each armored, each the same distance from the other. Their helmets gleamed deeply; the crests stood up black and white. Each wore a bronze corselet, each carried a short stabbing spear, and swords glinted at their sides. On their shields were emblazoned a most ironic portrait—a small, creeping black ant. And they were antlike themselves, marching to the beat of their drums with ant precision. But Corydon had seen how a nest of ants could strip a sheep to the bone in a day.

And then he saw who rode ahead of them.

He was alone, driving his own chariot, as if he despised having a driver as soft. Armored like the moon in silver, his helmet bitter with brilliance like the stars, his spears like sea light. A white light seemed to radiate from him. He stood and raked the battlefield with his silver eyes. Corydon saw the exact moment when he picked out the sally port opening. His eyes lit and he gave a sharp call: "Chelonia!"

The machine-like forces following him responded with terrifying swiftness. The whole formation swung around like an opening door, then coiled on itself, forming several small mounds. As one, they lofted their spears, and somehow each group lifted shields, too, to form a tight overlapping wall, like the shelly outer casing on a great reptile. Then Corydon realized that Akhilleus had shouted "tortoise" and that the men were obeying. Now they were equally impregnable. The multitude of ants had become seven vast, impregnable reptile creatures, lumbering toward Troy. Any attack would beat in vain against their heavy armor.

Corydon had expected the great man-tortoises to stop, but somehow the ants who made them kept moving toward the walls—slower than before, it was true, but keeping up a steady pace, exactly like ants carrying grains—staggering but persevering.

Then he saw the bright flash of Sthenno's and Euryale's wings in the sky. They had banked around to get themselves in line with the sun, increasing the surprise of their attack. They each swooped down upon one of the lumbering, prickly tortoises. The men hadn't noticed the menace, and Corydon saw Sthenno pounce, but she was rebuffed by the heavy shield wall, and Euryale fared no better with her tortoise.

The two Gorgons battered hopelessly against two of the armor-plated tortoises; they managed to slow progress and to kill a few men, but the other five tortoises crept inexorably on, waiting for the sortie to burst through the sally port.

It was evident that Akhilleus had devised the tortoises to defend against the Gorgons. And it was also obvious that it was working. Akhilleus came forward in his swift chariot and sent up a rain of spears at Sthenno; she was forced to dodge to and fro in the air as spears struck and loosened her bronze feathers. Corydon's heart was in his mouth, and he felt a black rage.

He lifted his slingshot. Akhilleus was very nearly under the walls now, and Corydon heard the hard twang of Sikandar's bow beside him, as he aimed arrow after arrow at the hero. But none found a secure mark. Corydon took aim, and a stone shot from his sling, straight at Akhilleus's eye.

His heart sang as he watched the stone's flight, curved, perfect. . . . It hit—and as it did, it crumbled into stony powder. Akhilleus looked up, his face showing the mild annoyance caused by a fly buzzing about one's head. His uninjured eyes met

Corydon's, and he smiled, a fierce battle smile. Then he turned back to the battle. Clearly he was under the protection of some god.

Euryale, infuriated, was still picking at a tortoise of men, darting to and fro, but they were not afraid of her. They kept their shields high, knowing she could not penetrate. She tried prizing the shields apart, using her strength, but the men had developed a strategy for that too; when her claw was inside the shields, they slammed their shields together. Bronze met bronze with a harsh scream of tormented metal. Their bronze was just as strong as hers. Her claw was bent and buckled in the collision, and she was forced to withdraw, nursing it.

Corydon's eye was caught by a small troop, obviously Greek, moving purposefully toward the walls. They were trying to avoid attracting attention; they were lightly armed, the poorest and weakest troops, peltasts with slingshots and archers. Leading them was a man hard to notice, harder to remember, a man with a patient, lined, ordinary face. Something about his plainness was oddly restful after one had gazed at glorious Akhilleus. Corydon looked at the man's solid comfortingness and thought he, too, had a little monster in him; he recalled the Minotaur, dark and furred and full of plans.

This man had a plan now, Corydon was sure. He was busy not being noticed, while the tortoises took up all the attention. A shepherd's eyes were useful in battle. Corydon decided to watch this seemingly ordinary man.

There was a grinding noise as the sally port opened to allow the Trojan sortie out. It was so narrow that only two fighters at a time could emerge.

At the front were the captain Corydon had noticed and a woman who looked familiar; her long silver hair was tightly braided, she wore a black pelt around her shoulders, and at her side paced a panther and a leopard, clearly battle cats; they lifted their heads at the smell of blood. The woman was plainly related to the Selene Amazons he had known in Atlantis. He turned to Sikandar, who was still raining arrows down on the Greek tortoises; he was such a good archer that he'd actually managed to find a few gaps in their defenses.

"Who is that man?" he asked.

"My older brother, Hektor," said Sikandar, his hands still busy fitting his bow with a fresh arrow. "He's bossy, but he's brave. In battle, he goes completely mad and screams at the enemy at a full charge." Corydon looked at Akhilleus and could see that this tactic was likely to lead only to death. "The other one is Penthesilea, the queen of the Amazons—they're our greatest allies. She's a warrior, but they also have witches and magewomen—you'll see in a minute."

"Are they Selene Amazons?"

"They worship the moon, if that's what you mean, but all its phases—the young goddess, the full moon, and"—his voice dropped to a whisper—"the dark moon. We do not like to speak her name." Corydon didn't like to speak it either because he knew only too much about Hecate, goddess of night and death. "We may need their powers," said Sikandar, then saw one of his arrows strike down an antman whose shield had slumped a fraction.

Corydon clapped him on the shoulder, then turned to him. "Sikandar," he said, "Atlantis fell by using the powers of the dark moon. You must not."

Sikandar shrugged. "It will not be my decision," he said. "And it would be worse to be overrun by men like that."

Corydon knew it would *not* be worse. But he also knew that it was he who must find a way of defeating the Olympians. As he looked at the masses of soldiers spread on the plain, he felt sure he could almost see the shadowy forms of the gods among them. There was Athene, her owl heavy on her shoulder, whispering to one of the heroes. He saw that the Olympians were *inside* men as well as out, that they were ambition and pride and lust for gold and women and a belief that anything you wanted was yours by right—Zeus's rule.

The sortie party was still slowly emerging from the sally port. They were forming up, ranks of Trojans and Amazons, and an array of fierce leopards and panthers. Nine Sphinxes flew from over the walls to join the attack group. As they all readied themselves, Corydon saw the tortoises changing to an attacking formation: bristling spears sprang out all over them, and the lumbering reptiles were suddenly sinuous silver snakes of men with fierce fangs.

Akhilleus was still at the fore, and Corydon saw his teeth flash in a smile, the happy smile of a farmer who is bringing in a good harvest. His men turned, and he gave a high cry. They ran forward suddenly with ferocious speed.

Elsewhere, Greeks were battering the gates, assaulting the walls of Troy with ladders. Almost every ladder that hit the wall was either too short or slithered from the brick. Defenders dropped buckets of burning sand on any Greeks who ventured up; it was work for the Trojan women and children not trained to arms, and they seemed to relish it. But Akhilleus was blind to all that. He saw only the sortie party, ripe for his sickle.

But then something happened to disrupt his plans. Corydon saw, along the inside of the wall to his right, a party of Trojans straining to lift some kind of war machine, a great ballista that could fire arrows at the attackers from above like a deadly rain. Accompanying it was the familiar furry figure of the Minotaur. Corydon gave a cry, but the great beast didn't hear him above the roaring of battle.

With the Minotaur were a small man in heavy, dark robes and a tiny girl. The man carried a brazier and lit it. Fierce black flames rose, piercing the hazy blue sky, and down the smoky spiral a god began to descend. Corydon was sure it was a god. It bore a man's head with thick curls and the body of a serpent, long and sinuous and golden.

"Come, Loxias!" cried the man. The girl held out her arms, and the snake god slid into them. Then he breathed on the bundle of arrows she held. Instantly, every arrow turned black as night. The arrows themselves seemed to tremble, as if terrified of what they had become. She and the Minotaur began loading them into the ballista. Then, at a signal, the ballista fired, and arrows flew over the wall and straight at a rushing platoon of Greeks trying to reach the walls with their ladder.

The sky was almost darkened by the arrows' flight. The men looked up, flung their shields over their heads. But these arrows seemed intelligent: like an angry swarm of wasps, they sought the joints in armor, swung and twisted, until each had stung a man. Then the arrows fell to the sparse shore grass, and where they landed, they dissolved into black puddles, then disappeared, leaving only a circle of burned grass to show where each had been.

At first, the men seemed unharmed. They reacted as if stung by insects, then smiled to find themselves still alive. They re-formed and began moving toward the walls once more. But it quickly became clear that something was wrong. Corydon could see that they were staggering, apparently weak. "Is it poison?" he asked.

"Of a kind," said Sikandar, his voice hard. "It is plague." As he spoke, Corydon saw that the air around the men was thickening into a black, buzzing dark. A stench drifted toward him on the wind. The stricken Greeks dropped to their knees; Corydon could see one turn a white face to the sky and stretch out his hands, as if asking the gods how they could do this to him. On the walls, the snake god gave a rustling sigh, like dry scales rubbing dust. The man apparently heard it somehow, over the din of battle. His face slumped into pain and despair. He slid to the ground, lying full length, and his eyes emptied of life as they turned to the indifferent heavens. Along the walls, Trojans were cheering

The sound made Corydon sick. He saw the people of Troy bend to pay homage to the god Loxias, and his heart was dead. Then something astonishing happened. Where Loxias had been, a shape reared up, tall and terrible. It was not a serpent but a hero shape, slender and strong and golden like sunlight. It was manifestly a god, and in his hand was a black bow, the arrows of pestilence clattering at his back. He held, too, a black lyre. The strings shook and gave out a vast discord as the god leapt to the slopes beyond the city, his feet making no sound but his terrible arrows booming on his back.

As the god abandoned the city, Corydon noticed the only one who had not bowed to his serpent form. The Minotaur sat with his great furred head on his knees, his arms shielding his face. Corydon's heart went out to his friend. He knew the Minotaur was deeply ashamed of helping a god even for a moment. He hurried to the great beast's side as the people around him began to straighten up, as cries of pain came faintly from the Greeks below the walls. He put a shy hand on the furry shoulder. The Minotaur looked up, and Corydon saw that his huge black eyes were dimmed with tears, which clung starlike to his long lashes.

"Corydon, old friend. It is not simple now," he said, his warm, dark voice as comforting as Corydon remembered. "The Trojans are not perfect, but they are better than their foes. And they deserve better than to be first robbed and then butchered. Even if they keep making mistakes. But though I know this," he said—and Corydon could hear a faint, low sob in his rich voice—"though I know this, I hate what I know. I want them to be perfect. So my hands will be clean. Clean of blood." They looked at each other with wordless sympathy. To Corydon it seemed as if the Minotaur and he had come via different roads to the same desolate destination. At least now neither was alone there. They clasped hands.

"I want only to destroy the Olympians," Corydon was saying, when a movement on the plain below caught his eye. The antmen were staggering, their skin growing black with death. Akhilleus was trying to rally them, and Corydon could see his grief for them in his desperate movements. But the other little group of men, under their seemingly ordinary leader, was untouched. They were creeping along, so close to the walls that arrows could not reach them. They crept on silent feet, ignoring the plague victims as sternly as if blind and deaf. Their moving glitter of eyes was all fixed on the sally port.

Where was Hektor? Corydon looked wildly around. Hektor and his forces were exultantly pursuing and slaughtering the plague-stricken Greeks. The plain-looking man and his men were on the point of breaking into the city! And if they got in, they would open the main gates to the rest of the Greek army . . . who would bring their plague in with them. . . . The plague had been a perfect diversion for this ordinary man. He was using the Trojans' own attack to surprise them.

Another hero with brains. Perfect.

He shouted to Sikandar, but the little group was too close to the walls for a bow shot. The Minotaur looked up, and Corydon saw him rallying his own men, but by the time they devised a weapon that could reach the group, it would be too late. Where were Sthenno and Euryale? He sent up a long, singing cry and saw a small golden dot wheel and begin to return. It was Sthenno, and he could see that the wind was against her and that she did not really see the need for hurry. Euryale was nowhere in sight. He called again, then saw that there was no one but himself. Telling Sikandar in a fierce shout to shut the sally port, he seized one of the ropes from the ballista, slashed it free with his knife, and clinging to its end like a monkey, swung himself out from the walls and then, taking a deep breath, slithered down its full length. . . .

And let go.

He thought that his fall might distract them long enough for Sikandar to shut the gate.

Then all the breath was driven out of his lungs as he landed right in their midst. What saved him was the men's surprise and the fact that he was only lightly armed. Seeing in dazzles of red and black, Corydon held up his slingshot, flung a pebble almost randomly, and ran in the direction of the sally port. The men followed.

But it had been enough. Sikandar and a group of guards were there. Corydon squeezed inside, and the doors snapped shut. Racing back up to the top of the wall, he watched the little Greek party resume its prowl. Even though they couldn't break down the gate, they kept close; they had no wish to be shot by plague arrows. The Trojans hurled spears but couldn't touch them. Corydon stood next to the Minotaur as he watched the dark man lead them carefully, like a father shepherding nervous children. "He reminds me of you," Corydon said to his old friend.

The Minotaur sighed, a long, warm breath. Then he spoke. "They call him Odysseus. He may be the greatest of them all."

Corydon looked at the ordinary man's plain, blunt face, his hunched shoulders, and he recalled the searing eyes of Akhilleus. Yet he did not disbelieve the Minotaur. How could the monsters hope to survive them both? He had no illusions that anything other than blind luck had helped him prevent Odysseus's cunning attack.

The battle was dying down for the day, the Greeks retreating and the Trojans moving back to the gates. But the war would begin again tomorrow.

And such was life in Troy.

N I N E

The Trojans held a council of war that evening. It did nothing to help.

The large throne room was crowded with a heaving mass of diverse humans and creatures. Corydon could smell the sweat of fear under the courtly incense and spices. It was the custom in Troy that every man or woman who wished could have a voice in momentous state affairs. Corydon had thought this sounded fine and fair until he saw the bitter reality. Frightened people do not judge justly. They don't reason wisely.

Some of them yelled and quarreled about their troubles: sons killed, farms outside the walls destroyed. Others expressed their grievances about Troy's rulers. A tall man complained that Sikandar did far too little. "He stands safe on the walls while we risk our necks on the plains!" he shouted.

"And it's all his fault!" screamed a citizen-woman. "He offended the goddesses. He chose Aphrodite. Which gained us what? That silly Helena? Who has inspired these armies to come retrieve her? The attackers have mighty Athene and renowned Hera, and we have a cowering—"

King Priam, looking very tired, silenced her with a wave of his hand. Raising his thin old voice to be heard over the tumult, he spoke out. "We are not here to discuss the causes of the war but how to win it!"

Prince Hektor spoke out, too. "We are not beaten yet, friends. As long as these walls hold out—"

"But the Greeks nearly got inside them today. Because of your foolhardy sortie, which achieved *nothing*," said a dark-faced man whose apron proclaimed him a smith.

"You forget the plague," shouted the priest and his daughter. "Did you not see how Loxias's magic brought them to their knees—yes, even the antmen?"

"The army of Agamemnon will not run because of a mere plague!" shouted another belligerent man, wearing the breeches of a laborer.

"And our hero Gorgos is on his quest to find Philoktetes and Herakles' bow," said Priam in his high voice.

At Gorgos's name, the angry people were briefly silent; it seemed they respected him. Then one of the citizens banged his goblet on the table. "The bow will do us little good if we are all dead when it arrives!" he said. The brief peace was shattered, and fresh outbursts of fear came from all present, together with fresh solutions.

Corydon's head rang. It was even worse than the councils of war the monsters had held when Perseus came to their island.

"We need to study their battle tactics," he said suddenly,

remembering the Sphinx's careful battle drawings in the sand, at Lady Nagaina's tower.

A cool voice from an unnoticed corner chimed in with his thoughts. "The boy shines, with his feet on the sands of prophecy," said a large silver Sphinx.

On the Sphinx's back was Penthesilea, queen of the Amazons. They had been so still in the noisy, hot room that Corydon hadn't seen them. Now the queen spoke. "They have new leaders," she said, her soft, precise voice somehow audible amid the hubbub. "Akhilleus, who is protected, and a man called Odysseus. I know little of him, but I do know that High King Agamemnon was so eager to have him fighting for the Greeks that he sent an argosy to his home in Ithaka. . . ." Her voice trailed off.

"Then," said Hektor, "we should aim to defeat these two in plain battle. Call each to single combat." Corydon's heart lurched. Single combat hadn't helped Medusa. He could see a little of her in this wiry young man, who had leapt onto the table to volunteer. "I will fight Akhilleus," Hektor cried.

"And you will die if you do," said Sthenno calmly. "The stars speak clearly. Akhilleus is virtually invincible. Have you not seen spear and arrow bounce off his flesh as if it were made of the metal of the stars themselves? His mother is a sea daimon, and she has made him proof against any weapons by holding him in the dark waters of the Styx; his body drank death there, and so it cannot be pierced by death."

"But Herakles' bow—"

Sthenno interrupted curtly. "That is nothing to place faith in."

"How did she hold him in the Styx?" Euryale asked. Sthenno

shrugged. Sikandar was sitting nearby; he seemed about to speak. But his great father had moved on.

"What is Akhilleus, what is Odysseus, without followers?" he said. "He may be impervious, but those who serve him are of flesh and blood. We do not need to destroy him. We need patiently to destroy his followers. This will break his heart. For indeed, I think he has one, this hero."

The wintry chill in his voice shook Corydon. Did Akhilleus really deserve to have his heart broken?

Perhaps the king saw him wince, for he gave a wry smile. "Little one," he said, "I do not seek any man's destruction lightly. But I do seek to keep my city."

Corydon bowed his head. But in his heart a rebellious wish for an end to all this continued to flicker like a wavering flame. "Sire," he said, "have any tried a peace embassy? Since all here think Helena a bad buy, why not return her? Then Agamemnon and the Greeks would have no excuse to attack."

There was a long silence. There were doubtful murmurs. Sikandar spoke. "I would gladly do this," he said, and then fell silent.

Hektor spoke. "But, friend, there is a disadvantage," he said. "If we return Helena, we will earn the hatred of the goddess who entrusted her to my brother. And have you ever seen what Aphrodite's wrath can do?"

"No," said Corydon staunchly, "but I have seen Hera's. And Athene's. And you yourselves were saying only a moment ago that their anger was worse."

Hektor turned his wine cup in his hand; the firelight swirled over the black figures of two wrestlers on its side. "Aphrodite can send men mad," he said. "There were once two cities on a great plain. Beautiful, with slender turrets piercing the blue sky. Someone offended Aphrodite, and the men of that city began running mad with love. Not even the children were safe. Eventually a great djinn of shriveling fire came, and the city was ash on a wind that blew for five years. The cities were called Sodom and Gomorrah. I have seen where they stood."

Corydon said no more. He still felt unreconciled. He wanted to tell them of what Hera's anger had done to Atlantis, to Tashkurgan. But what use was it to make them hopeless? He was still turning over in his mind the idea of some kind of truce with Aphrodite when the Snake-Girl, utterly silent till then, pressed his arm with her tail. She lowered her voice to a hiss so soft it was like shifting sand. "They are right. Neoptolemos is mad with Aphrodite's madness, and it is much more dreadful than you know."

Corydon noticed that she held her hands across her soft, scaly belly as she spoke. A sudden recollection of Medusa cupping her womb ripe with Gorgos pierced him.

She saw him staring and took his hand in hers and placed it on her belly. Faintly, his monster-sense felt the small insect-flutter of a life within. A rush of protective love welled up in him for this innocent monster, not yet born.

"Well, a battle plan is needed, then," said Penthesilea.

The Sphinx nodded. Corydon wondered how she had tamed it. The Sphinx heard his thought and swiveled her yellow eyes to his face. Then she spoke calmly, cutting across someone's long speech. "Little monster-boy, I do not serve. I am her companion. My people cast me out, long ago. The Amazons took me in. Now

I have persuaded some of them to help. We do little to avert doom."

Everyone stared, and Corydon felt shamed. But he spoke up. "Can you not use your magic powers?" he asked. "Enchant the army?"

"We cannot turn entire armies. An army has a will many times the weight of the individual men in it. Training, collective motivation . . ." Her voice was mocking.

"But what of the leaders?" Corydon persisted. He remembered all too well the Sphinxes charming the heroes on that cliff, only a few short weeks ago. "Could you not break that will by controlling those who lead it?"

The Sphinx was silent, and Corydon could see her turning over the plan. "It might be possible," she said. "The memory of my colleagues shows it would be possible if they were all separate and alone. But they are always near their troops." Her voice rose in song. "The silence, the deep quiet of all the stars . . . The love that moves the spheres and the glinting stars . . ."

Sthenno smiled in delight, but other people began drumming their fingers and sighing. Corydon wondered why she'd said it. Sphinxes usually meant something by their songs. He thought about the stars. . . . Was she talking of fate? Then he remembered. The daimons of the air . . . Could that be it?

"What of the daimons of the air?" he asked abruptly, interrupting a long speech much as the Sphinx had done. Some of the Trojan warriors were plainly wondering if all the monsters were more trouble than they were worth. But Hektor and Priam looked interested.

"Yes, the daimons!" Hektor said. "Our friend is right. They have power. Even now, they stir up winds that keep the airs around the Greek camp as a kind of wall, so that Loxias's plague may not menace Troy or its people."

"But the daimons have the pure power of the stars."

"Why can't they tell the stars to fall?" said Priam sadly. "Let us end in silver fire." Everyone was silent, but Corydon's whole body rebelled. Priam caught his eye and noted its fierce refusal. He smiled faintly. "Some still have the will to resist, it seems," he said.

"Many," said Hektor firmly. He caught Sikandar's eye, and he, too, nodded, though Corydon could see that he truly agreed with his father.

"I have an idea," said the old, grizzled man in the leather apron. "Did any of you ever see Gorgos's sword?"

There were some nods, and the smith continued. "Gorgos said it had been made from a star that fell from the sky. Its blade was black, and it was far harder than anything I have ever seen before."

"But philosophers say the stars are but matter like ourselves," said Sikandar quickly. He could foresee the next step, and he evidently disliked it.

"Perhaps they are transformed by flight, or perhaps philosophers are wrong. They have probably not been to look," said Hektor. "I see your plan, Eumenides. What if the daimons ask for *some* stars to fall? Then we, too, could have better blades." His eyes shone. "Then we could all wield star-swords."

Corydon was shocked and Sthenno outraged. "King Priam," she said, her high voice sweet. "King, you do not wish the stars to begin destroying themselves to preserve your city. You do not wish that. The years of men are few, but the stars go on forever. We cannot destroy the immortal to save the fleeting."

Priam nodded gravely, and Corydon could see that he respected Sthenno's words. But others murmured. "The Gorgons are immortals themselves," Corydon heard one man say. "We are but dust to them."

"No," Corydon said, "I have another plan. Friends of Troy, the Greeks are not your true enemies. You know not what is being done to you. Your true enemies are the Olympian gods themselves. It is they who have decided to destroy your city, because you are too wise. Because you have too many knowledges. Because you have poets singing in the streets and artists making paintings that are even more beautiful than they are. All this challenges their power, and they will kill you for it. The Greeks are but their weapon, like the spear in a man's hand. It is not the spear we should destroy but the man who wields it. Allow me to think of a plan to end the Olympians' reign. You must hold the Greeks off until I succeed. But do not bring more of the gods' enemies to destruction in the battle. The stars spell out the ending of the reign of Zeus. Sthenno has seen it. Haven't you, Sthenno?"

Sthenno bowed her head. There was a long silence.

"Even if that is true," said Priam at last, "what can mere men do against the gods?"

"Mere men, mere men! Do you not know the gods need you and not the other way around?" said Euryale impatiently. "Why be so humble? Without you they would fade into the common light of morning. It is you and your worship that burnish them and give them luster."

"But what of the old gods?" asked Sikandar. "They do us no

harm and much good. Can we still have faith in them? Can they have faith in us?"

Priam spoke from deep weariness. "We have invited our household gods many times to defend our homes, but they do nothing because they are not gods of war. They make our houses *homes;* they cannot make them citadels. And it is the same with the little chthonic gods of wood and stream and hill. They are mighty in their own domains. They have no might to oppose the will of the heavenly powers. To outlast them, perhaps. To survive them. But not to master them."

Corydon's thoughts ran deep, to his own father. Mighty in his own domain . . . "Then how," he asked, "how did the Olympians come to fill the sky? For it was not always so. Once they, too, were little gods. How do they now rule all?"

Priam sighed. Euryale spoke sternly. "It was men's doing," she said. "As men spread out over the earth, they took their little local gods with them. They wanted every place to be the same. So gradually the dominion of a few gods grew great. Men called the gods of others by the names they knew. Every sky god became King Zeus. Every hunter became Apollo. So a few gods came to rule more and more land. They longed to see their own extended lands, and so they ascended the mountain, becoming forever separate from the land. . . . And then there was nothing left to connect them with the men who loved them and feared them. Not even the earth under their feet."

"Spread out against the limitless sky, they block the light." The Sphinx's cool voice was assenting. "When the stars threw down their spears, and watered heaven with their tears, Zeus smiled his work to see." She smiled herself.

No one knew what she meant, but a germ of an idea was growing in Corydon, a cunning kleptis idea. The Olympians had become mighty by combining the strengths of many other little gods, by becoming supergods. What if the monsters and the little gods of the earth could do the same? He wasn't sure it was truly possible—and monsters were already precarious blends of snake and girl, boy and goat, metal and flesh. But wait! There was Gorgos, who was both monster and god, and whose body was less unstable than most. . . . Could the little gods of field and hill and river somehow come together in him? If so, he might be a champion for Troy. . . .

And repeat his mother's fate, said a voice in his head. But he squelched his dread. His mouth was open to tell his plan to the council when the Sphinx spoke again. "Out of the mouths of babes and sucklings," she said, "your young men will see visions." She looked directly at Corydon with her huge golden eyes. Corydon felt as if he were drowning in them. She withdrew her gaze. And now she spoke clearly. Corydon felt exposed, as if a wind had blown away all leaves from an autumnal tree. "He knows."

Priam looked at Corydon. He could see that the Sphinx's endorsement meant that he would be heard.

Haltingly, he explained his idea. Sikandar's face lit up, and Sthenno and Euryale began talking excitedly. Priam's face was full of hope, and he began eagerly questioning the Sphinx and the Gorgons. The priests and priestesses began arguing about how to proceed. One priestess asked how they might summon the wood and field gods, and another how wood, earth, water, and fire might occupy the same space. And whom should they occupy? Already the Trojan princes and heroes were outdoing each other, trying to volunteer to be the hero possessed by the gods, though most argued Gorgos was the best choice.

But the Minotaur was silent. Corydon put a hand on the great, softly furred arm and raised his eyebrows, hoping to hear his verdict.

"My friend," his soft voice rumbled, "the little gods combined may win. And then we will truly have made a monster. All that wildness . . . Then we may have to set about destroying our own creation. Have you not seen enough of that?" His great head drooped. Then he went on, his voice so soft it was like a faint murmur of wind. "And if we lose, the little gods will also be lost. And men will lose forever the sense of a home, the sense of their own place." He gave a great, bull-like roar. "It would be better for Troy to fall."

There was a shocked silence. Sthenno clashed her wings for attention. "If I read the stars rightly," she said, "this is Gorgos's destiny. But he cannot fight the Olympians, only Akhilleus. We must wait until Gorgos returns. And, in the meantime, we must think of a way to attack the Olympians themselves."

"And we must hold the Greeks from our doors," rumbled the Minotaur softly. "Kalkhas has a healing herb that will cure the plague. If we offer it to the Greeks in exchange for their withdrawal—"

"No!" Trojan voices broke out from all sides. Levelly, coldly, Hektor spoke. "Let them die," he said. "They have taken many a brave man's life. The more of them who die, the better."

The Minotaur bowed his head. It was clear that he was unhappy. And Corydon could see that they all resembled their foes too much already. He thought of the choking, screaming troops. This was no longer warfare. It was vengeance. But wasn't vengeance what he wanted himself? Vengeance for the lions ... for Medusa ... for Atlantis ...

No. He wanted a world in which evil no longer reigned. Not a world in which the only way to prevent wrong was to do wrong.

Corydon looked at Priam, at Hektor, and saw their fear, their pain, their frustration.

Priam stood up. "The council is over," he said. "Tomorrow the battle will begin again. My friend"—he turned to the Minotaur— "are your new machines ready?"

The Minotaur looked up and said simply, "Yes." It was clear that he did not see Priam as a king or as special.

There was some murmuring, but Priam didn't seem to mind. "We all rely on you, my dear friend," he said grimly.

The Minotaur looked down. Everyone else got to their feet, and the Minotaur took Corydon's hand.

"Come," he said. "I want to talk. But I must go and make sure my machines are all right. Will you come with me?"

Corydon smiled warmly, took leave of the others, and followed the shaggy form out of the great hall.

T E N

CORYDON FOLLOWED THE MINOTAUR THROUGH THE long, twisting corridors of Priam's palace. "It reminds me of my prison," said the great black monster. "It's very old. But I liked my own home much more. I could smell the thyme everywhere." His face was still, dreaming. "They've given me a room, though." Their way led them past many staring faces. Corydon felt the eyes upon him; was he friend or foe, good or ill omen? He kept his head bent. He didn't want to make any silent promises to the hopeful eyes.

They reached a series of storage rooms. Corydon saw that the food store was guarded and realized what it meant. "The corn dole is down to half a measure a day," said the Minotaur. "The Greeks have destroyed the harvest. The port is blockaded. Much came by sea. Now we rely on the slow land caravans. And last week the Greeks intercepted one of those, too. No one is starving yet, but the children begin to look hungry."

Corydon shivered. Though he had seen much, he had never before seen starvation or plague, the accompaniments of war.

"But my machines might help," said the Minotaur hopefully. "They are not only war machines. They may make it possible to gather food from farther away." He turned several keys and flung open the door to the last storeroom, an immense wood door with a complicated shutting mechanism.

But the room was utterly empty. The Minotaur looked around as if he couldn't believe it. Like a puzzled dog, he searched the room with his eyes. A roar broke from him, a mighty bellow of rage; then he sat down and put his great head in his hands.

"They're gone," he said, in a simple, hurt voice. "Gone. All of them. And my plans for using them. And the launchers. All gone."

Corydon was shocked. Quickly, he asked, "Could someone have moved them?"

The Minotaur shook his head, as if the question were a distracting fly. "I alone have the keys. It cannot be." The Minotaur examined the door lock. "All is well here," he said. Then he turned to one of the guards, who had heard his cry and come in to investigate. "What happened? Where were you?"

"I was sent to escort the royal ladies to the council chamber," said the guard, swallowing; it was clear he feared the Minotaur.

"How many people knew they were here?" Corydon asked.

Then Minotaur put his head in his hands again. "Each machine had two men trained to use it," he said. "And I had two assistants. Euryale sometimes came. Her paintings gave me ideas." He stood up. "We'll have to resolve the how and who later. I must go to Hektor so we can remake our plans for tomorrow." And with a sigh, he left the room.

Corydon stayed, searching for some clue. But the place was swept clear. The thief or thieves had left nothing behind.

It was obvious, however, that Troy had a new problem. There was a traitor within the gates.

Corydon hurried after the Minotaur. Grimly, they went to report to Priam and Hektor that the machines were gone and that it was possible the Greeks had them. Priam, his face set, called Sthenno, Euryale, and the Sphinxes to him and warned them of what they might now have to face.

Euryale tried to encourage him. "King," she said, "do not fear. We shall suffice. The Minotaur made them, so he can help us determine how to best them."

Priam sighed, but the others nodded, the Sphinxes keeping their heads lowered so their eyes would not enchant the king.

The Minotaur set to sketching the stolen machines, and all the flying monsters bent over him.

But Hektor, angry and flushed, insisted they search for the thief, and Corydon explained again that there were no clues at all. As he did so, he began to wonder if any mortal could have done this. Not a footprint, not even the dust disturbed . . . Maybe the daimons might know something? He suggested this, and Hektor clapped him on the shoulder, a little too hard. Corydon lurched slightly. "Good boy!" cried the prince. "A fine idea. They see everything."

"But they may not choose to reveal it," said Sthenno. "Like the stars." She was hunched over a sketch that showed a kind of giant wasp machine, with a stinger in its rear that could evidently spew out flame. As Corydon watched her, she gave a sudden shiver. He moved to put a hand on her shoulder. Her usually calm bronze face was somehow troubled. The Minotaur was explaining how to destroy the weapons on the various craft and how to block up their fuel pipes so that their flamethrowers would not work, and all the monsters listened attentively.

As they did so, an astonishing thing happened. The air in the room turned blue, like the sky of evening. Drifting about in it lazily was a series of shapes, like papery cutouts of men and birds, floating rather than flying in the smoky, torchlit air. One large shape detached itself from the others and was wafted toward Priam like a leaf on the wind. There was a sound like shrill song, not unlike the song of Sthenno herself—a kind of lark's song that eddied and swirled.

"That is their speech," said the Minotaur. "Only a few understand them. Priam is one; he was an acolyte in their temple as a boy."

Priam was singing to the blue daimons as he spoke, telling them the need. The tall one stood in front of him, and Corydon could tell it was angry; its bluishness had a hard shimmer, like the hot blue of a huge star.

Priam turned to the monsters. "They are angry about the plague," he said. "They say the work of Loxias has made miasmas in the air that is their food. They say that if we pollute the air, then they cannot be our friends. They also say they cannot fight for us. But they say they will try to disable the machines if they can do so without hurting other men."

He produced a burst of grateful-sounding song. No one else

felt especially pleased. It was plain that the daimons could eliminate the Greeks if they felt like it. Penthesilea, who had been summoned with the other war leaders to plan for the disaster, looked mutinous. She seemed on the verge of speech, but Sikandar plucked at her arm and she subsided.

"Ask them if they know who the thief was," said Hektor urgently.

Priam spoke, and a long, fluting birdlike song broke from the daimons. Priam turned.

"It was the god with winged feet, Hermes." He looked surprised. "But if the Greeks have the Olympians *running their errands*, we can have no hope. None."

Corydon thought of Hermes and his response to the death of the lions; which side was he on? Could he be trying to stop the war, prevent the machines from dealing out more death? Aloud, he said, "We, too, have gods, and ours will help us. And my plan may work. Tomorrow, however, our task is to keep the Minotaur's flying machines from landing in the city." It was abruptly clear that no one had quite realized that this was the greatest risk and that they now did. Priam and Hektor seemed silent from despair, so Corydon spoke again. "We must place a Sphinx on each tower," he said, "to intercept any machines that come near. Minotaur, how many machines are there?"

The Minotaur spoke softly. "There are ten. Though the Greeks may begin to build them themselves by copying my design. But I made ten." Corydon longed to hug him, his voice was so sad. He could feel the thoughts, so like his own. *I meant to help . . . only to help . . .*

Euryale spoke. "Sthenno and I, together with the other Sphinxes, will try to destroy these machines over the field of battle. And the daimons have promised to disable some if they can. But we must station buckets of water and sand about the city in case the Greeks manage to set fire to it. The men must also guard against smoke."

It was plain that the preparations would take all night. Corydon turned to Sthenno, who was unusually silent. "Is something wrong?" he asked.

Sthenno put her bronze wings around him and hugged him hard. "It is difficult for an immortal to face death," she said. "I have seen so many deaths. In parchments and on battlefields. Now I see something. . . . But it may be just fear. . . . I wish I could be on the island again with you, mormo."

Corydon felt a cold shudder down his spine. Was Sthenno truly saying she feared for herself? She had never said that before, despite the dangers she had faced. "This is not the place you will die," he said, "somewhere so far from home."

"Wherever there are stars," she said, "I am at home." She spoke briefly to the daimon leader, having plainly learned his speech. His response sounded like a mourning cry but died away peacefully. Sthenno turned resolutely. "And now we must help with buckets of water," she said.

As Corydon left the palace, he couldn't help thinking that Sthenno knew what might happen at the battle and that that was the reason she was so afraid. Maybe some of her parchments would help him understand. But he realized that although he had been to Euryale's studio-house, he had not seen Sthenno's parchments; she had obviously found somewhere else to study them. So he asked a guard simply and plainly where Sthenno worked.

"She lives up in that tower," he said, pointing to a rickety structure that leaned like a spear at ease. "But you had better be careful. She does not like being disturbed."

The tower was unlocked, and he climbed the wooden steps, carefully dodging the missing boards and gaping holes. Then he was at the top, a small, round room with its roof torn away to reveal icy stars and a jet-black sky. All about the room were piles of parchments, spread on a table and on the floor. In the center of the table were a round clay disk and a piece of parchment. Corydon moved closer and noticed four symbols—a whirlwind, a wave curling fiercely, a flame, and what looked like a lump of something—etched into the disk. Around the rim were some hastily scratched symbols. Corydon examined the parchment and decided that it was a kind of key: the same symbols appeared, but beside them was a Hellenic translation. He read, "Air . . . Water . . . Fire . . . Earth . . . These are life itself. When all life is done, the city must fall and rise again beyond the seas."

So the city must fall. . . . But what did it mean about rising again? He knitted his brows, and as he did, the air turned sharply blue. There was a cold gust and a light singing sound. He looked up to see one of the papery daimons floating above him. It sang a long, garbled phrase, and Corydon thought it was trying to tell him something, but he had no idea what. Then the creature began twirling rapidly in its place, like a spindle. As it twirled, it developed a sharp point; then, with a furious buzz, this point touched his ear, and the daimon vanished into his head. Corydon felt it buzzing there, and suddenly a clear bell-like voice spoke inside him.

"It is the prophecy of the city's fall. But you should not be here.

This room is that of great Sthenno, watcher of the stars. We honor her because she guards the secrets of the universe."

"I know she dreads the battle," said Corydon aloud. "So I decided to visit her room to find out why. I want only to protect her."

"Yes, I can see that," said the voice. "Very well. The stars show that the theft of the machines is the beginning of the end for Troy. There will be a battle in the air, and when there have been battles in air, water, earth, and finally fire, Troy, too, will be destroyed, as Atlantis was. But from that death, it will rise again, far greater than before; it will be reborn as an empire so great that all the gods will marvel at it."

"And will this empire last forever?" asked Corydon hopefully.

"No," said the spirit. "No. But its greatest city shall endure. It will last for thousands of years and will rule the lives of many countless millions."

"And will it be like Troy and Atlantis? A place of ideas? A menace to the gods?"

"The Olympian gods will fall," said the spirit. "And I see your dream. They will fall by your hand, Corydon Panfoot, though it will take some years for mortal men to see that the gods are mere eidolons."

By his hand! But how? He knew enough about prophecy to know he was unlikely to get a direct answer.

"You will find the way," said the daimon in his head.

Corydon had another, more pressing question. "Can you help in the battle?" he asked urgently.

"We are not warriors," said the voice firmly. "We do not fight. But we can help. Not by killing and not by knowing. We can awaken others who can help in the ways you hope." It was plain that it would say no more. It withdrew from Corydon's ear with a slight pop and floated away, just a leaf on an autumn wind.

Corydon sat down on the floor and pulled an old cloak over himself. The moon rose, hard and bony white. He fell asleep, his hands around his knees, and when Sthenno came in, she did not have the heart to wake him, though she felt a sharp longing for comfort tonight. She looked up at the stars and took cold comfort from them. Whatever happened on earth, they would continue their great and fiery dance.

The morning dawned chill and foggy. Corydon woke at first light and at once became aware of a terrible sound, like a dissonant version of Sthenno's clashing wings. Then there was a grinding sound, like metal wheels on stone.

The flying machines! Were they already overhead? Corydon looked up, and so did Sthenno, who sprang aloft.

"They come," she said grimly. "Go, Corydon. Help the peltasts and the Sphinxes." And she flew off.

Corydon tore down the stairs and ran through the streets. Already men and women were looking up fearfully. He took the stairs up to the walls three at a time. Ten machines droned in the air. Ahead, he could see Sthenno and Euryale flying out to meet them, the rising sun catching their wings.

The flying machines were long triangles like dragons, with tails hanging behind them. One of the tails somehow twitched itself over the creature's head, and a thin thread of flame came from it. So the daimons had not managed to disable all the weapons. The

Minotaur spoke beside him. "They stopped the ballistas," he said. "They stopped them from firing spears. And they told me they blocked the fire pipe with small stones and bent it. But the Greeks must have noticed and fixed it somehow." Now it was as if ten dragons were converging on Troy.

Sthenno and Euryale flew steadily toward them, but beside the great mechanical giants, even Euryale looked puny. The Gorgons suddenly swept upward to try to come down on the machines from above.

A piercing whistle sounded from one metallic dragon. All the tails turned forward, then swiveled upward. Ten bursts of conical flame combined and then shot toward the Gorgons.

Euryale swerved suddenly, crashing heavily onto a flying machine and managing to swipe another with her claw. Both lost height abruptly. The one she'd caught began hurtling toward the plain below, and the other was forced to land and bury itself in flying dirt. The Trojans cheered. That left eight.

But Sthenno had not fared so well. As she pounced hawklike on one clumsy beast, the pilot managed to turn his flamethrower toward her. At such close range, it emitted a fierce high-pressure geyser of flame, beating against her right wing. To his horror, Corydon could see the bronze melting like wax. Flapping desperately, she tried to reach the walls, but already she was below their rim. One of the guardian Sphinxes dived for her and managed to get beneath her, singeing herself on the melting metal. She shuddered, and Sthenno lost her precarious hold. She slid from the Sphinx's back, crashed to the ground, and lay exposed on the plain. She tried to rise, fell back, her eyes staring at the sky as if seeking a last sight of the stars she loved.

The flying machines closed in for the kill. Frantically, Euryale stood over Sthenno's body and tried to beat them off; she snatched one from the air, tore off another's wing. But there were still six of them. Four peeled off to attack the city. The others dive-bombed the Gorgons, evading Euryale's claws. It was plain that whoever was piloting them was becoming better with practice.

Corydon was frantic. The Sphinxes were less maneuverable than the Gorgons and would find it very hard to bring down the flying menace.

They tried. One Sphinx flew down to help Euryale defend Sthenno, while the others strove frantically to block the metal machines. One Sphinx used her hypnotic gaze on the pilot and managed to confound him, but thick, flickering flames from behind set her alight, and she fell as well, screaming horribly. Euryale rushed to put out the fire, exposing Sthenno. Sthenno gave a faint cry, and Corydon sensed that she was groping for a spell, but then pain made her lose consciousness and her head rolled— or was she dead? Corydon took aim at the nearest metal beast. Its gleam reminded him of Talos, who had destroyed another feathered creature by fire. So with all his hatred, he aimed, and his stone hit the pilot's hand; the man cursed, but his machine drove on, low, toward the walls. It dived over them into the city.

Troy's defenses had been breached.

ELEVEN

THERE WAS A LOW, THRUMMING WAIL. CORYDON FIRST thought it was the people of Troy, but as the sound increased, he realized it was the walls themselves. They were humming louder and louder, until it was impossible to hear anything above the shrill, hard sound. Men stood with their mouths open.

And an answering hum came from far away. Straining his eyes in the direction of the sound, Corydon could see something like golden rain gathering and massing and forming in the air. It grew larger, swelling with song and sound. And they came, seven djinns, golden cloud-kings of the desert, bringing their empires of sand with them. Each paused outside the city.

When they noticed the flying machine within its walls, each formed a thin golden thread and poured itself over the walls, which cried out in welcome to them. Then they ballooned into clouds again and closed in on the flying machine. It tried to fly beyond them, but it could not climb sharply enough.

The djinns drew closer and finally blotted the machine out altogether. The singing was so intense that Corydon could not even hear the machine crash to the streets of Troy. But now it lay, twisted and gnarled, its pilot turning his dead eyes to the thankless sky. The djinns gathered themselves together and withdrew, heading for the flying machines that still hovered outside the city.

No. One thin golden streamer remained. It hurtled toward the walls—toward Corydon himself—as if bringing some urgent message. It poured itself onto the ground in front of him. And slowly it grew into someone Corydon had not expected to see again.

Bin Khamal gave a wintry little smile. "I was near Wabar when we all heard the call. I knew it must have to do with you."

Together they looked down from the walls. Without, the remaining flying machines were now encased in sandstorms; within, people were running and cheering raggedly—but Corydon had eyes only for the limp form of Sthenno, carried from the field in Hektor's own war chariot.

"Is she dead?" he called.

"No," said Euryale. It was clear that she would not leave Sthenno's side. "Her wing is damaged, though. We must think how to reforge it. If we cannot, she will not be able to fly again. But she will not die of this wound."

Corydon gave out a long breath of relief. He felt certain that Euryale would find a way to reforge her sister's broken wing. "I'll come and see her soon," he promised. He thought with a jolt of Sthenno's own fear before the battle, of what the daimon had said. It was obvious she had had a prophecy about herself. He decided that he must ask her more when she was better. Waving to Euryale, he turned to Bin Khamal.

"What called you to Troy?"

"The walls of seven cities in the world were built by my people, the djinn. In each a djinnish sacrifice lives; when any enemy of the city breaches the walls, that djinn sends out a call to his brothers, and we hear it and come even from the ends of the earth. Troy is such a city, endowed with our magic."

"What are the others?" Corydon asked.

"Not all still stand; some are gone, like the Cittavecchia of old Atlantis. But some stand yet. Wabar, which I visited before rushing to Troy's aid, is another such. But I cannot reveal more. It is a secret of my people."

"And will you stay and help?"

"For a night and a day. Such is our vow. I am with my people now, though it is not the freedom of which I once dreamed. But I would like to see Sikandar again as well as you."

"I am here, old friend," said a voice from behind them. Sikandar seized his friend's hand.

They smiled at each other. The survivors of the kleptis gang were united, though Azil's absence was a wound. The Minotaur shambled past, his dark head bent. He looked sad and forlorn, so Corydon introduced him to Bin Khamal.

The Minotaur spoke in his low rumble. "I help with the machines. Those that you destroyed were stolen, and I am glad that you stopped them. But I can never forgive myself. . . ." His voice trailed off.

Corydon patted his arm. "You were right to make them, to want to help," he said. But truly he wasn't sure that the Minotaur had been right to want to save Troy at this cost; was it ever right to make a killing machine? And Sthenno . . . "Let's go and see Sthenno," he suggested.

"I shall keep watch," the Minotaur said. "The Greeks may have learned the secret of making them. I will watch them. They will not harm us again." Studying his face, Corydon saw its haunted sadness change to grim resolution. Then suddenly the great monster gave a bellow of fury and ran for the stairs.

Corydon watched in dread. It was plain that he had reached a deadly resolve.

The Minotaur emerged into the streets moments later, wearing his breastplate and carrying his ax and shield. He disappeared from sight, and Corydon thought he'd gone toward the sally port. He hurried to follow the huge beast, accompanied by Bin Khamal and Sikandar. The sally port was closed, but they flung it open and closed it behind them. The Minotaur was ahead of them, his great head lifted, as if he were trying to smell out the Greeks.

Then he lowered his head and charged, his legs pumping furiously. Corydon could see the bull was uppermost in him, the angry bull that had been goaded again and again until all he felt was a killing rage. He ran straight for a line of antmen, and with a fierce toss of his head, he scattered their ranks. He ran on, brought his ax down, swung and struck again and again and again. His horns were dark with the blood of men. The Greeks fled before his rushing charge like sheep fleeing a wolf.

A huge man turned to face him, a man as tall as the Minotaur and as thickset. He carried an enormous shield, bigger than any Corydon had ever seen, the size of a cartwheel. Beside him was a tiny, nimble man holding a bow. The Minotaur's ax flashed down, but the little man swerved elegantly and pivoted to arm his bow; it was so graceful that it could be mistaken for a dance. Corydon, seeing the danger, armed his sling and fired. The little man was hit on one elbow; it spoiled his aim, and his arrow went wide.

By now, the Minotaur had begun to fight the giant, and the plains rang with the clash of their weapons. The giant had a long stabbing spear, and he had already goaded the Minotaur with it; black blood ran down the monster's bare arm, its passage slowed by his thick black fur. Corydon saw Sikandar draw his bow and send a flight of arrows straight at the giant; one pierced his knee behind the greave, and he gave a howl but did not stop his fighting. His teeth were set in the fierce grin of battle.

A swift movement caught Corydon's eye. The small bowman behind the giant fired, catching Bin Khamal in the arm. Bin Khamal gave a cry and sank to his knees; though his djinn flesh closed up almost at once, he could still feel pain. Corydon bent to help him, but the fight was now all around them as Greeks and Trojans joined the fray.

Then Corydon heard it: the swift, unmistakable footfalls of Akhilleus, running toward them, deadly as a shore-bound wave bearing on its shining top a white crest foaming and free. His steps grew impossibly swift, and he planted his spear shaft and used it to vault over the combatants and reach Corydon and the wounded, cursing djinn-boy. Sikandar fitted an arrow to the string with a trembling hand. He fired, but Akhilleus's jump was far swifter than he had anticipated. Then Akhilleus struck the ground, as delicate and precise as a landing waterbird, his feet outstretched.

But one of them struck a spent arrow, and great Akhilleus gave a roar that silenced even the Minotaur as the arrow pierced his flesh—a roar of amazement at feeling any pain at all. He cursed and with his wounded foot began to limp back toward the camp, supported by the antmen who had come hurrying up to help their leader.

But now the big man saw his chance while the Minotaur stood dumbfounded. He thrust his swift and deadly spear at the great beast's throat, but reflex saved the Minotaur: his ax flashed down, and the spear fell in two pieces, its end bouncing on the sand. The giant was left holding a stump. He threw it down and ran into the camp, ran and ran as if heading for the ships themselves. With another bellow the Minotaur followed. Corydon started after him, but Sikandar spoke. "Corydon, it is his *aristeia*."

Corydon didn't know the word. Sikandar explained. "All warriors have a day or an hour when they are unbeatable and triumphant. It comes from virtue, *arete*. Your true nature. Then they are like gods, though only briefly. This is his *aristeia*. His time. We should leave him to it."

They began trying to fight their way out of the press, using their stones and arrows. When they were clear and making their way toward the walls, Corydon thought about it. An *aristeia* did not truly mean that the Minotaur was like a god. Or if he was like a god, perhaps he was like the wrong god. His virtue was not a warrior virtue but a dark, furry kindness and a gift for solitude. So in triumphing on the field of battle, he was not doing what he was born to do but something else.

*   *   *

The battle raged on for much of the day. Corydon saw most of it.

The Trojans had cleared the Greeks from the plains and confined them to a small line of beachhead around their ships. Corydon had seen the Greeks running all afternoon; without Akhilleus to lead them, they spent more time on the defensive. Eventually, after much fighting, the arrival of dusk forced the Trojans back into Troy.

The Minotaur came last, his head lowered. He did not look like a triumphant warrior but like one who had been defeated: his horns were stained with blood, his own and that of those he had killed; his fur was thick with it from wrist to elbow. He looked at his ax, its blade dripping with gore, as if wondering how he had come by it. Then he put it down softly. Corydon picked it up and was amazed by its weight. The Minotaur had been wielding it as if it were a light blade. Corydon began to wonder how strong he really was.

Wearily, Corydon resumed his place on the walls. No one had told him he must watch there, but he knew his monster-sight could see trouble farther off than human eyes could hope to do. Sikandar and Bin Khamal stood with him. After an hour of cold and tiredness and growing dark, Euryale came up to relieve them, saying that Sthenno was mending from the shock but that her wing would need careful remaking.

Just as they were turning to go, they heard a long, low horn call. It was a great sea horn, fierce and clear and true. Everyone rushed to look out into the darkness and at the Greeks' fires, more distant than before, piercing it like counterfeit stars.

A small group of horsemen was galloping toward the city. The leader blew his horn for aid, and Corydon could at once see why:

another and much larger group of horsemen was closing in on them fast. At their head, Corydon could see the white plume of Akhilleus shining in the darkness and his armor gleaming like the sea on the shore. He had not been disabled by the wound, then, unless . . .

There was something wrong. Corydon couldn't see the hero's strange silver eyes, but perhaps that was the dust lingering in the air. The pursuers raced toward the small party with the speed of a thrown spear. The horn bearer swung his horse around to face them, then set him to a full gallop, so that he seemed to fly over the plain.

The rider was Gorgos. Corydon couldn't see his face, but only a son of Poseidon could so manage a horse.

The two raced toward each other, their followers also charging but more slowly. Corydon saw the moment when Gorgos's spear left his hand; it flew in a perfect line straight at the white-plumed hero, who raised his shield only just in time. But Gorgos had another spear, and he flung it at the hero; to Corydon's amazement, it found the space between greave and saddle, and a gush of warm red blood stained the silver armor.

The hero looked down for a second, and Gorgos seized the moment to draw his sword. The hero's sword appeared in his hand, and the two blades clashed, like lightning in the sky. Gorgos's horse reared up suddenly so that his rider could rain down blows on his opponent from a height. Akhilleus had his shield over his head now. Gorgos's attention was fleetingly caught by one of his band falling, and it infuriated him. He drove his sword into the hero's throat. Black blood bubbled from his mouth, and the white plume began to tilt, then to fall, till the hero lay prostrate on the windy plain. Then a sortie appeared from Troy, and Hektor led it; he kicked the hero's body once, hard, and then plunged his spear time after time into the hero's belly, till it poked out from his back. Then he and the others began systematically stripping off the stained silver armor, the helmet, the shield.

Gorgos was indifferent to plunder. He was watching the fleeing Greeks riding to their camp with their terrible news. The Trojans all turned for the walls and rode back hard, passing through the sally port. Gorgos was mobbed by the many friends eager to congratulate him, to greet him, to tell him he had killed great Akhilleus. "And I have Philoktetes, and he brings Herakles' bow," said Gorgos happily. "Here he is."

He ran up to the walls to show Philoktetes the Greek camps. Corydon and the kleptis gang went, too, trying not to notice the peculiar smell that came from Philoktetes. "They say his wound never heals," whispered a Trojan boy. Corydon's heart was in turmoil; here was Gorgos again, as irresponsible as ever . . . but now a great hero, too.

Gorgos flung himself cheerfully at the Minotaur and gave him a hug, and everyone chattered and laughed. Corydon, as always, did not know what to say to Gorgos, or how to return the thump on the shoulder that Gorgos gave him, or how to respond to his cheerful "I knew you were safe, somehow." He watched Gorgos caught up in a cloud of merry greetings and hoped he didn't look sulky. The Minotaur, still shaking from his battle fury, stood close by. Neither found anything to say.

And because they were silent, they were the first to hear the sound from the Greek camp.

It was not a wail. It was not a scream. It was not a song. It was a cry, high and controlled and clear. As clear and defiant as Gorgos's horn call but bursting from a terrible grief. The Minotaur looked up as if it at last expressed what he felt. It was a series of sounds made by a naked anger fully controlled and turned like a spear at the throat of Troy. The poet in Corydon thought he had never heard a better lament for the painful mortality of all things.

"It is Akhilleus's war cry," said Priam behind them.

And as he said it, they all saw a sight that was the most dangerous any had ever seen. Akhilleus, naked, weaponless, stood in the Greek trench, his hair lit by a brilliant silver flame, as dazzling as lightning, which flickered and ran over his whole body. He did not even have a dagger. But everyone could see the murder in those silver eyes.

"But he died. . . . We all saw him die. . . . See, his corpse." They pointed to the stiffening body spread below them on the plain.

"Only his armor died," said Corydon. It was as clear as a written scroll. "He sent out a friend in his armor because he was wounded. His wound is healed, and now he is back. And he wants revenge on us all."

Gorgos smiled. "I can face him," he said easily.

"Not yet," said Corydon, finding words for Gorgos at last. "We have a plan. We will discuss it in council." He smiled. "You shall face him, my brother. But you cannot face him alone."

TWELVE

THE COUNCIL WAS THE SAME MUDDLE AS THE NIGHT before. The Snake-Girl slid in beside Corydon, looking white and ill. Corydon pressed her hand quickly. Then he banged imperiously on the table; he had had enough of the silliness of Trojan councils and the complaints and grumbles. "We need to talk of the old gods," he said. "All priests and priestesses must come to Sthenno's tower this evening to discuss how to summon their masters. Then we must invite them to the same place, where Gorgos will await them. And you must ask the Greeks to send forth their greatest warrior for single combat. We already know who it will be."

His tone was almost stern. He was amazed to find that the day of battle had left a thread of hard metal in him. He no longer feared to bend these people to his designs, though he knew—none better—that his plan might fail. And said as much. "Of course, we cannot be sure that Gorgos and the small gods can together defeat Akhilleus. But there is at least a chance. And if it fails, we can try other plans. And others and still others, until they weary of their work and go home. We cannot surrender, but we can make them stop."

The Minotaur nodded sturdily, his great head heavy. He was the toast of Troy tonight, and yet no one was more deeply unhappy than he. "Gorgos," he said, "are you willing? Consider. I myself had my own *aristeia* this day. It is not as you think. It is possession by another, a terrible burning from inside. If many gods possess you, you will be changed, your simplicity lost. You may be worn out. You may even die. Is Troy worth all this to you?"

It was a very long speech for the shy Minotaur to make. He sank back, ashamed. But his deep eyes met those of Gorgos unflinchingly.

Gorgos smiled. "I care not for bricks and stones," he said. "Troy is not worth all this to me, but my friends are. And if I choose this path, there is a good chance that I may also find a way to defeat the Olympians and avenge my mother."

"We do not even know if it is possible," said Priam.

But Kalkhas, priest of the goddess, spoke at once. "Oh, it is little more than most priests and prophets take on," he said. "All the gods can take possession of a willing man or woman, and most can force an entrance where none wish to receive them. The risk is that if he opens himself to many nameless little powers, then some evil spirits or evil gods may find a foothold, too. I can try to protect him by calling only upon those who can be named, but it is still possible to be mistaken. We know how the Olympians take and take the power of such little gods, just as King Agamemnon absorbs the kingdoms of little kings."

"It is especially risky that Gorgos is the son of a god, who, though not precisely an Olympian, is not exactly *not* an Olympian either," said Euryale thoughtfully.

"My father will not interfere," said Gorgos. "I am still on terms with him."

"But All-Father Zeus seeks dominion over Troy," said the Minotaur heavily. "And to blot from the earth all who dissent. He is cunning, as we know to our cost."

"I will safeguard Gorgos as I can, and Euryale will help me," said Kalkhas. "Any weapon we make may be turned against us, as this day showed only too well. Yet we cannot sit here and wait to be starved out; already the corn dole is down to half a measure, and the children in the streets beg for bread. We must try. Come, Gorgos. You must undergo a cleansing and a ritual before you can be offered to the gods. Are you decided?"

Gorgos got to his feet. With a little smile at Corydon, he followed Kalkhas. Corydon wondered if he would see his friend again in private; there was so much to say. He felt a familiar cold dread. Would Gorgos's life end in single combat with a hero, like his mother's? But he also felt a strange calm. If that must be so, then so be it.

Quickly, talk in the council turned to Sthenno. One short, stumpy man asked, "How are we going to reforge her wing? Is it possible?"

"I think that with the help of a blacksmith, the Minotaur and I could reforge it," said Euryale hesitantly. It was obvious to Corydon that she was scared that Sthenno might remain flightless forever. "Are you a blacksmith?" she asked. The stumpy man said he was, but he said that she should approach Volkos, the greatest of the Trojan smiths. He did not come to councils. *A sign of good sense,* thought Corydon. But he did make weapons for all of Troy. Euryale said she would go at once. Corydon followed her to the door, and Bin Khamal and Sikandar went with them. The Snake-Girl looked wistfully after them but remained in her seat. Corydon had felt a little usurped by Kalkhas, who was now overseeing the execution of his plan.

But in this he was wrong. Kalkhas was waiting for him outside. "Gorgos must have an esquire," he said in his stern priest voice. "You can serve as one, if you wish."

"I am no esquire," said Corydon. "I am a simple peltast and shepherd."

"But a leader," said the priest. "A leader of boys and also of men. I have marked you and your followers: one a djinn, one a prince of Troy. It takes a strong will to make a whole of such parts, and I have come to see that the will is yours." His deep eyes seemed to burn into Corydon's.

Bin Khamal laughed. "But Corydon does not always lead us," he said. "He has the most ideas, and so we fall in with them. His wits are good. You are doing the same. Falling in with his plan. Do not make a mystery of sense, good priest." His tone was ringed with dislike.

Kalkhas smiled, a smile full of knowledge held by men, as opposed to little boys. It irritated all of them. But Corydon laid a restraining hand on his friends' arms, then turned and addressed Kalkhas. "I will help Gorgos as I can. Has he gone to prepare already?"

The priest nodded.

"What ritual is needed?"

"First he must be bathed in seven waters. Then he must watch this night in the temple of the Great Goddess, to placate her and ask her assistance."

It sounded very boring, and Corydon couldn't imagine Gorgos sitting still for any of it. "Is all this truly necessary?" he asked.

Kalkhas nodded solemnly. "It is a courtesy a man does to the gods," he said. "Boredom, too, is a sacrifice." And here he smiled a little.

"Can you organize the priests and priestesses in time?" Corydon asked.

Kalkhas nodded, evidently enjoying himself. "Yes. I have already made contact with them through the daimons of the air."

Corydon questioned him no more. He took leave of his friends and allowed the priest to lead the way to a dark temple that Corydon hadn't seen yet. It reeked of earth-magic; he could smell the stink of pigs and the smell of gathered wheat. *Demeter,* he thought, remembering her daughter, the Lady of Flowers. He remembered, too, the tests he had undergone in the Land of the Many. He felt sure that Gorgos would be tested somehow, as well.

And he was right. After the ritual washing, Gorgos and Corydon were led into a large room. In it was a table, and on the table was the most complicated twisting of rope that Corydon had ever seen. No, not rope, but wheat. Lengths of it with the golden grain still attached in places. Impossible lengths of wheat tied and twisted together.

Kalkhas smiled. "You have an hour to observe this knot," he said to Gorgos. "When that time has passed, I will come and ask you to untie it." He glanced at Corydon. "Your companion may stay with you. But there is to be no talking. No noise. That will make you impure." With a swirl of purple cloak, he turned and left the room.

Gorgos looked at the knot. He probed it with his hands and tugged here and there. He picked it up and put it down on the floor. Then he smiled, curled up with his head on the knot, and went to sleep. Corydon didn't dare to wake him because he couldn't speak without making the test invalid. But how was Gorgos going to manage?

Eventually, Kalkhas came back into the room. When he saw that Gorgos was asleep and that Corydon was anxious and close to fury, he could not suppress a quiet smile of triumph. Corydon, already tense as a lyre's strings, couldn't help wondering if this man was truly on their side.

The priest woke Gorgos with a tap on his shoulder. Gorgos rolled over sleepily.

"Now," said Kalkhas, in his musical voice, "unlace the knot."

Gorgos looked calm. He placed the knot back on the table.

Then he drew his shining sword and swept it down on the tight mass of wheat.

The bright blade cleft the knot in two. It cleft the table in two as well, and the halves fell with a sharp clatter. Working briskly, Gorgos effortlessly untwisted the wheat ends until before him lay a mass of crinkled sheaf pieces.

Kalkhas scowled. It was obvious that Gorgos had passed a test meant to defeat someone of his abilities. In his sheer simplicity, he had proved more than a match for cunning.

"Very good," said the priest. "You must now face a second and harder task. You must enter the maze, and you must find its center. There you must perform a ritual in honor of the goddess. If you make any mistake, you will know her wrath, and if you do not find the center, you may wander forever, until the ending of the world. Will you try?"

"I will," said Gorgos.

"And, you, will you go with him?"

Corydon shrugged off a tiny reluctant stab. Then he smiled. "Yes," he said. "Gladly."

The priest led them to a low tunnel blocked by a stone. "Help me move this stone," he said. Gorgos lifted it clear easily. Gorgos and Corydon entered a dark tunnel.

"May we take a torch?" Corydon asked.

"Yes," said the priest. "But you may not speak to him, still."

Corydon took a pine torch from the wall and held it aloft. He and Gorgos saw a long tunnel curving away to their left. It had no corners and no junctions. To their right was a similar tunnel. Corydon didn't think the tunnel could really exist—he suspected they were stepping into another realm entirely. Gorgos stood still and lifted his head as if he were sniffing; all Corydon could smell was the damp, earthy smell of the goddess and a faint odor of pig. Then Gorgos, who appeared to be listening, turned right.

They walked for some time without passing any junctions, without making any choices, without seeing any living thing. The curve seemed to go on forever, like the curve of the earth itself. Perhaps they were to walk all around the world. Corydon could see the walls, slick with mud, and he felt hideously imprisoned, a grain of wheat caught in a furrow. He was not a farmer; he was a shepherd, and he longed for the pale sunlight on upland pastures, the clean winds of his home. What was more, his stomach had begun to rumble. It could not yet be reasonable to be so hungry, but Corydon found thoughts of roast pork and fresh barley bread with honey stalking his imagination.

Gorgos was still listening and smelling when the torch began to burn lower. Corydon knew he must say nothing, but he looked as imploring as he could. Gorgos shook his head, as if to brush off a fly. Then he stopped dead and suddenly began burrowing into the left-hand wall of the tunnel, as if he were a dog who had hidden a bone there. Earth flew from his fingers. As he scrabbled, he called, "It's all right, I'm coming." It was clear he was not talking to Corydon.

Corydon began to help him, dropping the spent torch. In the utter blackness, he was forced to rely on touch and smell, and to his surprise, he found it less terrifying than by the dim light of the torch. The echoing tunnel was reduced to a handful of earth, then another handful. It was as if the touch of the earth itself took away his fear. But he still felt wildly hungry, as if he had not eaten for days.

In a rush, they broke through the wall, to be all but dazzled by the glare of a thousand thousand torches.

They were in an immense cave, stretching upward into darkness farther than they could see. All around it stood women. Old women and young ones, pretty and plain. All wore gray robes daubed with ashes and dark red streaks of what looked horribly like blood. All wore their hair unbound. With one voice, they spoke.

"Men!"

"They shall die," said a tall woman.

"They shall die hard," said another. "And their bones will be thrown into the pit."

"You greasy, stinking zetas, you fat white leering lard-laden louts!" "You bad-breathed, snot-nosed liars!" "I was looking for fools when I met men!" "If we can send one man over the sea, why can we not send them all?" "You eat so much that women can smell your farts from a league away!" "You run so fast from battles that the ground bursts into flames behind you!" The insults broke out from everywhere. Gorgos grinned easily, Corydon uneasily.

Gorgos stepped forward. "Greetings," he said. "I have come to sacrifice a pig. I have spoken to her, and she goes consenting. I am the appointed slayer."

There was a roar. Then all the women rushed fiercely upon Gorgos, waving crude weapons—roasting irons and pig knives. But they were stopped by a shout from a gray-haired priestess. "Wait, Sisters, for he speaks the truth!"

"If he can find the pig," said another slyly, "then we will let him go."

The women began chanting softly. "Find the pig, find the pig, find the pig." They eddied around Gorgos, their clothes stinking of blood and earth and pig. Corydon saw that *they* were the true maze.

Gorgos closed his eyes and seemed to be concentrating. Then he opened them again and walked straight forward, jinked suddenly sideways, shoved aside four women, and emerged from their midst with a small piglet in his arms. She squealed frantically. Corydon could see the stripes on her back, the huge eyes; she was a wild-boar piglet, and that explained why Gorgos could find her—he had the gift of understanding wild creatures' speech.

Now the women drew aside, making a narrow pathway for Gorgos. Corydon followed him. As he walked forward, the pig still bleating, the women threw blood and ashes at them. Corydon was nearly blinded and choked by the terrible iron smell, the press of unwashed bodies. Nevertheless his belly roared with furious hunger.

Gorgos stopped, very suddenly. And Corydon saw why.

In front of them was a chasm in the earth. Cautiously Corydon looked over the edge. It seemed to go down forever and forever, and he took a stone from his pouch to check. It seemed an hour before he heard the faintest plink as it hit the ground.

He looked a query. Gorgos nodded. He held the pigling over the terrible drop. The piglet looked calm, her large and liquid eyes fixed on his face. It might have been a last plea or gratitude.

Gorgos opened his hands. Soundlessly, the piglet dropped. Corydon heard a soft crunch when she landed and turned his face away. He could only hope that Gorgos had been right when he said that the pig had consented to her death. But there was a low hum of approval from the women.

"She will be reborn as corn . . . ," said the priestess. "Reborn, corn, corn, reborn . . ."

All the women took up the chant. Suddenly it was all like a dream.

Gorgos waved a friendly hand, shouldered some women out of the way, and began to move toward the opposite wall from where they had entered. They emerged into a new passageway, this one straight and lit by torches in wall cressets.

To his disappointment, Corydon found he'd brought his hunger with him. He could have eaten the earth itself.

With a faint bursting noise, something green and wriggling exploded out of the ground. At first, Corydon thought it was a green shoot, growing at a magical rate. But as a second and a third burst out, too, he saw their heads. He saw the glossy black eyes.

Snakes. Green ones, with black lines running down their backs. Some were thinner than string, others fatter than a ship's cable. Most looked hungry.

As the thirteenth snake erupted, Gorgos spoke in a low, hissing voice, evidently talking to them. Then he seized Corydon's arm and began running. Corydon kept up without difficulty but glanced back to see that most of the snakes were wriggling away. A few larger ones were sitting peacefully, but the largest was on the move. It shoved several smaller snakes out of its way and bit one who was not fast enough to escape in time.

The small snake gave a pathetic hiss, then sped toward Gorgos. Perhaps it sensed his sympathy. He had always loved lizards, and snakes reminded him of his mother. Delighted, he paused and picked the little creature up. It twined itself lovingly around his arm.

Slowly the other snakes emerged again and slid toward them. All of them made for Gorgos, who was soon engulfed in a happy mass of hissing and slithering as the snakes expressed their adoration of him and claimed his attention.

Gorgos stroked as many of the snakes as he could, then set off festooned with them. Corydon thought how pleased the Snake-Girl would be if he could somehow get them back to Troy.

But now the passageway was widening, its walls stone instead of raw, gleaming earth. Corydon could make out faint drawings on the wall, ancient ones like Euryale's hunting pictures. He saw a full-breasted goddess suckling a baby, a field of stiff wheat, a woman crouched over an oven.

And he smelled something different from the reek of earth and pig and snake. He smelled the most glorious and appetizing smell.

It was roasting pork. Plainly the sacrificed pig was somehow to be consumed.

Corydon was used to inhaling delectable scents from feasts to which he had not been invited. But this smell seemed to tear at his body. He could not give up hope that it might be for them. And when he saw a table laid out before them, with a fair white cloth and a lordly bronze dish and pottery goblets as fine as those in Priam's hall, he felt a rising excitement.

Then two of the priestesses, now changed into clean and seemly white robes, bore in a dish, and on it was the small body of the piglet Gorgos had sacrificed—or if that was impossible, a creature of the same size. Its rich brown flesh caught the light.

Corydon could have died for a taste of that piglet. He leaned forward eagerly. . . . Water rushed into his mouth.

He was stopped by Gorgos's restraining glare. The snakes were hissing a warning, a wail of horror. Corydon frowned. Why shouldn't he eat it? Everything was laid out for them. For them.

An old, old priestess moved out of the shadows. Her face was so wrinkled that Corydon could not even see her eyes. She beamed a toothless smile. "Eat," she said. "I know boys get hungry."

And suddenly, despite his roaring belly, Corydon felt a sense of warning tingling in him. He remembered the Kingdom of the Many, where he had been told not to eat. This, too, felt like a realm of the dead. As well as the delicious scent of pork, there was a dank earth smell, like an open grave. And the reek of old blood under that.

And he looked at the pig, its bronzy skin, its delicate little upturned nose. He could imagine it running and playing. Did he really want to eat it? His stomach said an eager yes. But now his head was awake.

"No, thank you," he said.

Gorgos squeezed his arm. He meant it kindly, though Corydon knew there would be a bruise tomorrow.

"Then leave us, you feeble sons of whores, you sniveling relics of what should have been men!" The old woman's voice rose to a scream, and she flung the roast piglet down on the table. It broke apart before their eyes. Then the illusion broke, and with a heavy lurch of his stomach, Corydon could see that it was no pig.

It was a baby. A roasted baby. Its skin was still bronzy, its nose still sweetly upturned. But it was a baby. A little girl baby.

"It is the goddess's daughter," the old woman said. "And when she is eaten, she is later renewed. But only if she is eaten by the goddess herself." With that, she tore off a hunk of meat—Corydon turned aside to retch—and crammed it into her mouth.

One of the other priestesses spoke. "Do not fear. This is as old as the world. Older than men. But it is not for you. Had you eaten, it would have been a curse to you. For her it is a blessing, and the babe will live." The firm, clear voice held certainty, and Corydon believed it. So did Gorgos. They had both seen stranger things.

"Now you must face one more test," said the younger priestess. The old woman was still cackling and mumbling and nibbling. Corydon still felt sick at the sight. But Gorgos turned to her.

"You are the goddess," he said. "You are a monster. You are of our kind. We offer you our homage."

Corydon was astounded. Suddenly Gorgos was learning true wisdom and discernment. Truer than his. It was his turn to squeeze Gorgos's arm.

The old woman slowly put down the bone she was gnawing.

"Yes, you are of my kind," she said. "All food is a monster. Men fear the loss of food more than a three-headed dog, and food has more power over them than love. Your friend Euryale knows all this. It fuels her art. She, too, is of my kind." She chuckled. "I will help you if you pass the final test. You must meet three old women and wrest from them a secret. If you can do that, you will be free." She laughed again. "Do not tell Kalkhas what you have seen," she said. "He does not have the wisdom to understand it. He would hate you for your knowledge."

Now she moved forward, a tiny bone still in her hand. She moved toward Corydon. "It is you who must remember," she said. "You must remember." And she touched his forehead with the bone.

For a few seconds, he was caught in a vision that seemed to burst onto the stone walls.

The terrible sacrifice was reduced to a heap of chewed bones, and now all three priestesses circled about the pitiful heap, throwing on herbs: the gingery smell of rosemary pierced him, and he saw the rich purple flowers of hyssop and the yellow of ragwort. They chanted, strewing the mass with something Corydon couldn't see. Then one of the women took a lump of pinewood, lit it, and used it to set fire to the pile. It burned with a strange sweet smell, and all the women cried out. At first, Corydon could not understand a single word of their song. Then it changed, and he heard "Let the goddess-child be whole! Let the goddess-child be whole! Let the goddess-child be whole!" At the third cry, the fire died abruptly, and in its center, glowing like a rose, Corydon saw a live baby. It was naked and crying with hunger, and one of the women picked it up and opened her robes to give it food. "Feed and keep, feed and stay, feed and live," they crooned. All were smiling.

The vision faded. It had taken only a moment. Gorgos had not even noticed.

The old woman pointed to a long corridor stretching away into the blackness of another room.

"Go. Find the women. Do as I said."

Still wreathed with snakes, Gorgos strode toward the archway into the next passage. Corydon followed him, tracking the noise of happy snakes, purring like cats.

Corydon wished he felt so contented. The vision had made him uneasy. What did it mean? And what was this secret that they were meant to discover? He was still musing on these things when he heard the muttering.

It sounded like birds fluttering for nesting space—sharp-beaked seabirds on a cliff edge, not sweet little hedge birds.

To Corydon's amazement, he could hear the sound of waves, too, and smell a rough saltiness in the air. The light grew stronger, grayer, bleaker. It was not torchlight but the cold light of day. He burst out into it.

He stood in a huge cave hollowed out from the soft sandstone by the groping fingers of the sea. The walls were pitted by long generations of hungry waves, sculpted so that they made homes for shells and seaweed and other denizens of Poseidon's kingdom. Gorgos, stroking the suddenly chilly snakes, took a deep, happy breath. But Corydon had noticed what looked like a bundle of seaweed or driftwood in the corner, a black tangle of ragged fragments. The muttering came from there.

He touched Gorgos on the arm. Gorgos turned. The muttering grew a little louder.

Corydon could hear individual words, but he couldn't understand them. *"Farra deae micaeque licet salientis honorem / detis et in veteres turea grana focos,"* said one voice. What tongue was it?

He looked a question. Gorgos shrugged eloquently.

From the untidy heap of sea wrack, a figure drew itself up. Corydon caught a glimpse of a face so terrible, it dwarfed all monstrosity. This face was old age itself. It made the ancient priestess of Demeter look like a young girl. The face was like the cave, worn to smoothness and folds by the beating waves, but these were waves of time, not sea. The eyes were blind, shut by eyelids with a thousand creases. The voice was a low, shifting mumble, coming from an ancient, soft mouth with no teeth: *"Et, si tura aberunt, unctas accendite taedas: / parva bonae Cereri, sint modo casta, placent."* If Corydon had not been a poet, he would never have been able to hear words in it at all.

Now another ragged shape rose up. It, too, sang. *"Venerat ad sacras et dea flava dapes."* It swayed softly to and fro, and Corydon noticed the bristles on its chin, which nearly met the nose. But this—woman?—gnawed something with one tooth in her mumbling mouth.

Finally, a third shape rose. *"Est specus exesi structura pumicis asper, / non homini regio, non adeunda ferae,"* it sang. And Corydon saw the face. This one was not blind. It—she—had an enormous eye, blue-white and rheumy with age, but huge, set in one socket. And the eye roved and saw them.

Laughing maniacally, she flung up her garments in the kind of obscene gesture a child might make. Bending, she showed them her bottom. Gorgos and Corydon made faces of disgust, and she laughed again, a cracked old cackle. The muttering rose, and it was plain the others were asking what their sister saw.

"Two boys come here," she said. She at least knew the language of the Hellenes. Corydon felt a rush of relief.

"Give me the eye," said another. "I want to see them. Give it to me."

The ancient woman who had been speaking sighed, then put her long, gnarled fingers up to her face. Using her talon-like nails, she prized the eye out of her head, as one pulls a cork out of a bottle. It came out with a thick, slithery pop. Corydon saw it lying in her hand, jelly-like and slimed with rheum. Corydon's still-hungry stomach heaved. Then the woman bent and offered it to the first shabby black figure, who grasped the air several times, muttering, "Where is it? Give it me, Sister!" before closing her fist on the eye. She held her hand up to her collapsed eye socket. With a sucking sound, like a sea creature slurping, the eye slid into her face. She swiveled it to look at Corydon.

"Oh, a boy. Give me the tooth, Sister. I have been hungry lately. The bones we gnaw are old. Fresh meat would taste sweet. Yes, juicy . . ." She smiled, a child's happy, toothless grin when offered a sweet.

"Come here, little friends," said the one with the tooth. She held out a bone. "See, we have food to share...." She tried to make her voice sound coaxing, but the greed under it was only too obvious. Her grayish tongue came out and licked her lips.

"No, not just now," said Corydon, feeling ridiculous. "We need to ask you a question." He paused. How could he ask them anything? What could he say?

Gorgos had no such qualms. Smiling, he said simply, "Tell us your secret."

There was a terrible silence.

"Only if you let us gnaw off your hand first," said one, in a quavering voice.

"And your head, too," said the one with the eye, fixing them with a steely glare.

"Give me the eye, Sister," said the second. "Let me look upon this sweet meat that asks us so impertinently for our treasure."

"I have only had it for a moment," whined the first old woman, but the others began long, querulous moans, and at last she reached up and began to loosen it, then held it out.

Quick as a panther, Corydon pounced on it. He felt he might die of fright if those terrible old fingers caught him, but he danced silently out of range before any of them were even aware he had been there. Then they began calling out and begging for the eye. "Sister, I cannot find it. Where is it?"

"You've dropped it, you stupid old woman. You're in your dotage. Feel for it on the ground." They all began a dreadful, groping hunt for it. Gorgos drew his sword with a sharp slither and stood in front of Corydon; neither wanted the hunt to discover them. At last, when the old women were wailing more and more frantically, Gorgos spoke.

"We have your eye," he said. "And I will crush it under my foot unless you tell us your secret. Now."

"No, no!" one of them cried out. "The secret is in our song, that is all. In our song."

Corydon spoke gently. "But we cannot understand your tongue," he said.

They cackled. "It will be the language of the world," said one. "One day. And the language of the gods. It is a light that comes from Troy. From Troy to light the world. But you do not understand it now. Not now. Of course not." She blew a long, rude raspberry.

"You wish us to destroy it?" Gorgos said. The eye gave a small, terrified leap in Corydon's hand.

An idea struck Corydon. Taking a burned stick from the center of the cave, where the old women had once had a fire, he began to write down the letters of the words he had heard as best he could. Then he held the quivering eyeball—not without a shudder of revulsion—to his own eye.

At once, the letters rearranged themselves into Hellenic words. Corydon did his best to read them, though the letters were as blurry as the ones he had scrawled. "There is a cave, rough-formed, of corroded pumice, a place neither man nor beast may enter. . . . You may honor the goddess with spelt and dancing salt and grains of ancient hearths. . . . Light some pitchy torches. Little things, if pure, please the good goddess-mother Demeter."

They must find a cave, then, and make an offering. And that would open Gorgos to the little gods. It was cryptic but not impossible.

But there were two immediate problems. One was what to do with the eye. The second was how to get out of the cave.

"Gray women," Corydon said, "I have found out your secret. I will restore your eye if you tell us the way out from here. A safe way, a quick way. No other will do."

There was a furious scrabbling and a kind of clacking sound, like the fighting of angry birds. Then one of the sisters spoke.

"We must tell him or be blind forever. We must. And besides," she said, "I can see that their destiny is already marked out for them without any eye to help me. Mormo-boy, you will die of the high places. Snake-boy, you will die on the ringing plains. You will both die. But you will also be victorious. As you have been today." She pointed to the wall behind Corydon. "Place all four of your mortal hands on it, and a way will open," she said. "Go with the blessing of the goddess."

Carefully, Corydon crept over to them and placed the eye on the floor in front of them. The eye immediately began hopping frantically, as if trying to reach their faces. It made a noise like a plopping frog, and the one who had last spoken captured it quickly. Even from a distance, Corydon could see that it was quaking with pleasure. She inserted it and gave them a last appraising glare, blue-white and spare.

"Go," she said. "Troy's need is very great." For a second, Corydon thought her voice was different, younger and firmer, the voice of Demeter. But he did not remain to find out. He and Gorgos placed their hands on the wall and at once felt them reaching into darkness. They fled down a short corridor and emerged abruptly into the temple.

THIRTEEN

The torches in the temple had barely burned. Corydon and Gorgos's trials in the maze and the cave must have been outside time. Or in many different times but not this one.

Gorgos settled himself in front of the altar. His eyes were open and he was glassily calm, talking to his snakes and hearing their songs. Corydon was less at ease. Had they done enough? He paced restlessly, unable to give way to sleep; he must watch beside Gorgos despite his tiredness. Luckily he was no longer hungry. No one could stay hungry after seeing a baby being devoured and an eye being passed from hand to hand.

They were still there at dawn, grimy and very tired, when Kalkhas came in.

"Well done," he said. It meant nothing to Gorgos, who knew that Kalkhas's approval made no difference now that he had done as Demeter wished. She was the mother of all the gods of earth— not literally but spiritually. Kalkhas gave a little shriek and drew back when he saw Gorgos's snakes, who had all found warm places to sleep while the boys remained awake. Now they poured out and crept up to Gorgos, climbing him as if he were a tree. Corydon looked tiredly at the man before him.

"Did you ever pass those tests yourself?" he asked bluntly. It was a Gorgos kind of question, he knew, but he felt irritated by the man's air of knowingness.

"No," said Kalkhas. Corydon saw that he was ashamed. "I am acceptable to the goddess as her priest," he said with a sigh. "And I can speak with her and with other gods. But that is all." Sudden tears came to his eyes. Corydon and Gorgos moved toward him, and Corydon awkwardly patted his arm.

"Try," urged Gorgos. "We can give you knowledge of what you must do. Not much knowledge, because the goddess forbids it. But some. You must seize the adventure before you."

The priest looked up hopefully, then nodded. "For now, the adventure is yours, and I will help you as I can. You must go and see your other friends; they have been anxious about you." He smiled.

Outside the temple, Sthenno was waiting. Corydon and Gorgos hurled themselves at her. The snakes, too, entwined themselves around her, sensing Gorgos's love. Her bronzy wings went around them with a crisp rattle.

"Your wing!" It seemed as good as new, though now that Corydon looked, he could see that the feathers were a little smoother and sleeker than on the other wing.

"Yes, I am remade," she said encouragingly. Her claws stroked their hair.

But then Sthenno broke off the joyful hug. "Gorgos," she said, "there is a prophecy. . . ."

"I know. That I will die tomorrow. I know I may. But it will only mean that I am in Elysium. All heroes long to be in Elysium. And I will see my great mother. And be truly my father's son."

He seemed genuinely calm. But Sthenno fluttered. "Yes, I know the prophecy of which you speak," she said. "But that was not the one I meant. I wished to speak of the four battles of Troy. It says that Troy will fall when it has endured the battles of the air, of water, of earth, and of fire. I have a clay disk that shows it all."

She pulled a disk from her bag. Corydon examined it; it was indeed the same disk that he had seen in her room—but wait! The whirlwind symbol had vanished. And Sthenno, too, was frowning at it. "There should be a fourth symbol. Where did it go?" She caught her breath. "Of course! The battle of the air is over and done. So its symbol has gone, too."

"And soon Troy may be gone," said Corydon. "We must learn from the fate of Atlantis and make a plan to rescue as many of its people as we can and lead them to safety.

"We should ask the Snake-Girl. Her powers might be useful. If she can enchant people and tell them where to go . . ." But Corydon felt no confidence in his suggestion.

He and Gorgos went to Euryale's studio, and Sthenno retired to her tower to consult more scrolls.

The Snake-Girl was sitting at a table, surrounded by a mess of feathers and small bones. Before her was a tray on which Corydon could see at least a hundred songbirds. They had been spelled and struggled pathetically to be free, their wings flapping weakly. As Corydon watched, the Snake-Girl picked one off the tray and, without even bothering with its song, popped it into her mouth and crunched hard. Then she picked up another and shoved it in, too, spitting out bones and fragments of feathers.

She looked around. "Aroo Cooydong," she said. Her mouth was too full of bird to make much sound. Swallowing hastily, she added apologetically, "I'm so hungry, I need to eat them all." Sitting on a chair beside her were two empty trays. Corydon could see that birdsong was unlikely to wake the city early for many a long day. He could also see her swollen belly for the first time. It was now very clear that she was expecting a child.

She crunched up a protesting robin. A wren on the tray made panicky tweets. It gave an abrupt squawk when she grabbed it.

"What happened to singing with them? To burying them and laying wreaths on their graves?"

She shrugged. "I'm just hungry," she said.

Euryale bustled in with twelve boiled, stuffed dormice to tempt her; she knew the Snake-Girl would be full of regret in a few minutes' or a few hours' time.

She looked at them. Then she grabbed three screaming larks at once and bit their heads off. Corydon saw her chewing.

But she was still the same in other ways. When Gorgos brought in his snakes, she gave a soft, welcoming hiss and forgot the birds completely. The snakes folded themselves around her, hissing back.

"They are hungry," she said reproachfully. "You should have

fed them, Gorgos." Now she picked dormice off the tray to feed the new pets, who responded eagerly; then all went to sleep in a contented warm huddle.

But the Snake-Girl woke after a quick nap and joined them at *their* meal. Corydon told her that the fall of the city could not be prevented forever. He asked her to help assemble people and plan an escape when the end came.

"But this is the royal family's business, King Priam's business," she said. It was clear that she did not like the idea of leading, nor of leaving the city. "And I cannot control so many people."

"If King Priam tells people to leave, it will be seen as surrender," said Euryale. "You can show people the way."

She had laid out a wonderful feast—a rare thing in this besieged city. There were hunks of cheese, cold lamb, an egg apiece, a spoonful each of precious honey, plenty of bread she had made. It was crisp and caramel-crusted, and somehow its savor seemed to recall Demeter herself, as if she were blessing their feast. She was the corn-woman—and suddenly Corydon thought of an old song about the corn as a king who ruled for a day and then was cut down, then beaten down, then buried—only to spring up into the light. Resurrection . . . corn was resurrection. And the bread made with fresh, rich wheat gave life. He took another huge bite. It was as if it strengthened him magically. Gorgos laughed, and Corydon saw the same bright vitality in his friend's eyes.

"Euryale," said Gorgos, "what did you put in the food?"

"Food always makes me feel like this," said Euryale calmly. "But it's better when you are really hungry. Look, Gorgos. What is going to happen to you is what happens to every artist. You have to empty yourself to be possessed by the work. And you were empty with hunger, too, and now you are becoming full. It's the same kind of thing."

"Is it?" Gorgos looked doubtful. "If you say it is."

Euryale fetched a painting she'd been working on. "It's called *The Goddess's Spring*," she said. It showed a pink girl lying on the ground, surrounded by blurring flowers. She lay under a softly painted apple tree. One huge apple hung down over the girl's head.

"But if the apple is ripe," said Gorgos, "then it cannot be spring. It must be *The Goddess's Autumn*."

"Things can happen in art that are against the rules in real life," said Corydon.

Euryale beamed. "And in the realm of the gods, too," she said. "There, too, life is like art."

Taking another healthy draft of the honey-sweet wine that seemed so much a part of Troy, Corydon found a million ideas revolving in his head. He thought of art and the gods . . . of how artists tried to capture a god in their works so that they might harness some of his or her power.

Then he thought of the djinn and how one had sacrificed himself to become part of the wall he had created, to be part of the city's defenses. The djinn unleashed were like gods, but they could be held in a bottle the size of a man's hand. He thought of how Gorgos was to be a vessel for all the little gods who each dwelled in one fountain, one riverlet, one tiny tree, one family hearth. And he thought of how the good seemed always limited by being tied to the earth, while the wicked were free to stride over it and call it theirs. They could rule life because they stood outside it. So they gained power.

"What a pity," said Corydon, "that you can't put the Olympians in bottles. Like djinns."

"Perhaps you could," said Euryale. "If you knew how to. It would make an interesting installation. Live gods in glass bottles."

"It would make them as they once were," said Corydon. "Little gods of hill and river. No god should rule the whole world, and no man either. And it would be fun to see them struggling to get out."

"Beating the sides of the bottles with their hands," agreed Euryale, smiling.

"Maybe even trying to push out the stopper," added the Snake-Girl.

They all stared dreamily into the fire, enjoying the thought of a world where the Olympians were in bottles. Perhaps it was the wine, but their own spirits felt freer and more released than at any time in Troy. But there was also the knowledge of tomorrow. Euryale and the Snake-Girl, as well as Corydon, found themselves noticing things about Gorgos they had never noticed before. He was full-grown now: a tall man, lean and very strong. But his dark skin had kept a boy's softness, his eyes a boy's brightness.

When Sthenno clattered in again, she made for Gorgos and hugged him; she had been at work on prophecies in her tower. It was plain that this was an act of love. She also had a small spell to offer. "It will make your weapons sharp," she said shyly. Gorgos's sword was always sharp, but he didn't say so for once; he was learning a kind of care with people's feelings. He thanked Sthenno warmly. But the old Gorgos was still there. At the end of the meal, he pushed back his stool and said, yawning, "Well, I'm going to sleep. If I die tomorrow, please don't worry. Corydon knows what to do."

"What do you mean?" asked Corydon desperately.

"You'll know," said Gorgos. "The little gods will help, and so will their mother." The Snake-Girl looked puzzled, and Sthenno scrabbled for a parchment that spoke of the fight. But Gorgos, with another wide yawn, was already heading for bed.

None of the others could sleep. Corydon dozed and tossed, fragments of dream reaching him: the dead baby . . . the live baby . . . the smell of earth and blood. When the dawn trumpets sounded, he was deeply asleep for the first time in the night and woke with a horrified start.

Gorgos was already up and was putting on his armor. "I have to take it with me, and on is the easiest way to carry it," he explained. "I'll take it off when we get to the cave."

Corydon noticed Gorgos assumed he was coming, too, which was warming. "Shall I wake the others?" he asked. The Snake-Girl was snoring softly, and as he looked at her tired and tender face, he felt a wave of protectiveness.

"No," said Gorgos. "Let's just go."

The Greeks had readily agreed to the challenge of single combat, and the fight was scheduled for high noon, on a dusty roadway on the plains south of Troy. No one wanted to let Akhilleus into Troy, even for a fight they hoped he would lose. But Corydon felt he could sense Akhilleus's rage and impatience licking at the strong stone walls like a fire.

He and Gorgos found Kalkhas waiting for them, and together they slipped out of the south gate. Stiff green grass remained on this side of Troy, though the cattle and sheep had been pillaged by

Gorgon and Greek. A few wildflowers lined the path with bright pinks and purples. On the mountain was a morning mist, turned to faint pink by the sun's dawn light. The river Skamandros shone and twisted nearby, and a few birds that the Snake-Girl had spared sang. Gorgos began to climb, and Corydon and Kalkhas followed. The knowledge of where to find the cave of pumice seemed embedded in Gorgos, like he was following some inner direction.

They reached a narrow slit in the rock. "We are neither men nor beasts," said Gorgos, and ducked his head to insinuate himself into the slot. Corydon followed suit. It was dim and gray in the cave, damp and shaley, though the walls were full of giant holes blasted by some wrath of the earth's. The ceiling had a huge gap torn in it, mainly overgrown by vines and cyclamens but giving faint light. Through this gap appeared the anxious face of Kalkhas.

"I cannot enter," he said. "I am but a man. But I will be here. Stand in the cave entrance, Gorgos. And you must be naked. You will resume your armor later."

Gorgos smiled. Kalkhas had to feel as if he were in charge. But he was not.

Glistening, dark, naked, Gorgos took up a loaf of bread he'd brought with him. A simple, pure gift to please the goddess. He broke it and set down his offering. "Lady," he said simply, "fill me."

There was a long, deep rumble of thunder.

And Corydon heard the sound of many thousands of feet moving toward the cave. He went over to Gorgos and stood by his side.

They streamed up the hill in the mist, taking shape as they grew closer, and the shapes were strange—the shadow of a blossoming tree with long hair like a girl, little squat faun-men with stout goatlegs, tall half horses, some satyrs swishing long tails. Here was Faunus, with his thick pelt of fur. Pales came with her fleecy shepherdess's coat, giving Corydon a fleeting smile. Maiden huntresses of the desert came, tawny and golden-eyed like lions. The rivers flowed uphill, took shape as solid beings, and poured themselves into Gorgos like long drinks. Out of the city came a new flood of beings. These were the family gods, the Lares; and since every family had a Lar, there were every kind of people: glossy blue-black Lares and russet Lares and Lares with golden skin, pale pink Lares with linty hair, male and female and everything in between.

As each god or goddess arrived, he or she saluted Gorgos and then somehow merged with him.

Gorgos stood bolt upright, as if someone were holding him by the hair. He looked just the same, but he radiated a new kind of power.

A sort of fight seemed to be going on over the surface of Gorgos's skin. First Faunus's soft fur seemed to be mirrored in it; then it turned to a reflection of soft petals, then to tree branches. Then a raging waterfall seemed to erase him altogether. Then his own dark skin emerged like a black, wet rock, and he seemed to step out of the water. Gorgos's expression was thoughtful and concentrated, as if he were trying out weapons or armor.

"Are you all right?" asked Corydon anxiously.

Gorgos paused. "My own form is best," he said. "Their strength is in me. I can take their forms, too." His voice sounded odd, as if he were speaking in a vast and echoing cave. But he bent to his armor.

"Are you ready?" Corydon asked when they had strapped on his armor and his sword.

For answer, Gorgos picked up the heavy plumed helmet that he normally didn't like to wear.

As he turned toward the cave's doorway, the old woman in black whom he had been half expecting came and put her hand on his arm. Immediately, an ear of corn erupted from his skin. His hair turned to straw. Then it all went back to normal.

"You carry my powers, too," she said. "Though they are not really a warrior's powers. The power to make things grow is not of immediate use in battle, but it is the only reply to battle. Without that power, it would not matter who won or lost." She took his hand again, and briefly Corydon saw that his face was made of small loaves of bread. And then she was gone.

Gorgos stepped out of the cave and ran swiftly down the hillside, burdened though he was. Corydon followed. Already the sun had melted the morning dew, and the hillside grew pale. The air was very clear up here, above Troy, powdery with dust.

"It's like the monsters' island," said Gorgos wonderingly. "I wonder how Mother Wolf is. And your sheep," he added kindly.

Corydon had long since resigned himself to the fact that Mother Wolf had eaten his sheep, but it didn't seem the right moment to say so. "I miss our home," he said.

As he spoke, he felt a fresh new wind, which brought a scent of thyme and crushed herbs with it, a scent of the island. A swirl of dust built up, and from it stepped his father, Pan. Corydon ran to him, feeling his usual mix of love and dread.

"I am not truly here," his father warned. "This is only my

image, and it is only for this place, which is pasturage, my domain. The other gods have been willing to sacrifice themselves to be Troy's defenders, but I am not willing. I must be what I am." His face was both sad and comical. "I wish you well, Gorgos," he said, "though you are none of mine."

"Join us!" Gorgos's face was bright. "We fight for Troy."

"She is not mine either," said Pan. "I cannot take what is not mine."

"Everyone else has," said Gorgos simply. He raised his hand. Millions of tiny faces swarmed in it like ants.

Pan laughed his sly laugh. "If you have so many, then you do not need me," he said.

"I do not know what I need," said Gorgos. "In Troy—in all my life, in truth—we are like men piling up defenses against a sudden flood, building the wall of sand high lest the tides overwhelm us."

Corydon thought this idea wasn't at all Gorgos-like, nor was the language. Plainly, his passengers moved in his brain and heart as well as in his body.

"You do not need me now," said Pan. "You need me later. To make a threnody for the fallen." And again his face was sly.

"Who will fall? You know and I know. But you also know what will happen next."

Now Pan was serious. "Yes, I know. But do you understand what it means? You will be cut off from normal human joy. You will be an exile."

Gorgos laughed. "So have I always been," he said. "So are we all. And I do not really care if my joys are normal or not."

Now Pan smiled. "And what of you, my son?"

Corydon spoke sturdily. "We must save something of this land. You yourself said it. If its defeat is swift, more of what it stands for will be lost. If the battles for it are worth a song or two, men may remember it forever. That is the best way to defeat the Olympians."

"Not the best way," said his father. "Remember that songs can lie."

"What is the best way, then? Show me!" begged Corydon.

His father's eyes were deep green wells of sadness as he said, "Do not run, my son. In a few days, you will know. You will know. And you will act. I will see you again, soon," he promised. "For now, I leave you an additional weapon."

A man appeared who walked as if he were old. He wore a robe of a blue so dark it was almost black, a precious color, but it was as plain as ash. He carried a black staff, and Corydon saw that he was using it to feel his way. "Where is my boy?" he asked in a high, shrill voice, a voice of power that didn't sound like a human voice but like one of the daimons of the air.

"Your boy is here," said Pan. "A new boy to lead you to this day's great battle." The man shuffled over, and Pan placed his hand on Corydon's arm.

Corydon looked in amazement at the softly folded old face. The man was blind, his eyes sealed as if by some giant hand.

"Has he always been blind?" asked Gorgos.

"I have not always been blind," said the man clearly and directly. "But it is only since I was blinded that I have been a singer of wars and heroes. My sight was taken in order that I might have other gifts." His voice rose sweetly in a song: "Sing to me, Muse,

156

of the courage of the swift-footed son of Poseidon, the ebony-skinned one, Medusa's boy. . . ."

"How do you know about me?" Gorgos demanded.

"I know everything that I need to know," said the blind man. "That is my gift. And now you, too, are large, and you, too, contain multitudes." His smile was not sly like Pan's but open and direct like Gorgos's own.

Pan himself gave Corydon a last smile and melted into the hillside.

"Are you ready?" Corydon asked Gorgos.

But the old man replied: "He is ready. So am I. Now for the battle. Already the eagles have gathered, and the fat wolves of the woods, swollen with the bodies of dead men. You contain their powers. Their wildness."

Corydon looked around nervously. He could see no wolves. Then he looked at Gorgos and could see what the old man must mean. Gorgos himself was the wolf and the eagle. . . . "You see well," he said.

"You do, too," said the old man. "You are of my kind. Not his. It is your métier not to fight the Olympians but to sing songs about those who do." His voice was hypnotic. Corydon thought he sounded more and more like Pan, and like the daimons, too. The old voice ran up in a strong arc. "Sing, Muse, of the shepherd boy who saved the dead, of his hurt when he could not save a city. Sing of his vow, great Muse. Sing of his war against the Olympians. How he sent many men to the realm of the dead, where the kites picked their bones."

Corydon shuddered. The song had caught perfectly his own

sense of who he was, the melody weakening under the weight of the words, just as he felt himself weak in the face of the gods. Then the man grinned.

"Sing, Muse, of the boy who hates himself," he said. Corydon forced himself to smile back. "But, first, I shall sing of another. Of Gorgos. Of the rivers of gods who pour through his veins, course through his heart. He is mighty beyond the lot of mortal men, but this day's battle will not be lucky for him. You have invoked your gods. So, too, has the Greek champion."

FOURTEEN

THEY HAD BEEN MOVING AT THE OLD MAN'S SLOW
pace down a road, now white with dust in the late-morning light.
And it was through a hot white haze that they saw Akhilleus in his
chariot.

His armor was all black now, the hard black of obsidian. His
helmet still bore a silver crest, but the plumes of light were inter-
woven with black feathers, and even at this distance Corydon
could see the plumes were dyed with blood. He bore a new shield,
splendid in painting and carving, but he bore it as a weak impedi-
ment, one he did not want or need. His true shield was his eyes.
Corydon had thought their silver fierce before. Now they had the
ferocity of burning sunlight on metal; they gave off silver lightnings like great storm clouds. His mouth looked as if he had never
smiled.

As they approached, he was absolutely still, as if he were truly
made of stone.

Gorgos greeted him when they reached hailing distance.

"You are the champion of the Greeks, I of the Trojans. I fight to save my city."

The severe mouth opened. "I care nothing for Troy. I fight you because you killed my friend and stabbed him where he lay. For that I will gladly tear out your lungs."

Gorgos was silent. He had killed many on the field. "Which one was your friend?" he said.

"He wanted to wear my armor into battle. He took my place when I was hurt. Now I take his place. Enough words. We are warriors, not actors." He jumped nimbly down from his chariot.

He and Gorgos began circling each other, like stags who fight in springtime. Slowly.

Corydon led the poet a safe distance away.

Then Akhilleus reached down his spear and threw it swifter than eye could see, all in one movement. Gorgos leapt aside. Corydon saw the spent spear on the dry ground, a flash of black at its tip.

Now Gorgos flung his own light spear, and it hit Akhilleus's shield and broke.

Next the two swords clashed, and it looked as if they were animate, fighting each other while the strong men watched. The blades were equally strong; again and again they drove against each other. Akhilleus's golden blade thrust to and fro, and Gorgos's blue-black blade leapt to meet it. It was as if the swords were friends or lovers who could not bear to be apart. Akhilleus tried to overbear Gorgos by strength, but Gorgos pushed him away. He tried speed, but Gorgos was equally quick. Akhilleus leapt to the top of a small, tufty hillock to rain blows down on Gorgos, but Gorgos managed to trip him and he stumbled. The Trojans cheered frantically from the walls. But Akhilleus recovered his balance as swiftly as a cat.

It was plain that neither man could easily overcome the other. The battle might come down to sheer luck. Or the will of the gods.

Now the gods within Gorgos did seem to take a hand. Corydon saw the shadows of their forms and faces passing over his friend's face. A cunning little Lar looked out and in the next second, Gorgos had somehow jerked Akhilleus's sword around so it twisted, and then he brought his second spear down on the blade with a thud like a falling tree. The blade shivered. It did not break but a splinter shattered from its side. It was very slightly weakened.

In a burst of white light, a young man appeared at Akhilleus's side. He held out a new sword, exactly like the old one. Gorgos tried to keep the Greek so busy he didn't have time to grab it. But at last, Akhilleus managed to land a blow on Gorgos's shield arm, and he used the precious second to make the switch. The boy who had held it gave a satisfied smile. In that smile, Corydon recognized Athene. She vanished to the sound of boos from the watching Trojans—the Olympians were always cheats.

Now Akhilleus pressed forward eagerly, hitting at Gorgos repeatedly. Gorgos parried again and again with his sword, but Corydon could sense some of the gods in him turning away, horrified and afraid. He thought about it: trees and rocks and woods had some power to resist battle, but not much. Eventually, if men fought over and over in the same place, the pleasant landscape would become a blasted wild with wizened trees and no clean water.

Now fragile landscapes were trying to stand against the face of War itself.

As Corydon looked at Akhilleus, he saw a terrible grinning rictus, far uglier than Medusa, more dead than any resident of Hades. His horror was shared by some of the gods who inhabited Gorgos. As he watched, a sobbing dryad distended Gorgos's skin. With a soft popping sound, she materialized beside him, her leafy hair dripping with tears, and then stumbled away, searching for her tree.

And now his heart was black with a sense of disaster. For after the dryad's defection, other gods had begun to leave Gorgos. Corydon saw some small Lares patter back toward the city, crying with fright.

Akhilleus's grin widened. But Gorgos's strokes grew swifter. Was he getting too desperate—might he blunder?

There was a flick of Akhilleus's sword, and everyone saw a trickle of blood running down Gorgos's arm. Gorgos himself stared at it in disbelief. He, who had withstood lava and seas and monsters of the deep, had at last had his skin broken by a man's sword. He looked up and met Akhilleus's eyes. They stared at each other for a long time. And slowly a smile curved on Gorgos's face. A death smile. A smile that made the two terrible faces, streaked with dust and sweat, strangely alike.

Then he turned, twisted on the spot, seemed to stretch, his armor slipping off him, his arms slowly merging into his sides and his legs cleaving together. Again and again he wrapped himself around Akhilleus as his skin turned into watery scales. His face became that of a shimmering snake, his eyes two blue pools with shells for eyelids. His hair grew long and weedy, greener than his mother's snakes had been, and in it gasped little fish lice.

Corydon realized that Gorgos had allowed one of the river gods to possess him completely. It must be Skamandros, the chief river of Troy.

The serpent-river flung many coils about the hero's body, trying to trap his arms against his sides, then trying to choke him. Akhilleus managed to free his sword arm, and the Gorgos-river roared with fury and tried to squeeze his arm so that he would be forced to drop the sword. But Akhilleus held the sword aloft and brought it down against the watery body. It was silly, like a child angrily hitting a tree with a stick. But it kept his head above water, and the Gorgos-body within the watery carapace felt the blow resonate and shivered.

Plainly, the river could not overcome the hero like this. He tried a new tactic. Skamandros's waters had run red with blood as he meandered into Poseidon's realm. He felt polluted. And now he heaved up from his whole being those dead who wallowed in his waters.

A tidal wave of half-decaying corpses surged at Akhilleus as the river rose and charged against him, churning, surging, all his rapids rising in white fury. Then the river drove the mass of corpses against the shield of Akhilleus. Skamandros—or Gorgos—was bellowing like a bull as the river flung out its dead.

To the amazement of the onlookers, the dead were animate; they thrust broken spears and swords at the great hero, impelled by the riverine frenzy. Akhilleus beat them off, but now his eyes were staring with horror as men he himself had killed strove for revenge, strove to force him, too, into muddy, bloody death. Thrashing over Akhilleus's shoulders, the river formed itself into a wall, a wave that hurled itself at his head. The tremendous thrust of it slammed into his shield. He staggered and lost his footing. A corpse was on him, shoving him deeper into the water. He managed to grab a tree, but the branch was ripped from his grasp by an avalanche of dead, mud, and water.

Akhilleus fled, with Gorgos-Skamandros at his heels, roaring and immense. "Gods are stronger than men!" roared the voice of the river. "Gods are stronger than men!"

Now Akhilleus turned. His brilliant eyes flashed. "I see that there are many gods in you," he cried. "Fight me as a man and we shall see who will triumph." Again and again, the mighty crest of the river kept coming, but Akhilleus leapt and ran, desperately, as the river kept on dragging his knees down, cutting the ground from under his legs. He looked at the sky. "Why have you abandoned me, Lords of Olympos?" he cried.

Instantly, the youth who was truly Athene was at his side. "Do not be afraid," she said contemptuously. "I bring the blessings of Zeus. That river will subside. You know it is not your fate to die in the embrace of a little local mud god. You chose glory, Akhilleus. Glory rather than length of days."

"Help me!" The words were torn from Akhilleus. Corydon could see that he hated to ask even the gods for help, and Athene smiled. Suddenly Hera stood beside her.

Hera's voice was shrill and severe. Corydon shuddered as she called, "My son! Hephaistos!"

And a little man came running on his lame leg, his body black and sooty. He came limping down from the mountains, running so fast that the ground behind him was bursting into flames as he ran. "Mother, I come!" he cried eagerly. Corydon remembered his love, and hate, for his mother.

"Burn that river!" his mother screamed. "Destroy it!"

The little man somehow lifted the flame of his own running and flung it directly at Gorgos-Skamandros.

The fire poured over the whole plain like water. The dead burned, the living dead crying out in pain. And the bright coils of Skamandros shrank, turning to billowing clouds of steam. The earth shrank, too, its moisture drying out; cracks appeared in the ground, arid and hard. Trees by the river caught, too—elm and willow and tamarisk and lotus—and Corydon heard many dryads shriek in agony and crumble into ashes from within his friend, who stood in the midst of the turmoil, bewildered. But no doubts held Akhilleus, his foe. As plain Gorgos emerged from the steam and the water, Akhilleus wasted no time.

"You will die now," he said in a low, soft voice that carried to the watchers over the crackle of flames. Soon they were at it again.

Hephaistos was running desperately toward his already vanishing mother. "Mother! Don't go!" he cried. But it was too late. The dwarf god gave a wail like an abandoned baby. Athene turned away in distaste. Hephaistos huddled small on the ground where his mother had stood.

Then he turned to look at the contesting heroes. "I made both swords," he said to the air, since no one was beside him. "I made them both. I think it will be difficult for either to triumph."

But it was plain to everyone else that Akhilleus was winning. Steadily he drove Gorgos back. Gorgos was somehow depleted by the magical energies he had exerted. It was as if he were stretched thin by Skamandros's use of him. And then Athene intervened again.

She slid out a foot and tripped Gorgos. All the Trojans booed, but Gorgos fell.

"Get up," said Akhilleus. "I will kill you on your feet."

Gorgos got up, smeared with mud and blood and ash. He did not know how to stop fighting or how to despair. Or how to die. It had to go on. And it did. From time to time, a little god would appear in Gorgos with a plan. Faunus with his strength. The wild cunning of a hunter staring out of a boy's eyes. But Akhilleus was always still standing. Still there. He killed the hopes of a thousand gods, but he could not seem to die.

Now Gorgos looked tired. He wasn't as quick. He didn't look as strong; his blows lacked force. Akhilleus was wearing out that godlike confidence. Fighting the Greek hero was like attacking a statue; every time Gorgos managed to land a blow, there was a dull clang, and the weapon bounced off.

"Gorgos!" Corydon shouted it. "Gorgos! Retreat!"

Sthenno and Euryale stood nearby, ready to sweep him away.

But Gorgos didn't even turn his head. Beside Corydon a dark-haired woman said in a low voice, "It must be now." Corydon turned and saw it was Demeter. He began a rebellious protest but was silenced by her seriousness. "Do not fear," she said. "It does not end here."

As she spoke, Akhilleus finally saw the opening in Gorgos's defenses that he had been seeking all day. His sword flashed forward. And Gorgos was on it.

Gorgos looked down and saw the black blood of his death. More black blood gushed from his mouth. He made a choking sound.

The little gods gibbered and bubbled inside him.

Gorgos looked at Akhilleus's sword, still incredulous. He drew the sword from him and threw it at Akhilleus, who caught it easily. And smiled. And smiled and smiled as Gorgos's knees gave way, as he fell to the ground like a wave collapsing. Corydon ran over to him, withstanding Akhilleus's silver glare.

"Do you wish to die, too?"

"Rather than let him die alone, I would oblige you," Corydon shouted recklessly.

This seemed to give Akhilleus pause; a shadow crossed his silver eyes, as if he was remembering. Sthenno and Euryale moved forward protectively, but Akhilleus didn't fear them. Instead, his eyes were all for Gorgos. He bent toward the body, still with that terrible smile. "Little king of monsters," he said, "you are for the dark. Find my friend there. His name is Patroklos. Tell him Akhilleus sends him a slave, the man who killed him." He clapped the dying Gorgos sardonically on the shoulder.

Corydon took no notice. His eyes, too, were all for Gorgos. He took his hand; it was slick and sticky with blood. To his amazement, he felt the Snake-Girl slither up beside him, under the defiant shelter of Sthenno's and Euryale's wings.

"Can you help?" Corydon asked desperately.

She shook her head. "He's dying, Corydon. There's nothing we can do." Gorgos's breath was rasping through the blood that was choking him. The Snake-Girl wiped it away, but it bubbled back. She was joined by the dark-haired, dark-robed woman, who wiped Gorgos's brow.

Gorgos found enough breath to speak. "Corydon . . . ," he said. "Remember. Remember."

Corydon nodded and pressed his hand. His own tears were falling fast, but he barely noticed because he was so busy drinking in Gorgos. Imprinting him on his mind. Sealing him there forever. Even now, he could hardly believe his friend, his brother, was dying. Had been defeated. It seemed impossible.

Gorgos tried to give him a final smile, but death caught him and his eyes rolled backward. His head flopped into the lap of the woman in the dark robes. She stroked his hair and very gently closed his eyes.

He was gone.

Akhilleus was exultant. He split the skies with a shriek of triumph.

"Now Troy will fall at my feet," he said. "And I shall be remembered forever."

FIFTEEN

T HEY BORE GORGOS HOME, SHOULDER-HIGH. HIS BODY lay in state in Priam's palace. And all Troy came to visit him. For hours people walked slowly down the long corridor, then into the receiving room where he lay. Huge piles of flowers furtively gathered from gardens and hillsides piled up around him, and they smelled not of scent but of rot and decay.

Corydon had not left him for an instant. It was for him to brush away the flies that came.

At last the city quieted. And Gorgos still lay motionless.

Corydon knew he had to try now. Try something impossible. He had to try to raise the dead.

Resurrection was what the little gods did, after the small annual death of winter. This was Gorgos's winter. Corydon was a shepherd, and this would be like moving his flock from pasture to pasture. But he said all that to himself because he knew he was breaking a law that was far older than the Olympians. Man is mortal.

Sthenno understood. She, too, had stayed. She knew what had to be done.

She took Gorgos in her arms; he was stiff, like a wooden doll. She called Euryale, shrill and birdlike; it was like the cry of a hunting nightjar. Now Euryale came and took Corydon, and together they flew.

They landed on the bare hillside just beyond the cave of the goddess shrine.

They gathered wood in silence. Sthenno spoke only once. She drew the clay disk of prophecy from her wings. "See," she said to Corydon. "The water has gone. There are still earth and fire to come."

Then they laid Gorgos on the pyre.

They flung on rosemary, hyssop, ragwort, and a knot of pine. Gorgos was buried in an avalanche of flowers. Then Corydon bent and looked at his face. It might be the last time, and he wanted to make sure he did not forget.

Then he lit the pyre. He spoke the words he had heard in his vision of Demeter's priestesses resurrecting the baby. "Let him be whole! Let him be whole! Let him be whole!" The fire sprang into greedy life, and its glow lit the entire hillside, so that grass and flowers stood out, their long shadows black behind them. From somewhere, a ring of dancers appeared and flickered around the pyre—or were they nothing but the shadows of the flames? Corydon's heart was full of a terrible mixture of unbearable hope and ashy despair. He remembered the burning of Gorgos's mother. He wanted to fling himself onto the pyre, but the wide, greedy turrets of fire also terrified him with their heat.

Out of the pyre poured more of the little gods; not all of them had left Gorgos alone in death. Some sleepy pasture gods didn't seem to know he had died and only now awoke with the pain of burning at their backs. A few left nursing bruises or burns. It was clear that they could never make a force to rival the Olympians. It was also clear that no one would ever persuade them to take action again. A pastoral nymph of a spring shook her fist at Corydon as she fled.

The flames closed around Gorgos after these exoduses. And then the fire stopped giving out heat or crackling. And its center slowly changed color, like a cloud filling with rain. It had been red and orange and gold; now it deepened to a dawn green, and then—slowly—to blue, the clear, pale blue of winter skies. Gorgos was invisible inside it; this flame was not transparent but a cloak behind which the gods were at work.

The flame turned rosy. And inside it Gorgos stood up, and with flame shining on his skin and spurts of flame clinging to his hair, he walked out of his own funeral pyre and stood on the hillside before them.

The dark-haired goddess stood beside him. Had she been in the fire, too?

She held out her hand. "Bread," she said. "It will hold you to earth." She broke the bread and gave a piece to Gorgos, who took it and ate it solemnly.

"Hear me," she said, "I do not do this so that you may fight. That would break the laws of battle. I do this that you may save the idea of the city. It must fall, and you cannot prevent it. But you must lead the Trojans to a new place. And it is there that your destiny will be fulfilled. For now," she said, "you must remain with me. In my temple." She turned to the others. "And when the city falls, he will return to Troy, to lead the people." She took Gorgos's hand and led him away.

Corydon was stupefied. Now, indeed, Gorgos belonged to someone other than the monsters. They had not even had the chance to talk to him.

They had brought him back, but somehow Corydon felt more unsure than ever.

They went to King Priam's palace, where the blind man was singing a long account of the battle to the king. Corydon listened for a while, his heart stirred by the marvelous weaving of words—though he noticed that the man had not mentioned Gorgos at all, seeming to think Akhilleus had just fought a river. Priam looked up with tears streaming down his face.

"What of Gorgos?" Corydon asked the old man fiercely.

"You do not truly want the Olympians to know your plans," said the man serenely.

Corydon was reminded only that he had no plan, and the monsters went home and gathered around the table, morose, feeling prickly and uncomfortable. Gorgos was a card they had played. And the loss—even though it had been predicted—was more than they could bear.

No one said, "What now?" They all thought it but rejected half-formed plans. No one wanted to do more than meet what might come with stoic courage.

Euryale was working on a bronze sculpture, slowly carving the wax form that would be destroyed when the hot bronze was poured into it. It seemed depressingly symbolic of their failed plans: working on a shape that would melt away to nothing.

Sthenno hated to see everyone so defeated. She scuttled to and fro, talking eagerly of the plan to evacuate the people of Troy. She had already organized muster points for key Trojans: priests and artists "and, of course, about fifty astronomers," said Euryale rudely. But Corydon felt pleased that this small idea was in hand. It made the struggle to raise Gorgos seem more valid.

"How does that work, Euryale?" he asked idly, watching her press the wax with her scraper.

She explained, "Well, I will encase the wax in clay and fire it slowly. Then I'll pour in molten bronze, which melts the wax and hardens in its place. You can't carve or change bronze because it's so strong. But wax is weak, and you can change it."

"What is it? A statue of what?"

Euryale looked down. "It's Gorgos when he was full of the gods."

She showed Corydon how, on the wax, faint shapes of the other gods could be discerned—a shadowy nymph peering from his chest, a satyr in the line of his belly, a thousand dryads caught in his curly hair. Corydon admired the conception. Gorgos would truly look full of the little gods.

And yet it seemed ironic for Gorgos-and-the-gods to be so . . . fixed. The reality had been so malleable, full to overflowing, full . . .

Full of the gods . . . The phrase rang in Corydon's ears. And then he remembered their silly conversation about trapping Olympians in bottles, like djinns.

Then suddenly he stood up, pushed back his chair, and, seizing his cloak, went out of the house. He had an idea, and it was vital to think it through thoroughly. Using one of the small tunnels, he crept out of Troy and sped up the hillside. Sitting where he could see the Great Hunter spiraling toward the earth, he thought hard.

The idea he had had was to catch Zeus himself in a kind of bottle. A statue maybe, an eidolon. Something unbreakable. This would ground him, hem him in, make him as he had once been, as the little harmless local gods still were. He would be not destroyed but *limited*.

What he needed was a vessel and the power to persuade or force the king of the gods to enter it.

Euryale! She could make a beautiful Zeus sculpture, and Corydon could suggest he inhabit it to delight his loyal followers. Could it really be that simple? No. He suspected not. He might have some powers of persuasion, but they weren't likely to work on such as Zeus.

His thoughts were rushing now, like the tumbling river he sat beside.

Someone else would need to lure Zeus. Who? Gorgos would be too tactless even if he were available. So would Euryale herself. He wished Fee were with them; she could get anyone to do anything. Would the Snake-Girl do it, with her hypnotic powers? She might be too timid. What was likely to tempt this god?

"I think you need my help," said a voice beside him.

Aphrodite! Corydon had almost forgotten her, but here she stood, still looking sulky and pretty but uninspiring. "Excuse me?" he managed to stammer.

"You don't see me as beautiful because you have not yet learned to want what I offer," she said. "You are young, and your heart is full of more innocent dreams. Later you will know me as part of your heart, and then I will seem much lovelier—much more irresistible."

Corydon didn't like the idea much. . . . He thought of the Snake-Girl, of his warm and tender feelings for her, his longing to protect her, and couldn't imagine himself becoming like the man who had hurt her. . . . But he recognized Aphrodite's power. The Olympians were extreme about love: Zeus seemed to want every nymph, while Athene refused all desire. Perhaps moderation would be wiser.

"I will help you, young boy." She said again, "Just ask."

But Corydon was wary. "Why?"

She laughed. "Because I hate them, too. They spoil all my fun," she said lightly, but then her gaze turned more menacing. "Sikandar chose me as the fairest, and now Athene and Hera are here interfering in my affairs as usual. I've had enough. And"—she paused for a breath—"they killed my father. Well, their father killed my father. That stupid old man in his stupid old library."

"So . . . you remember before there were Olympians?"

"The gods did not always live on Olympos. And I like being a goddess on earth, not all cold among the snows." She laughed again. "Though the cold, hard snows certainly suit those frumps Hera and Athene."

Corydon wasn't sure he wanted her on his side. Except . . . she was like Medusa, in some ways. Fierce and vivid and passionate. Somehow it made him feel fond of her.

"What is the price?" he asked her cautiously.

"Well"—she smiled coquettishly—"I'm sure I will think of something." And her smile chilled him because it was so greedy. Then she drifted off into the brightening morning mist. Corydon saw her give a little skip at the end, a skip of glee and triumph, and it made his blood freeze.

SIXTEEN

He RETURNED TO THE CITY GRIMLY PREPARED TO FACE
the day. The thing was to find Euryale and persuade her to work
on a vessel—a god catcher.

Over breakfast he explained. Both Gorgons looked startled,
then more and more thoughtful. Sthenno felt a surprising prickle
of affection for Corydon. Her dear mormoluke. Always seeking to
heal the universe.

"There is no prophecy of this," she said severely.

"But that's the whole point," said Corydon. "Zeus won't
know we're coming. If there was something written across the
stars, the Olympians could find it out as well as you. Also, don't
you think this is a moment when monsters might free themselves
from their fixed fates? Can we not say 'This shall be so because I
will it'?"

"We do not have as much power as that."

"Are you sure? Is it truly our stars that are at fault, or ourselves,
that we believe we are underlings?"

"Akhilleus would agree with you," said Sthenno very dryly.

"He would." Corydon nodded. "Because he is the most monster-like hero we have ever met. I can sense some kind of conflict in him, as if there is something in him that shames him."

"Perhaps his *agony* will end today," said Sthenno. "Philoktetes has given Herakles' bow to the House of Priam in honor of Gorgos. The princes of Troy will try to destroy Akhilleus. The battles will continue. Gorgos's death meant nothing."

Corydon groaned. "We hold these desperate last stands about the city, knowing it will fall nevertheless. Is it not obvious why we do it?"

"No, or not to me," said Euryale.

Corydon noticed that she was not eating her pottage of stewed grain. Admittedly, it tasted like glue, but the city had become used to it after the flour grew scarce. It was not like Euryale not to eat.

"It is because of duty and necessity," said Sthenno. "And if you do away with them entirely, men will be less than animals."

"It may be, but it is also because the Olympians use all that is good in us to make us their sport, so that they can watch us fall and suffer and strive. For nothing."

"For something," Sthenno corrected. "For our homes. For our friends. For this bowl of tasteless gum that sustains life. These, too, are necessary."

"And I have thought of a new way to protect them," said Corydon. "Let me try."

"I will try, too," said Euryale. "I will make you a vessel of astounding beauty, one that will tempt a god with an exaggerated reflection. One that will convince him he will be loved."

"Is that what Zeus wants?"

"I do not know. But I shall guess as I work," said Euryale. "Sister, I must leave the war to you."

"No," said Sthenno. "I will go to my tower and think on the enchantments that will be needed to make your sculpture into a god catcher. This will require powerful magics. And I will also look out on the battle. And join it if I must."

"And I will go with Corydon to Olympos," said a deep voice from the doorway. "I heard your talk. And I understand what you have not yet said—this task will involve a journey, a pilgrimage—to the very summit of Olympos. I will travel with you again, as I did to the Underworld."

Corydon smiled and put his hand on the Minotaur's furred hand. With him at his side, any journey seemed possible. It was good to see him again; he had been aloof, recovering from his *aristeia*, helping by caring for the children of Troy.

"There is something else, though," Corydon added.

"What?" said Sthenno.

"Well, Aphrodite."

Sthenno flapped her wing in a gesture the peasants used to avoid the evil eye. Then her face tried to look kind. "Oh, poor Corydon. I suppose we forget you're growing up." She patted his arm.

Corydon laughed. "No, not like that! I mean she's offered to help us."

"Help us?" asked Euryale after a startled pause.

"She seems to want to thwart Athene and Hera. But I don't trust her."

"No, I don't think you should. Take care in what you tell her, Corydon," warned Euryale.

"I will," Corydon promised. "But there are the battle trumpets. Euryale, can you start work on the sculpture today?"

"I have already made a plan in my head," she said. "Sister, call me if the battle gets too hot. Corydon, go with her. Don't let her do anything silly."

Corydon wondered how he was supposed to stop a ten-foot metal Gorgon from doing anything that occurred to her, but he remained silent.

A hiccup came from the end of the table. It came from the Snake-Girl. She had just eaten everyone's pottage. "Oh, I am sorry," she said. "Did you want it?" Then her eyes bulged, and she slid to the door. Hideous sick noises were heard. When she returned, she was marble white, and her eyes were full of tears.

"I keep doing that," she said. Then her tongue flickered. "I hate this stupid baby," she said, and burst into tears. Corydon put an awkward arm around her shaking shoulders. Savagely, she turned away, then seemed to relent and let him hug her.

"I promise I'll look after you," he said uncertainly.

Through her tears, she almost laughed. "But, Corydon, you can't protect me from something that's already happened."

The trumpets were still blaring. The city was full of hurrying feet. Sthenno stood in a huddle with Euryale, then brushed apologetically past them and took off with a brassy rattle. Euryale bustled off to her art room. Yet Corydon still held the Snake-Girl in his arms. His chin touched the top of her head. Daring, he stroked her soft scales. She looked up at him, and he kissed her, just as he had once kissed a girl he thought was her. It was a quiet, sad kiss.

"I shall like the baby," he said. "It's your baby, too."

"You are very sweet, Corydon," she said. "But I'm not a girl anymore, really. I've been spoiled."

"Shhh. Things might have been spoiled for you. That doesn't mean *you've* been spoiled. You're still you."

"It's as if my feelings are worn out. Worn thin."

Corydon said gently, "We all feel that way. We saw a city fall. You yourself are a kind of fallen city. But one day, in the kingdom of Hades, Atlantis will rise again. If people want it badly enough. As Gorgos has. And so will you."

He hugged her again. This time both knew they were clinging together for warmth against the terrible sucking cold of dread that had invaded their lives.

The trumpets sounded their final call. Corydon let her go, giving her rounding belly a pat. She smiled at him, and he thought that her smile was a small, warm miracle.

"I go," he said.

"I wish I could help," she said. "But I can't seem to make snakes anymore. It's the baby, I think."

"You can help if the city falls," he said reassuringly. "Rest now." And he ran off into the hurrying, frightened city.

Even from the street, Corydon could hear the approach of the Greeks and their antmen. The ground seemed to shake with the rhythmic, disciplined pounding of their feet. The sounds from inside the city were frantic and chaotic. But that was why his heart was suddenly full of a longing to defend the place. Chaos was better than that unnatural rhythm.

Reaching the top of the wall, he saw that Hektor was leading a defensive force that had formed a shieldline in front of the broad wooden gates. On the walls stood Sikandar, who was organizing the archers so that all could fire together. They were dipping their arrows in a vat of Hydra poison.

"Look," said Sikandar, smiling. "I have it! Herakles' bow."

They were interrupted as a large silvery Sphinx landed beside them, the one who bore the queen of the Amazons. Penthesilea was astride the monster, holding a long, sickle-bladed spear; its point was like the horn of the new moon. "I bring you our bows of the moon," she said, gesturing behind her. Perhaps two dozen women in brightly colored doeskin tunics were readying their bows. "We have our own poison," said Penthesilea. "Do not touch our weapons. The poison paralyzes instantly."

To prove her point, she drew her own slender bow, took aim, and fired at a Greek who had run out ahead of his regimented shieldline. The arrow pierced his forearm where the greave didn't cover the skin, and the man looked down in surprise. Then he stiffened, as if he had been turned to stone, gave a gasp, and fell backward clutching his throat. "They have also been blessed by my father, Ares, the god of war. He often helps me."

Looking at Penthesilea, Corydon wasn't surprised that her father was so violent; he could sense the same raging blood in her. He turned once more to watch the man as he finally stopped twitching.

Sikandar winced and grabbed Corydon's arm. "My brother's chariot just tipped over. A spear knocked one wheel off."

Corydon looked over the wall and could see that he was right: Hektor's chariot lay on its back, the horses standing surprised by the wreck. But Hektor stood firm, wearing Akhilleus's old armor, his hate-filled eyes turning to the chariot constantly circling him. Akhilleus's chariot.

As they watched, Akhilleus leapt out of the chariot and threw his second spear all in one fluid moment. A sudden wind blew the spear straight into a passing bird, killing it instantly. Corydon could see that this was not fair play, that a god was taking a hand. Beside the wreckage stood the semitransparent form of Aphrodite, smiling girlishly. Hektor shouted an insult as he prepared to throw his spear: "Hunting birds, are we, my friend?"

But a fog encircled Akhilleus, and a silvery, smiling Athene stood behind it weaving it stronger. Hektor shouted in frustration and lost his temper. He flung his spear into the center of the dense cloud. There was no thump of a body falling. Then Hektor seemed to go berserk. Drawing his bright sword, he rushed into the cloud, shrieking, "Akhilleus! Coward! Come out and fight!"

The cloud turned silver, the hard silver of Akhilleus's eyes. It burned away like a tattered piece of paper. In the center stood Akhilleus, a faint smile on his lips, his black sword shining. He waited for Hektor as a lion waits for a wounded deer to stumble into its path. It waits and waits, then springs, and the deer is no more. So great Akhilleus waited.

And Hektor ran straight at him. All Akhilleus needed to do was raise his sword. And Hektor ran right onto the blade.

Akhilleus laughed as he gripped the prince of Troy, drinking in his death like a long draft of cold water in a desert.

Then he flung great Hektor's corpse into the dust. And again his war cry sounded and sounded. And he cried out in a voice clearer and fiercer than a hawk's: "Have you any more of these little princelings of Troy? They are my meat and drink."

Sikandar gaped in horror at the sudden death of his brother.

But Penthesilea cried out in answer, "Nay, but I am a princess of the moon and a daughter of Ares. Will you give battle?"

Akhilleus's face closed, as the helmet of control replaced his momentary exultation. "I will."

Penthesilea gave a slight tap on the Sphinx's shoulder.

The Sphinx rose into the air, wings spread, and drifted down to land in front of the mightiest of the heroes. Corydon pressed his knuckles to his mouth as the warrior queen sprang from the Sphinx's back. She was an Amazon, but still, Akhilleus was taller. His arms were three times the size of hers, bulging with muscles that were sickeningly visible through his golden tanned skin.

But the queen did not seem to have noticed that she was overmatched. She looked directly into Akhilleus's eyes. Even from the wall, Corydon could see her eyes were blazing, her mouth a tight line.

"You stupid bully! How can we go into Troy and say that Hektor's dead? King Priam will be struck to stone. Hekabe will weep so much she will be a fountain, not a queen. How can I say it? Better that they say that Penthesilea died, too, and lies beside him. But before I die"—and here she sucked in breath between her teeth and fumbled with her helmet strap—"beforehand I shall see you, too, lying in the dust, coward and bully. Die now upon the spear of an Amazon!"

She flung her helmet from her, and her long hair poured down, a torrent of gleaming silver.

Akhilleus was still, just for a moment. Corydon could almost have thought him tangled in that net of shining hair.

And in that moment, the great spear given to her by her father flashed upward. It caught Akhilleus's face, slashing his cheek; only an enchanted blade could have marked his skin with a thin line of red blood. But the blade could not withstand the contact; it jagged, as if the queen had driven it against a hard stone, and its crisp edge was blunted. Penthesilea snatched it back in horror. And Akhilleus used that moment to bring his sword around in a swift sweep, and the blade sank deeply into her throat. She sank like a slender tree felled by a woodman's ax and lay in the dust beside Hektor.

Her silver Sphinx swooped in desperate rage on her slayer. He waited, poised; he seemed immune to her eyes and her magic. Then his spear arced upward and caught her between her forepaws as she wheeled over her mistress's body. She fell like a hunted bird and lay in agony beside her still mistress. Akhilleus left her to die slowly, ignoring her cries of pain. But he seemed less callous than preoccupied. To the surprise of the horrified watchers on the walls, Akhilleus remained beside Penthesilea's body as her last breaths gurgled in her lungs. He unpinned the dark cloak from his shoulders and dropped it over her. The gesture was like a man throwing away an old coat he doesn't need. And yet the man had done it, had singled Penthesilea out from the nameless dead on the field. He stood still for a moment, his head bent. If Corydon hadn't known better, he might have thought the hero about to weep.

Then his head snapped up again, and he looked at the sky, like a man staring down a foe. A silver flame flickered over his bare head.

The Trojans remaining on the battlefield were terrified; they ran back toward Troy like frightened babies seeking their mothers.

Akhilleus didn't even turn to see them run. The Trojans were routed, but the hero was too preoccupied to enter the city. As the sun went down, he was still standing there; occasional silver flares of his anger shot up into the night sky.

By then he was alone: the Greeks had returned to camp through a sea of Trojan blood. And in front of the city lay shining Hektor down in the dust and the Amazon queen with her silver Sphinx dead beside her.

It was then that Corydon had his second idea to defeat the Olympians.

Hastily, he put his cloak over his head, clattered down from the walls, tore a branch from an olive tree, groped his way to the sally port tunnel, and crept out onto the plain. The stench of death was overwhelming. His hood well down over his head, he crept toward the still, dark figure that was Akhilleus.

He stood next to the hero, and what struck him was Akhilleus's great stillness. Usually, he was a man who moved as fast as a striking snake, but now he had the snake's hunting immobility. He was watching Penthesilea as if he were hoping that she might come back to life.

Akhilleus didn't turn his head to look at Corydon, but he spoke. "I would rather be the lowest serf on my father's fields than king of all the restless dead," he said.

"It's not like that anymore," said Corydon. "I have been to the

Land of the Many. It is now what men and women choose to make it. No longer a land of shrieking shades."

"My mother told me of that. But what will befall me, small goat-boy, when I enter the realm to which I have sent so many before their time? Will they greet me with joy? I think not. And you. What will the dead of Atlantis say to you?"

Corydon said, "I have seen them in a vision. They were angry at first, but now they are reconciled. You will see."

Akhilleus smiled. "But will I? Am I not immortal, like the great bronze-winged creatures who fight for Troy? Am I not capable of resurrection, like your friend whom I sent screaming to his death? Suppose for me there is no death?"

"There is death for everyone. For me, too. But I do not fear it. It will be for me a meeting place with old friends."

"I have no friends anymore," said Akhilleus. "Patroklos was killed because of me."

"And some of my friends were killed because of me. But it doesn't matter. Your friends will still be your friends."

Now the hero turned and looked at him. The light eyes went through him like daggers. "You have something I do not, boy," he said. "Hope. I have no hope for myself. I do only what I must."

"You don't have to make war on the city," said Corydon steadily. "You could go home."

"Home? To what? I have no home. I want to be remembered forever as the greatest of the Greeks. Because it is just, for I am indeed the greatest. And if I must die, I wish to die on the rubble of Troy, killed by the last Trojan as I kill him."

"You are the greatest hero," said Corydon truthfully. "And I see that you are also a monster. I see that you kill as my friend Euryale did, because you truly wish to kill something in yourself. I once knew a hero, but he was a coward. Now I see that not all heroes are so."

"That was Perseus," said Akhilleus. "A coward. Yes. But a son of Zeus." He said the name Zeus thoughtfully.

"Do you serve Zeus?" Corydon asked curiously. "I have seen Athene at your side."

"I see that you do not altogether understand the Sky Father," said Akhilleus. "I do not serve him. He serves *me* because I am going to win. Thus he gains prestige. He never helps the helpless." He smiled. "And neither does the Gray-Eyed Lady of Victories."

"Will you help me fight him?" asked Corydon suddenly.

Now Akhilleus turned his head toward him. The stars burned blue and silver overhead. There was a long silence.

"You are going to fight the king of the gods?" His head went back, not in a laugh but in true amusement. His smile became a grin. "Oh, I like you, goat-boy, I truly do. You have enough courage for a regiment of my antmen. I shall give you the command of a group of them, and after the war a farm of your own. I do not like to see courage wasted." He looked briefly down again at Penthesilea and her Sphinx.

Corydon found himself smiling back but then became serious again. "Lord," he said, surprising himself, "I cannot forgo this quest. Soon there will be none of us left. Monsters, I mean. We have lost so many. And soon, too, Troy will fall, and it has become our last refuge. I must act now to save my friends, however rash and foolish it seems to a hero."

"You must," said Akhilleus. "And I must die here, it seems. But before I do, I would like to help you. You have a plan? Do not tell me. But listen. Zeus wins men to his side because they do not want to be forgotten. To be forgotten is a kind of double death. I am a man like this, too. Zeus promises the immortality of fame. Do not be entranced by it. To beat him, you must give up the idea that your name will echo down the years. The story will be twisted, as the story of Medusa was twisted. You must be content with your quest. No laurel, no bays. Do you see?"

It was a long speech for Akhilleus, and to his dismay, Corydon found himself unnerved. Did he want laurels and bays?

"I just want to go back to my sheep," he blurted out.

Akhilleus smiled. "Such simplicity! Do you truly think you can go back? You yourself are not the same."

Corydon pondered. It was true. But he held on stubbornly. "I do not want anything but my sheep, and friends to visit. What do you want?" he asked curiously.

"I wish to be remembered forever, but I no longer know why I hold to that wish. It has caused so many deaths. I have swum in blood. I hate the high king of men and the high king of the gods. All kings I damn. I now seek only an end to it all. And yet I do not want to die." He shook his head. "What a fool I sound. And this day my folly cut down beauty and valor and worth." He looked sharply at Corydon. "When I die," he said, "I wonder. Do you think they will forgive me?"

For just a second, his face was naked with a child's need for reassurance.

"You do not want fame," said Corydon suddenly. "You want absolution. You are trying to drown the memory of blood in blood. Give it up. Go home. Embrace your father. End it now."

Akhilleus hesitated. Then his back straightened. "That would be dishonor," he said simply. "I honor your quest. Honor mine."

"I'm sorry, I cannot. You need the healing only the Lady of Flowers can now bring. I leave you to seek her." Corydon put out a hand that was no longer tentative and clasped Akhilleus's arm. In a rush, he said, "Thanks. Goodbye. Maybe we will meet in Hades' realm." Then he turned and ran back to the city just as the first rosy fingers of dawn light arrowed across the sky.

SEVENTEEN

As Corydon ran through the city, he noticed an unusual sound: great drums beating instead of the shrill bray of trumpets. And as he turned into the wider main street, he saw an extraordinary sight. Riding along on stubby, stripy horses were tall men with skin the same color as Gorgos's, glossy black. In their right hands, they carried long eye-shaped shields made out of the same hide as that of their mounts, with bronze rims. In their left hands, they held long, fine-pointed spears. They wore little armor, just a kind of kilt made of more hide, studded with metal.

Behind them marched more men of the same kind, this time on foot. And more men. By what magic had this whole army appeared in Troy? Corydon shuddered to think.

Among them, too, were men dressed entirely in skins, with huge masks to cover their faces. They were priests, perhaps. At their head, on a larger stripy horse, rode one who was wearing Greek armor, but it was festooned with the skins of strange striped and spotted beasts, and he bore a great darkwood spear hung with the tails of beasts and birds. Corydon was astonished. Here were men who seemed to want to be monsters; they liked the blend of animal and man. They were also heroes, though: slender and upright and very proud.

The tall man in the Greek armor was looking around, puzzled, as if searching for a missing face in the welcoming crowd. As the army got closer to Priam's palace, he came to look almost hurt. And Corydon, running along through the crowds, had a thudding moment of understanding. *He's looking for Hektor,* he thought. He squirmed his way to the front and caught the man's bridle.

"If you seek Hektor, I'm sorry—he is dead," he said. "He was killed yesterday."

The man's face went still. Then a great howl of fury and lamentation rose from his lips. He turned to his men, ordered them to halt, and dismounted, handing his strangely marked beast to his squire and striding into the palace. Corydon followed.

Another council? No. This man was stamping along, bellowing, calling on Priam and Kalkhas. Sikandar, his light armor half on, came running out. "Memnon!" And Memnon grasped his arm. "Old friend," Sikandar sobbed. "How can we bear it?" Corydon could see Sikandar was torn by grief. His hair stood on end, rumpled from a night of sleepless tears. And something kind had gone from his face.

The man put an arm around his shoulders, firm and quiet now. "Then it's true? As this boy said?"

"Yes, Hektor lies dead in the dust. But none have been able to perform the rites of burial. Akhilleus stands on the plain as if he were a lover longing to court the city. He, too, lost a friend."

"And now this day he shall lose his life," said a high, clear voice behind them. Memnon swung around and looked up in some awe at ten-foot Sthenno.

"I came to tell you," she said. "The stars are clear. He will die today."

"And by my hand," said Memnon grimly.

Sikandar looked grim, too. "If not by mine first."

Somehow Corydon couldn't bring himself to offer them help. How could he conspire to kill a man he'd come to know and—yes—like? Akhilleus was . . . well, difficult . . . but Corydon had come to understand how he'd become what he was.

He felt like a traitor. But no one noticed him. They were all too busy eagerly planning the attack. Corydon, listening, found himself tired of wars between the Olympians' victims. He patted Sikandar on the arm, smiled at Sthenno, and went off to see how Euryale was doing.

Euryale was carving a layer of wax on an immense clay statue. It looked horrible, obscene, and blobby and was thickly smeared with a kind of yellow snot. Surely no Olympian could want to inhabit it. As he watched, she began sticking little tubes and pipes all over it. Then she took an armful of clay and slapped it on over the yellow gobs. It spread smooth and thin, but just as Corydon was thinking it looked better, she pulled out much stiffer clay and began covering it with that. The thing looked as monstrous and crude as the Olympians were inside their hearts.

"You will see," promised Euryale. "When it is fired."

"Euryale," said Corydon gently, "isn't it a bit big?"

"It will need to be big for Zeus. He has that kind of mind. Sthenno's enchantments will make it small so you may carry it. Now we will fire it. Very slowly. Then we will pour the bronze and polish it. I have also asked the women in the palace to make a silken robe for the god to wear, with much gold stitching. They are working on it now."

Corydon tried to conceal his impatience. "How long?"

"Art is slow, little mormo. We must have courage to hold on until all is ready."

Corydon realized as she spoke that it was a long time since he had made any songs. The old blind man was making the songs for this war. But he missed the making. It had not been quiet enough to make songs. He needed the stillness of a grassy hillside. Thinking this, he understood Euryale's need to take her time and smiled. "I do see," he said. "Your work is good."

Then he told Euryale about the coming of Memnon and his strange stripy beasts, his proud men. "I wish I could paint them!" she exclaimed. "A few sketches. Just while the clay is baking slowly. When it is fired, I must be there, ready with the bronze."

When she had set the sculpture to baking, they flew to the top of the wall to see Memnon and his troops assembling in a spear-pointed formation. They were not waiting for the Greeks to attack but preparing to attack them. The head of the spear point was formed by the men riding on their stripy horses, but with them were men riding on gray animals the size of oxen, with two gray horns sticking like knives out of their foreheads, one small, one so great it looked fit to cleave anyone open.

"It is a monoceros," said Euryale. "Some men call it rhinoceros. I never saw one before. How wide the world becomes."

And now they saw the most astounding creatures of all.

They were gray, taller than the monoceros, with the most amazing noses, longer than tails, longer than their legs, noses that twisted like serpents. Their weight shook the ground, and yet they trod as delicately as girls. There were ten of them, and each on his back carried a little tent of fighting men. The men carried spears, and bows, too, but the beasts had their own weapons: two long, curving fangs of ivory that stood out from their faces. They were much stranger than any monster. As he watched, Corydon saw a Sphinx fly down to greet one she evidently thought of as a friend.

"What are they?" The question burst from Corydon and Euryale at once.

"Pakhudermos," said a Sphinx as she vaned past their turret.

When he had seen his fill of the great beasts, Corydon scanned the wall top for Sikandar. Corydon had become used to fighting alongside him and his archers. But he was nowhere to be seen.

"Down there," said Euryale, spotting him. "He is leading now Hektor is gone."

It felt wrong. How could an archer lead armed men? He would be killed.

"Get me down there," said Corydon tersely to Euryale. He could not let Sikandar go out like this.

Euryale swooped down in front of the army. Sikandar had acquired armor from somewhere, but it really looked no more fitting than it would have on Corydon; he looked like a boy dressing up in his father's things. A squire held one of the great, heavy helmets that made men into birds of prey. Corydon called to him, "Sikandar!" But when he turned, Corydon could see that his friend the shepherd boy had gone forever. The face he saw was set hard, all his smiles buried in the grave of his brother.

"Sikandar, don't—" But he stopped. It would be no use. This

man had never known him, had never galloped wildly on camels through sliding sands. This man was a prince of Troy, nothing else. He looked like the kind of man who might find the sweetness of forgetting more important than anything else.

"I have the bow," said Sikandar in a hard, dry voice. "I shall kill him, Corydon."

Corydon could find no words. And he was no longer certain of what he wanted. Was it Sikandar he wanted to save or Akhilleus? Or both?

But Sikandar was already lost.

He turned his back on Corydon. Without apology. He took a flaming torch from a servant, waved it in the air. "Memnon!" he cried in a shrill voice that carried to every corner of the field. "Ethiops! Men of Troy! Today we will put an end to this war! We shall kill Akhilleus! And after that we will burn their ships! They will die on our spear shafts, on our swords! We shall attack them, not defend ourselves! Are you with me?" A large chorus of eager shouts answered him. The strange gray pakhudermos trumpeted ferociously. "Charge!" cried Sikandar.

And they did. Euryale flew Corydon back to the wall, where they watched the destruction unfold. First came the monoceros. Two men were impaled swiftly on the leader's horn, their purple blood maddening the beast. The stripy horses followed, the wild creatures fighting and kicking while the men were using spears and darts, holding up their huge oval shields to deflect the blows of the Greek spears and arrows.

The pakhudermos ran right into the Greek camp itself. With a hard rain of arrows hailing down from their backs, their enormous feet crushed everything in their path. Tents and pavilions went down. One creature's nose snapped out and snatched a running man, then flung him aside like a broken twig.

But suddenly one of the great beasts stumbled and then toppled forward. It crashed into another pakhudermos, which gave a great squeal of fury and ran wildly, causing its own side to flee from it.

The man who had cut the pakhudermos's tendons and caused it to fall was gleaming in his shining black armor. He gave a quick, harsh shout. For the first time, Corydon noticed his long hair: it had escaped from his helmet, so that he was like an ill-omened, streaming comet. In his wake came his hard-running antmen, and they scattered the Ethiops like leaves in autumn.

Fierce fights erupted everywhere, and for a time it was not clear who had the upper hand. But with a sinking heart, Corydon saw that the antmen's steady attacks were wearing even the strange beasts. The plain seemed strewn with bodies. Then Corydon noticed Memnon. His mount was gone, but he went on with wild courage, jabbing with his spear. He would not give ground.

He was fighting his way toward the man he had come to kill, the man who ran dealing out death in his black armor, a storm cloud lit with silver lightnings. Memnon leapt through the circle of dying attackers and defenders who surrounded his quarry and thrust with his spear. Akhilleus knocked it away with his shield and thrust his own great spear at Memnon's throat.

The spear juddered, as if he had pushed it into a rock. Akhilleus frowned to discover one who shared his own invulnerability. Memnon gave a great laugh, his teeth showing, and spun round to force his own spear into the hero's throat. But his spear, too, was rebuffed as if he had hit a tree. He grinned again. "I will enjoy finding your weak spot," he said. "I know you have one."

"I know you have one, too," said Akhilleus evenly. Now they circled each other slowly, delicately. They had dropped their spears, swept out swords. Each watched the other's eyes. Then each would make a sharp thrust at a different part of the other's body, frowning as his weapon met rock-hard skin. The shocks jarred their arms—stabbing a rock hurt the stabber.

Memnon's rage could find no outlet. He stopped and picked up a huge boulder, bigger than a man. Holding it in his immense arms, he flung it at Akhilleus's head. But it was no use. Akhilleus simply head-butted it away. It broke into millions of pieces, some tiny as insects, some bigger than wild wolves. One of the large pieces struck Memnon himself squarely in the belly, and he fell over with a cry of surprise and pain.

Akhilleus smiled coldly.

"I have you now," he said evenly. He paced calmly toward Memnon. And bringing his sword down in a shining arc, he stabbed him in the belly, choosing the spot marked red from the impact of the stone, just where there was a gap between corselet and kilt. Black blood gurgled out, and Memnon looked down in astonishment. His Ethiopian warriors gave deep cries of mourning; many of them, too, had been struck down, and the plain was littered with the fierce and outlandish bodies of their beasts. Corydon heard the great drums beating for a retreat.

And still above Memnon stood his conqueror, methodically cleaning his blackened sword.

The sight was too much for Sikandar. Ignoring the drums'

command, he charged forward, entirely alone. Corydon saw him putting an arrow to the string, his hands sure and steady. Hardly knowing what he did, Corydon shouted to Sikandar to stop, but he lifted his bow, and as he did so, Corydon saw his quarry look up. Akhilleus's silver eyes lit, but he didn't move. Then he closed his eyes.

Sikandar's arrow flew, swift, and it found the mark. He had seen Akhilleus's weakness in the hero's battle with the Minotaur. Now his arrow sped like a hound for that very place on his left foot, the place where his goddess mother had held him as a baby when she dipped him in the Styx to make him like iron. The arrow plunged in, ripping a path through tender mortal flesh and delivering the deadly poison of a Hydra.

Akhilleus gave one cry, one hard cry, as the arrow hit. Then he fell forward.

Sikandar was so absorbed in his glory that he didn't notice the Greeks behind him. They were led by Odysseus.

Without any fuss, Odysseus took in the sight: Akhilleus dying, Sikandar standing over him triumphantly. He said something to one of his men. Then he scuttled sideways, like a crab, until he could get to Akhilleus directly. Meanwhile, four of his men's bows twanged. Corydon shouted, but Sikandar didn't even turn as four Greek arrows pierced his body, finding every joint in his ill-fitting armor. He toppled onto the sands, plucking feebly at one of the arrows. Once more, Euryale flew Corydon to his side. He took the dying man's head into his lap, but Sikandar was already past speech. He had just time to hear Corydon's "Farewell, my friend," before his head rolled in death.

Corydon looked at Odysseus, cradling Akhilleus's head as he himself held Sikandar.

Their eyes met. In the hero's dark face, he saw, as in a mirror, the image of his own anger and sick bewilderment. But when the man spoke, his words were light, having nothing to say to the glittering tears in his eyes.

"You do seem to love leaping from high places when I am in sight," said Odysseus. Despite his casual words, there was a sadness in his voice, as if he found the entire war sad, even hopeless. "Who are you, leaping boy?"

"I am Corydon Panfoot, and I come from the Island of Monsters."

Odysseus smiled. "Then Perseus did not conquer you," he said. "Ah, well. I suspected not. Now I must lead the Greeks against the city, Panfoot. Perhaps we shall meet again, before the end."

He lifted the dead body of Akhilleus to his shoulders and strode off, toward the Greek camp. The hero's arm flopped down from under Odysseus's cloak, and Odysseus bundled it up again as if it were a piece of stray laundry. It was comic and undignified and unimaginable. Euryale and Corydon carried the body of Sikandar—no, he must always be Alekhandros now—back to his city. The Trojans had cheered the fall of Akhilleus, but Memnon's troops were spent without their leader. And the last of the princes of Troy lay dead. The city looked at a future blank as a wall.

EIGHTEEN

CORYDON WAS AMONG THOSE WHO MOURNED BY HIS friend's bier most of the night. The wind howled outside the city like the voice of a crying djinn. Was it Bin Khamal? Thinking of the djinns, Corydon began to compose a little threnody, a lament for his friend the shepherd boy; the song said that the boy had had to die long ago. But he also put in the triumph of killing Akhilleus and a few lines of lonely lament for the hero as well.

He was going back to Euryale's studio to see how she had progressed when he saw a hooded and cloaked woman coming out of one of the houses, her sobs ringing out on the night air, unabashed, hiccupping sobs loud as a toddler's. She collided with him, and her hood fell back, revealing a face glistening with tears. At first, Corydon thought she was some girl who had lost her man in the war. Then he recognized her. It was Aphrodite.

With a gulp, she said in a voice blurry with tears, "Such waste. All gone. Who will be left to love me?"

Corydon asked, "Are you still going to help me?"

"More than ever. Did you see those arrows? Guided by cold-hearted Athene." She almost spat the word. "She's always favored Odysseus." Corydon was surprised. Odysseus didn't look too carried away by the Olympians. Odysseus seemed to him more like the Minotaur—a man who would rather be at home. Corydon also thought of his father when he thought of Odysseus: they both had a simple delight in tricks.

"I hate him, too," said Aphrodite bitterly. "But don't worry. I have many plans for him. And I will help you with Zeus. I will." She put her hand on his arm. He wanted to snatch his arm away but prudently made no move. Drawing her cloak over her head again, she drifted off into the street, one among many mourning women whose sobs filled the night air.

Euryale was at work, cursing the bronze, cursing her assistant, cursing the statue. It was an inferno of heat in there: kiln fire and melting metal. It also stank because Euryale was keeping herself going with bites from a deer she had taken that morning and hadn't had time to cook properly.

"Shouldn't you share that?" Corydon asked.

"Not *now*," she snapped, taking another mouthful. "Come back in a few hours and I'll show you something." She moved around to steady her slave as she began to pour the bronze into the vent. A river of liquid metal, brighter than the sun, lit the room.

"Where's the Snake-Girl?"

"On the roof," screamed Euryale. "Go away, Corydon."

So he did. He climbed the ladder to the rooftop, to find the Snake-Girl coiled in a corner, wrapped in an old quilt, watching the fading stars. She looked up as she heard Corydon's step. "It can't go on much longer," she said softly. "One way or another. Akhilleus is dead. Sikandar is dead. Hektor and Penthesilea and in a way Gorgos. Is there anyone left to fight?"

Corydon thought of Sthenno's disk. There would still be a battle of earth and a battle of fire. But Sthenno had sometimes misread things. . . . He sat down beside her, and they stared at the sky. Corydon felt the light touch of her shoulder against his. Awkwardly, feeling he was soothing a scared animal, he patted it. "Why don't you go?" he asked. "Go back to the island and look after the baby. There are still boats farther down the coast."

She was silent for a while. "I think of it," she said. "But I want to stay with you." Corydon felt a huge warmth invade him. He put an arm around her. She hurried on. "It's not only you, it's the Gorgons. And the Minotaur, too; he brought me some honey only yesterday, and he's so unhappy here. And the Sphinxes. I feel . . . not at home, but befriended."

He felt the warmth spread still farther—her thoughts so closely mirrored his own. She settled into the crook of his arm, spreading the quilt over them both. The pink light of dawn found them asleep. Corydon was sleeping so deeply that at first not even the loud thudding noises woke him. Then he sprang into wakefulness; was it the gates? What was it?

He ran to the street side of the roof, followed by the sleepy Snake-Girl. At first, he saw little; the light was still grayish.

But then he spotted something.

A small mound of what looked like sand, moving. Was it a wounded djinn? How could sand move? Then an arm with a spear burst out of the mound. A second arm with a shield. And a fully armored Greek soldier leapt out, followed by another. More Greeks emerged as Corydon watched; he saw that they were Akhilleus's antmen, now truly running like ants from an anthill.

Somehow they had tunneled in! Instinctively, he crouched beneath the parapet, then began working his way along to the ladder.

"Get down," he whispered fiercely to the Snake-Girl. "I must warn the army."

"Be careful," she said. "They are right outside."

"I'll get Euryale," he said. "It will be all right."

Perhaps it would have been. But when they reached the studio, Euryale was nowhere to be seen. Perhaps she had gone out for more onyx stones; a half-finished eye for Zeus lay on the table in her workroom, uncanny and staring.

"I'll have to risk the streets," he said grimly.

"I want to come!"

"No, please. I still have plenty of kleptis skills. I'll be fine."

He opened the great wooden door a crack. As they peered out, the noise increased. A last hoplite, resplendent in glossy black armor, seemed to pour out like a snake slithering from a hole, rearing up to strike as it emerges. Corydon caught a glimpse of furious eyes, *red* eyes. And the Snake-Girl froze beside him. It was the man she feared, the father of her child: Akhilleus's son, Neoptolemos.

"Hide yourself, Lamia. Hide!" Corydon whispered fiercely.

Stealthily he crept out. The Greeks, including Neoptolemos, were heading to the right. So Corydon went left, sliding silently from doorway to doorway.

He was almost at the end of the street when he slipped and

set a door gate rattling hard. Corydon didn't even need to see; he could feel Neoptolemos turn, feel the hard red stare piercing the street. "Men, go ahead!" he called. "Remember, open the gates. No more for now. I will make sure no one warns the palace."

He began moving down the street toward him.

Corydon frantically grabbed the door handle, but it was locked. He would have to run for it, chased by that terrible tower of metal. Corydon tore off down the street, then saw a narrow alleyway. He turned, hoping against hope that it was not a dead end, and the hard metal feet came on fast. The alley led to the main street, which was full of anxious Trojans. Corydon burst out into a whole group of them and clutched them with relief.

"The Greeks are in the city!" cried Corydon. "A tunnel or something. Go protect the gates! One of them is right behind me. Akhilleus's son."

But when he turned, Neoptolemos had vanished. The Trojans began hunting through the streets, seeking out antmen and dispatching them angrily. But not their leader. He had simply vanished.

Had he gone back into the hole? Or was he hiding in the city?

They heard the trumpets blare as Agamemnon's forces attacked the gates from outside. Corydon saw boys younger than himself strapping on plaything bows to answer the call to fight. He feared for the Snake-Girl with her former master abroad in the streets and ran for the Minotaur to help him search.

The Minotaur was sitting alone in his small garden, ignoring the chaos. When he saw Corydon, he stood up. "Is it time?" he asked, sounding worried.

"Not yet," said Corydon. "But we have another task. We

must find Neoptolemos. He has concealed himself somewhere in the city."

The Minotaur was already hurrying into the street. "We need the dogs from the palace to help. I can scent as I must, and so can you. Do you have anything of his?"

Only his child, thought Corydon. *And the babe is not yet born.* Had he come for that? Somehow Corydon didn't think so. He thought Neoptolemos was the kind of man to forget the Snake-Girl when he had used her. Aloud, he said, "No."

They went back to the earth-floored street where Corydon had seen the Greeks first emerge. They tracked Neoptolemos easily until the large, strong feet reached the cobbles. Then the footprints vanished. It was as if Neoptolemos himself had also vanished.

They combed the street for signs. But there was no trace of a Greek hero. Corydon was exploring the edges of the cobbles for the ninth time when he idly noticed the curving trail of a small snake as it slithered through sand.

A sudden hiss alerted Corydon to its presence: it was slithering toward him down the street. It was an asp; its fangs glistened, and its eyes were . . .

Corydon halted. Could it be? . . . But that would mean that . . .

The black-scaled snake reared up, twisting higher and growing arms and legs, its tail shrinking, armor bursting out from its body, and the red eyes glinting, glinting with satisfaction at seeing the horror and amazement in Corydon's eyes as it prepared to thrust its spear. Corydon leapt aside and called for the Minotaur.

The bull-monster turned and ran toward Corydon, seeing Neoptolemos complete his transformation from snake into man.

The man in front of Corydon grinned. "When she blinded me, I was healed by bonding with snakes. There were some useful side effects."

The Minotaur charged him from the side. He was flung through the air but, with a graceful twist, found his feet again. Corydon saw his arms fasten to his sides as he shrank back into a snake again. *Quick!* With bursting lungs, he flung a market vendor's basket over the snaky, writhing form.

Neoptolemos was trapped, apparently unable to make whatever writhings were required for his transmogrification back into human form. Breathing hard, the two monsters faced each other across the basket.

"What shall we do with him?" asked the Minotaur.

Corydon was silent. He thought about killing the hateful hero while he was vulnerable but dismissed the idea. No. There had been enough death. He eyed the glossy black snake through the small chinks in the wickerwork.

"Throw him from the walls," said Corydon reluctantly.

"The fall would kill him."

"Not from the gate side. You saw how well he jumped."

"All right." They carried the basket hastily up to the wall and flung the contents as far as they could. The advancing Greeks were amazed to see Neoptolemos rise up before them like an angry basilisk . . . with a broken basket on his head. Corydon saw him shake it off furiously and knew that they had further roused the rage of an already angry man.

"We must fill the tunnel so they can't send more men through the earth— Oh!" Corydon stopped suddenly. "Was that the earth battle?"

"Maybe." The Minotaur shook his great head. "Maybe." He looked grim. "And then let us go and see if Euryale has done her work," said the Minotaur. "I do not think there is much time left."

When they entered the studio, they saw two bronze wonders. The first was Euryale, curled up asleep in a ruffle of sharp feathers. When had he ever seen Euryale sleep unless enspelled? He hadn't thought she could.

The second was the statue: gleaming, silky, robed in green and white. Its eyes dominated the room, their hard onyx stare and long gold lashes seeming to hypnotize everyone.

The Minotaur shook Euryale's shoulder. "Wake," he said in his soft rumble. Euryale did wake. Her own bronze lashes lifted.

"That was remarkable," she said. "Mortal sleep! A whole new subject for art. Well, what do you think of him?"

"It's awesome," said Corydon. "It will fill everyone with amazement. And so . . . big."

"Do not fear, mormo," said Euryale with a wide yawn. "It has been enchanted. Sthenno has wrought greatly. You may make it shrink to a size you may carry, and with another word, you may make it grow to godlike dimensions again. Look!" She said a word, then lunged for a piece of dried barley bread Sthenno had left behind.

The statue shrank to the size of Corydon's forearm in a great rush, like a fountain going backward. Corydon picked it up. It was heavy, but it did not carry its full-sized weight. The Minotaur took it from his hand. "This I will carry," he said, and Corydon was grateful. He was grateful to Euryale, too. Sthenno had written down the magical words to make the statue shrink and grow, and the sisters had also prepared a pack of food and a waterskin for each of them; some wrinkled apples in another bag were the last of their store.

Now Sthenno herself fluttered in, feathers stiff. "Mormo," she said sharply. "Mormo. Listen. The city will fall. Look at the disk." Only the fire battle was left. "And that may be the fall of the city itself," she said. "Do not fear for Gorgos," she added kindly. "He is with the goddess."

"Where is Lamia? She should know that Neoptolemos is gone from the city."

"Find her quickly, and then we must go," the Minotaur rumbled softly. "A ship is ready at its moorings, south of the city."

Corydon ran to say goodbye to the Snake-Girl, but he found her asleep and saw that she slept with a terrible stillness that told of her exhaustion. There were blue circles under her eyes. So he bent and kissed her, very softly so as not to wake her.

He knew he would probably never see her, or any of them, again.

As he and the Minotaur moved through the streets of Troy, Corydon found his gaze sharpened by his awareness that he was looking on a great city for the last time. He noticed the ornate fountains in which soldiers would wash themselves after battle. He noticed the way the smallest children's limbs had grown sticklike with hunger, though their faces still smiled with a cheer that couldn't be quenched. One was carrying a tiny bunch of weed-flowers, which she placed carefully at the feet of a Lar who stood in the gateway of her house. Corydon saw the Lar smile and wave. It was hard to imagine that Zeus had once been like that gentle house god.

The city was looking neglected; some houses were dilapidated because their owners had been killed. And there were so many lone women, watching the children play from under black veils of mourning. But it was still precious. He wished he could save it.

"You can save something," said the Minotaur comfortingly, and Corydon saw that he, too, had been watching the children. "We can save the idea of a great city. Or so Sthenno says."

"Gorgos will lead some of them away," said Corydon as they walked. "And the others will help. They will build again some-where else."

"Faunus told me of his country," said the Minotaur. "It lies many leagues from Hellenic lands. It would serve. It has vines and olive trees. It would be a beginning."

Now they had reached the tiny side gate of the city, guarded night and day. Corydon looked up at the walls and put his hand on them, wondering if Bin Khamal's relative slept within, also cease-lessly watching. Or had his power been exhausted?

The guards stood still, not talking, their eyes watchful. Their armor was battered and it did not shine much, and they looked lean and hungry, but their discipline had not relaxed; they had not surrendered.

Then the gate was opened, and he and the Minotaur left Troy behind.

Neither looked back.

Neither could bear it.

NINETEEN

On the sea again . . . The small fishing smack was very like the boat that had taken Corydon to Atlantis. But now they were heading due west, the setting sun in their eyes every day like a streak of blood. Four days from Troy, Corydon saw stiff billows of cloud on the horizon. Was it a storm?

"That is Olympos," said the Minotaur "It is a lonely mountain. And always shrouded in cloud."

"Can they see us?"

"If they wish," said the Minotaur. "But their eyes may be turned elsewhere."

With a jolt, Corydon wondered if Aphrodite would be looking away when he needed her. He fingered his Pan-pipes. He had the beginnings of other ideas if she failed them, as he half expected her to do.

The cloud was a solid wall of white ahead of them. It was a fluffy cloud, not a storm, but it was utterly still; it should have been blowing and shifting in the light wind, but instead it was a fortress around the mountains of the gods. Its soft surface belied an unnatural strength.

He could see no mountain within, but the cloud was itself shaped like a mountain. The boat sailed into a shallow bay. Both Corydon and the Minotaur leapt onto the land and pulled the boat up as far as they could on the smooth stretch of sand. No seabirds sang. The beach rose sharply, and after assembling their packs, they labored up the soft slope. At the top they could see a path, which led into the cloud. Along it were small, crude altars, on which men had sacrificed oxen. The piles of skin and fat for the gods stank a little in the warm sun.

"It's that stink of death they feed on," muttered the Minotaur.

The cloud-wall was directly ahead—it seemed to lean over them.

The Minotaur extended his walking stick and prodded the cloud-wall. It did not seem solid. And so they walked into the cloud. A moment of drenching gray. A sense of pent forces. A faint flicker of blue lightning. And then they were, astonishingly, through the cloud.

They came out into the hard yellow-white light of a brilliant sun. The grass was spangled with dew. Tiny wildflowers, rich purple, clambered over rocks. A few pale primrose orchids drowsed in the sun. The Minotaur saw a bee, its belly heavy with pollen, swooping on a flower cup. The silence was near complete. No birds sang. There was no wind to shake the green grasses or disturb the flowers. Only the droning bee could be heard.

They looked up. The mountain was like a dream above them, its wall looming over their heads, its peak capped by glinting snow. There were no clouds to blur its terrible outline.

No clouds anywhere. What had become of the mountain's thick cloak? Corydon looked around, his gaze sweeping the clear horizons. The clouds through which they had come were gone. Walking backward, he retrod his own steps until he had taken double the number that had brought him out of the cloud.

But there was no cloud. There was not even the memory of cloud. The grass was dry under his feet.

Which meant that they were trapped. There could be no going back. They were held in Zeus's fist of cloud, and they could not return unless they defeated him—or he them.

Where was Aphrodite?

Corydon turned his eyes to the heavy wall of mountain again, splurges of snow spilled on its flanks. There was no point in waiting. A little path ran toward the peak, stony and obscure, a goat track. *For me*, thought Corydon ironically. Along its way they could see stone altars, very like the ones they had passed just before they had plunged into the cloud. But these bore no meat. They were as bare as the peak that rose above them. They had, however, been tended: the grass had been pulled away from them, leaving bare circles.

Without a word, Corydon and the Minotaur began to walk toward the mountain. Neither wanted to break the thick silence.

Even their feet made little sound on the stony track. Keeping their eyes fixed on the peak, they plodded on. Their packs, which the Minotaur had filled with climbing tools, already felt heavy. The grass smelled sweet, though, and the scent of flowers drifted up to them. It was a place so calm that Corydon felt more than ever a monster, as if his Pan-leg were an unwarrantable disturbance. The Minotaur's shaggy head and furred body looked wrong in the smooth, enameled landscape. And although it was like a dream of pasture, there were no browsing animals—no goats, no sheep, and no men or girls to guard them. It was perfectly clean and neat. The heat of the sun was ideally pleasant without being oppressive.

And yet somehow its very perfection became a kind of burden. Corydon began to long for something real—some dung, some flies, a dead bush. Anything that wasn't manicured. This was not natural: it was a terrible garden, a smug parody of the wild pastures he loved. He began to hate it.

And the mountain's baldness cowed the landscape before it. It was as if all the life of the landscape had been sucked into its powerful, sheer slopes. As they grew nearer, Corydon began to sense a menace, as if the mountain had eyes.

It also looked impossible to climb. It was virtually a sheer wall of rock. Corydon knew about climbing—it was one of his goatish skills, and it had been honed on the Island of Monsters, which contained its share of rotten rock and chimneys and exposed walls. But this mountain was far larger than anything in his experience. It seemed to stretch forever. It was a shining pinnacle of impossibility.

He pointed and turned left. Perhaps there would be an easier ascent on the other side. Or on one of the flanks. The Minotaur plodded after him dutifully.

After an hour or more of roaming through the same jeweled meadow of purple and yellow flowers, he was forced to give in to his rising sense of hopelessness. The mountain was like a catalog of difficult climbing. As well as the fierce face they had rejected at first, they had managed to discern an avalanche funnel bigger than any he had ever seen; a whole packet of overhanging ledges;

and a cluster of couloirs, deep gorges surrounded by vertical rock, green ice making the surfaces gleam slick in the sun.

There was no easy way up this mountain. And the sun was westering. It was time to make camp for the night. They could not build a fire; there was nothing to burn. So they ate some hard biscuits, drank from a mountain stream so cold it made their teeth shriek in agony, and pulled their sheepskins around themselves.

Corydon was glad of his skin; it smelled real. He and the Minotaur slept back to back. But it was obvious that nobody would come, neither animal nor man. The land was empty.

The next morning they woke at dawn. It was a rich pink flush that made the mountain snows look as if they were stained with blood. But they must now attempt to climb.

They reached the mountain's foot only an hour after first light. They unrolled a rope and tied it around their waists, connecting them so that if one fell, the other could try to pull him back. Corydon knew he would have little hope of saving the heavy Minotaur if there was a disaster; he also knew that the great monster's weight could bring him to his death. But the rope at least gave both a chance.

Corydon knew, too, that his Panfoot could find vital holds. It acted almost like a hook, securing him to rock and ice. His other foot he therefore safeguarded with a special shoe that Euryale had made: it was light, thin bronze, very hard, and covered in sharp, hooklike spikes. It tied onto a snowboot made of soft leather. The Minotaur had similar devices for each of his huge feet.

They began to climb. Each step was a calculation: find a spur of rock, reach it with a hand, hold on, place a foot near the hand, swing forward, swing out, swing down. Place the next foot. The next hand. Confront the next problem: a bulge in the mountain's face. Work out how to traverse it. The next: an overhang. The next. The next. Slowly, but with rhythm. Slowly, but with grace. With momentum. With cunning.

It was tiring. It was hard work. And it was also a mere nothing. It required only application. Due diligence. There was nothing impossible here. And Corydon knew that there would be impossibilities to come.

They met their first real difficulty after they had been climbing steadily for three hours, ascending dizzyingly above the smooth grasses. There was no wind, but there was no cloud either to soften the spectacle of the sheer precipice below. They came to an overhead ledge; Corydon pulled himself up, then helped the heavier Minotaur to use his strength to reach it, too.

From this perch, they could see into the mountain's secrets. Ahead of them and to the left was the sleeping ice bulk of a glacier. Its surface was not smooth: it was split by countless crevasses. Some of them would be hundreds of feet deep and dozens of feet wide.

But they could not go to the right. Beside the glacier, rock had been pushed out to form an overhang that couldn't even be reached from their precarious ledge. It was impossible to traverse it.

They would have to attempt the glacier.

They set out. The first dozen or so crevasses they walked around, treading carefully on slippery ice. The next half dozen or so involved nothing worse than a long step across a deep darkness.

But then they came to wider crevasses, too wide for a step. The first was bridged by a terrifyingly thin span of snow and ice;

Corydon ran lightly across, but the Minotaur's greater bulk made the bridge shift with leathery groans. Cracks appeared. As the bridge collapsed, the Minotaur flung himself onto the other side of the great gulf's gape. His bronze-spiked foot found a secure hold, and he levered himself gasping onto the damp snow.

Still neither spoke.

But now Corydon realized that they were inside a deadly maze of wide crevasses. The nearest one bore another light snow bridge, thinner than the previous bridge. It could not be attempted; the risk to the Minotaur was too great.

Instead, Corydon and the Minotaur chose to try to find a way through the maze: they walked on their spiked feet in a wild world of emerald and turquoise ice, seeing dizzying vistas to the mountain's heart opening before their feet, swerving, dodging, weaving. It took over two hours to travel a hundred feet in the direction of the summit, because they had to cross and crisscross their line of direction. The hard sun beat down. And there was still no sound except the dripping of the ice. Corydon began to feel as if he had gone deaf.

At last, legs aching, nerves in shreds, they staggered off the glacier's edge, but what lay ahead was something far more deadly than the ice maze they had just survived.

It was a couloir, a narrow chute bounded by rocky cliffs on either side. It was tilted at a ferocious angle and slick with ice, bluish green and glossy. Here and there rocks protruded from places where the snow had thinned in the brilliant sunlight, then refroze into a fragile coating of ice too delicate for the small ice ax each held to get a good hold. It would simply shatter when a spiked tool was applied to it.

Again, neither said a word. It had become an unspoken superstition. If they did not speak, they might survive.

Each looked hopelessly at what lay ahead. At last, they sat down on the ridge at the top of the glacier. The Minotaur reached into his pack and brought out a hunk of bread. Corydon shared his waterskin, which was almost frozen. Still neither spoke.

Then Corydon drew in a deep breath. And as the mountain glowered above their heads, shining and terrible, he suddenly felt a bubbling impulse he didn't try to deny. He began to sing. It was a song about the mountain itself, a song that told of its splendor, its ferocity, its hardness. Its cold. A song of death in snow, of lonely climbers buried in its deep and icy heart.

In putting the mountain into words, he captured its strength. And the mountain seemed to know it. He couldn't say it looked docile now, but the dread of its awful silence was broken, dissipated. It was not conquered, perhaps would never be conquered. But it was less, well, monstrous. Suddenly he sang of Sthenno and Euryale, condemned to live for years out of mind. The mountain was like them. Gods rose and fell, men were begotten, born, and died. The mountain was almost immortal. And yet it was fighting its own slow battles—against the rotting of rock, the collapse of stones. One day it would be level with the plain. Corydon remembered that Gorgos had once said that stone had its own impossibly slow language, taking centuries to utter a syllable. Was he in danger of mistaking that long, slow word for silence?

But the word this mountain was saying sounded like a fierce word. His song helped him, but it did not make for communication.

He stood up. It was time to attempt the couloir.

They progressed with agonizing slowness. Each step had to be cut in ice with the axes. After a few laborious hours of jagged ice steps that gave when they put their feet on them, splinters of ice that seemed aimed at their eyes, fierce shards of ice that stuck in clothes and boots, feet that slipped treacherously, things got worse.

The slope grew steeper. Now it was not a slope at all. It was a cliff of ice. Now they had to use small bronze pegs to secure handholds, attach rope to them, and haul themselves up. Inch by inch. Below them the glacier crevasses yawned.

Each bronze peg had to be retrieved after use. They had only twelve—"one for each Olympian," Euryale had said lightly—and they could not afford to lose even one.

Then, just as Corydon felt his hands and feet would never stop aching or uncramp themselves, they were almost at the top, and he drew a deep breath.

Here, however, things got worse. Again.

The ice below had been hard, crisp. That had made driving the pegs into it with only a small hammer an ordeal, especially when dangling by one hand. But now they reached a patch of softer ice that didn't hold the pegs at all. Melting ice from the top of the ridge had softened the ice here, making it into unstable slush. They tried driving pegs into the rock itself, but it was granite, and the pegs simply bent and buckled.

Corydon had no idea what to do.

They couldn't traverse to somewhere better. The couloir was a narrow shaft between rocks they couldn't climb.

Then he had an idea. He wasn't sure it would work, and it was very risky, especially with the Minotaur. He tied one of the bronze pegs to the end of a slender skein of rope. Then he flung the peg end desperately at the ridgetop he could see, frustratingly, only a body's length above him. He gripped the other end of the rope tightly. His first throw missed; the peg didn't lodge. His second was also a failure. After repeated tries, however, he felt the bronze peg grip the ice; the rope, once slack, went taut. He tugged it. It seemed secure.

Now he had to trust his weight to it. With a glance at the Minotaur that bade him hold his position, he slowly detached feet and hands. Now he was dangling from the rope. It reminded him of the time Gorgos had rescued him on a cliff edge. But here there was no irritating Gorgos to help.

Slowly, painfully, his shoulders screaming, he began to inch his way up the rope. Hand over hand. It held, but it also burned his palms with icy pain. Inch by inch. One hand. Another. His feet desperate for a hold. Hand. Over. Hand.

The ridge had one final test for him. Its edge was an overhang, and he had to maneuver desperately to get his foot up past it. At last, though, his toothed boot caught on snow. He managed in one wriggle to hurl himself onto a narrow ridge. And lay, panting, winded, ignoring everything but his laboring lungs. After much longer than usual, his breathing returned to normal. He peered down. There was the Minotaur, waiting, patient. Corydon knew the great monster was not agile enough to do what he himself had just done. Nor was he strong enough to pull the other monster up.

Quickly he attached the bronze pegs to the rope he had used, at intervals. He lowered it down to the Minotaur, having checked that its pegged end was firmly embedded. The Minotaur began to try to climb, but it was obvious to Corydon that it wasn't going to work. He couldn't make any use of his legs; he dangled helplessly, and not even his great arms were strong enough to pull him up.

"This can't work," he gasped. Corydon could see his great labored breaths forming clouds of vapor.

"Wait—" Corydon tugged at his pack, pulled out his sheepskin, and began tying together his ropes to form a crude sling. He drove another spike into the ledge and attached the rope to it. Then, carefully, he lowered the sling. The Minotaur eyed it.

"Can you?" Corydon saw that he was close to being paralyzed by the vertiginous drop behind him.

"Just climb onto it," Corydon said, trying to sound encouraging. With a desperate heave, the Minotaur flung himself into the sling. The weight tugged hard, but the rope held.

Now how was he going to pull up his friend?

The Minotaur would have to help himself. The sling would stop him from falling, but he needed to dig his spiked feet and hands into the ice to lever himself upward.

"You have to climb!" he shouted. "It's not far! I'll pull you as well!"

The Minotaur gritted his teeth; Corydon saw them flash. Then he swung himself closer to the ice and pressed a spiked toe into its blue sheen, a hand. Corydon pulled, and the Minotaur raised himself along the ice. Another careful climbed step. Another.

It was working. The Minotaur's foot slipped once, and they lost some of the height they'd gained, but then he took another giant step, another. Corydon could see his furry head, his eyes bulging in fear. Then his arm shot out and took a hold on the top of the ridge. And with a scramble and a cry, he rolled himself out of the sling and onto the icy shelf so quickly that Corydon had to clutch at him to stop him sliding on the ice.

They gave each other brief, hard hugs. Neither wanted to give way to the tears welling inside or even to the relief flooding them. There was still far too much to do. And the sun was shedding red light over the snows. Corydon realized now that the whole mountain was a blood altar, with himself and all those who aspired to its summit as the sacrifices.

As the chariot of Apollo Helios galloped for home, streaking the slopes with scarlet streamers, it was getting colder. While once Corydon had been able to see his breath in clouds, he now noticed that it froze as soon as it touched his pack or his clothes. His clothes themselves were so stiff and heavy with ice that he felt as if he were wearing armor. The Minotaur's fur grew stiff with white ice, too. His thickly furred chin was hung with a long white beard of ice, so that he looked like a parody of Zeus himself. As Corydon watched, he saw the great monster give a shiver. A few small icicles fell off him. Corydon's ears were searingly painful, his nose a deep ache.

"Must . . . dig . . . shelter," said the Minotaur, reluctant to open his mouth because the cold set his teeth aching.

Corydon began to dig, but it was soon obvious that the ridge was no place for a shelter. The unnatural stillness of Olympos meant there was no wind, but it was exposed nonetheless. The ice, too, was impenetrable. It was obvious that they must go farther to find shelter.

They labored up the steep ice cliff with fingers too frozen to test holds. There were many heart-stopping slips. Just as Corydon felt his feet had no sensation left, he saw a small outcrop of rock, and in its lee was a patch of snow warmed to blood-red by Apollo's last glance. He shouted, his cracked lips splitting, stinging. And at last, as the mountainside turned blue, they reached the rock and found a wall of soft snow behind it.

Almost exhausted, their monster-strength drained, they dug themselves into it, made a hole big enough for both. Their warmth filled it with the drip of melting snow, and they caught some of the moisture and poured it down dry throats. Then they found harsh, stale lumps of food in their packs and wolfed them down. It was pitch-dark: they could not see their hands or each other. They hunkered into their sheepskins, which felt as thin as Sthenno's parchments, frail against the onslaught of ferocious cold. The air, too, seemed somehow thin; it hurt to breathe. They lay close, needing each other's warmth, and finally fell asleep.

TWENTY

Corydon dreamed. Zeus Almighty laughed as puny monsters tried to scale him, fleas attacking a great shaggy lion. Could they reach him? The mountain *was* him, and it was huge and strong beyond imagining. The mountain was too big to fear the little things that assailed it. But one day it would fall—to the small drips of water, the burrowing of plant roots, the gentle grip of frost and ice on its severe rock. Its power would erode. Its song was a song of loss, of failure. So would Zeus's be.

But then the dream changed. Corydon seemed to plunge down through layer after layer of ice and snow, searching, searching for something . . . a faint crying. . . . As the darkness deepened, the last rays of greenish light illuminated the face of a child, crying as if his heart were breaking—deep sobs, choking, tearing. The child put a hand over his mouth, as if he were frightened of being heard, then gulped out another sob. Before Corydon could put a comforting hand on his arm, the child vanished. But Corydon could hear his cries change to terrified screams somewhere,

somewhere in the mountain. . . . He himself turned for the surface again.

He woke with his heart full of hope, only to find himself caged by the ice created by their own breath, which had formed a solid blue wall before them. Corydon felt panicky at first, but then, as he turned to rouse the Minotaur, he put his ice ax effortlessly through the wall; it was thin, like an ice leaf, and no snow had fallen to reinforce it. Did new snow ever fall here? Or was this ice everlasting?

The Minotaur rumbled softly and woke, too. Rummaging in his pack, he pulled out a crushed honey cake wrapped in a leaf and held it out mutely to Corydon. Corydon took it but broke it carefully in half and gave half of it to his friend. The simplicity of sharing their meager food was enough for now to raise his spirits.

"Do you think it ever snows here?" he asked. He recalled the swirling flakes of Hades' lands.

"I think it did once," said the Minotaur. "Long ago. But this isn't the real Olympos. It's Zeus's idea of a mountain. Because it is all mountains, it is in truth none of them."

Corydon pondered as he made his teeth scream by drinking slushy snow. "Was the real Olympos his land?"

"It was first the seat of the king of the Titans," said the Minotaur. "Zeus's father. You have met him. Kronos."

Kronos! Corydon remembered the old man and all his books. "How did Zeus take his father's place?"

"It is a long story. Do you not know it?"

Corydon knew some, but both felt a disinclination to leave the snug snow cave, and so the Minotaur told the tale.

"Kronos and Rhea had many children. But Kronos was given a

prophecy that one of his own children would kill him; it was given by the Furies, who love strife. So he ate every single one of his children, or so he thought. Rhea managed to hide one, who was kept safe on an island. The boy was made to hide whenever the Titans came in sight. He grew up in shivering fear. Then one day his mother told him what had become of his brothers and sisters. And so he poisoned his father with a deadly herb. His father was in agony, and in his pain he vomited up four of Zeus's siblings: his sister Hera, his brother Poseidon, his brother Hades, and his sister Demeter.

"So began the war between the Titans and the children of Kronos. The Titans were mighty—remember Vreckan!—and many thousands of men died. Then Zeus learned that Kronos had imprisoned an army of monstrous smiths because they had refused to serve him. Zeus decided to free them and win their allegiance."

"So he wanted to free monsters?" Corydon was amazed. "Was he kinder then?"

"Yes. He was once the great leader he now only believes himself to be," said the Minotaur. "Zeus and his brothers descended to the deepest pits of Tartaros to free them. The monsters had great cunning, and they offered to make him and his brothers invincible weapons: a helmet for Hades, a trident for Poseidon, and for Zeus the lightning itself, the power of storm.

"You remember Hades' helmet. That is the means by which Medusa died." For a moment, his soft voice caught on an old grief. "Poseidon's trident gave him dominion over the seas. And Zeus was given rule over all the air and all that lives in the air. All. It was too much for him. Too much power, and he used it to dispose of enemies and allies alike. The monster-smiths were freshly penned in a volcano, forced to labor night and day to make weapons for the Olympians. They had to make crowns and jewels and regalia and thrones, so that Zeus might seem rich in his own eyes. Now he will not feel safe unless he is the only power remaining on earth."

Hidden in a snow cave, Corydon could understand Zeus's longing for security. He felt certain it was the child Zeus whose crying he had heard, deep in the heart of the mountain.

"So he *did* once truly rule on Olympos. What was it like then?"

"It was his country. As each Lar has a family. As each dryad has a tree. It was a real mountain. It was not as clean, nor as deadly. Once he loved it, too. But he tried to make it too safe, and to do that, he had to kill everything about it that mattered to him."

Corydon and the Minotaur crawled out of the cave. It was already morning. The rock face loomed above them, a vertical wall of gray, with no snow or ice. And Corydon saw why. This stretch of rock had a slight overhang at the top. The rock was solid and smooth, the worst possible rock to climb up. But they would have to do it.

At least it didn't look crumbly.

Out on the mountain again, Corydon and the Minotaur were once more reduced to silence by the enormous landscape. Looking down, they found they could see all the way to the verdant grass far below, its gloss paled by distance. The grass stretched to the horizon, its enamel interrupted only by what looked like clouds but were actually flowers. Only two kinds. Yellow and purple. Not a cloud broke the blue monotony, not a tree interrupted the green grass, not a hill, not a tussock.

It chilled Corydon's heart. It was like a bad painting of a

much-loved face. Impatiently, he almost called out "Father!" his heart aching for the shaggy roughness of Pan's lands, his own thick fur and beard. The Minotaur understood and put a warm arm briefly around him. Corydon saw for the first time that the great beast did resemble his father in his wild, rough, loving friendliness.

"We shall go," he said, his soft rumble the warmest thing in that hard and hating land.

Their bronze spikes were useless once more; the hard rock defeated them, bent them back and refused their entry. Corydon saw that the only way was to climb using natural fissures and cracks in the rock.

There were plenty once you were close enough. There almost always were. Clinging to the wall like a lichen, fingers spread, Corydon found he could manage well if he used his Panfoot as a kind of anchor while he searched for other holds. He led the way, telling the Minotaur to follow exactly in his steps, climbing as slowly as he safely could to give his friend time. Sometimes, though, a hold was too small for more than a second's rest of finger or hoof, and then he had to move on quickly. "Do just as I do!" he ordered. "Same speed. Everything."

The Minotaur was not tiring; his strength had always been immense. But the test of nerve and skill was telling on him. When they were about two-thirds of the way up the sheer wall, his foot slipped, and only Corydon's lightning reflexes saved him from falling. A few hundred yards later, and it happened again; this time he fell the length of his body before he could stop his descent, and Corydon had to climb back to where he clung grimly to the wall in order to lead him upward again.

Then they came to an easier patch, with a narrow ledge on which they could rest. They looked down the long cliff and drew in their breath and stretched cramped fingers and toes. Corydon's Panfoot was aching.

The Minotaur spoke in a whisper, as if he had little breath to spare.

"I hinder you," he said somberly. "You would be safer alone."

"I would despair alone," Corydon whispered back.

"I think I should leave you," the Minotaur whispered.

"NO!" Corydon had not meant to shout. But he had suddenly felt as helpless and abandoned as the baby in his dreams.

There was a sudden sound. Afterward, Corydon thought that it had been like a crack, as when a stick breaks when you stand on it, but very much louder. As loud as a drumroll. It was followed by a whooshing noise. And above them they saw it coming. The ice-white end of everything. A thick roll of snow, roaring like a beast. Was it miles wide?

They watched it advance. There was nowhere to run. No way to hide. The only hope was to hold fast to the mountain's face; perhaps it might slide over and past them. Perhaps. They could feel the aching, ice cold wind it blew already. They could feel the mountain at their faces. They braced themselves.

Luckily, there was a slight outcropping above them when the stinging power of the avalanche struck. Most of it billowed around them, blinding and choking them. But the ledge protected them from its full might. What they felt was merely its eddies and surges.

These were bad enough. Corydon's face and eyes were thickly coated in snow. Snow was in his hair, his eyelashes. The Minotaur's fur was so thick with snow that he looked like a snow demon. Both were heavy with the pouring waves of snow. But it did not dislodge them. They had managed to hang on. And now the snow made their upward progress worse. The incline was coated with unstable powder that made handholds almost impossible to find. When they did reach out cautiously, their fingers slid on the soft snow.

But they kept on, their bodies cold and aching. What choice was there? Corydon felt as if he had been climbing this face for days. For years. Each hand- and foothold took minutes. And already the sun was westering, diving behind the mountain. The shadows blued. And the snow began to ice in the shadows. Corydon kept going. They must reach shelter before full dark. Shelter. There was no shelter up here. Nothing but the mountain's own bareness. It did not want them. Its absoluteness defeated their blundering monster-bodies. It was icily perfect. They could never climb it. Never.

Left foot. Right hand. And then they were at the top, and Corydon could see the bleak, bald summit just above them, flat as an unfriendly face.

He would have given anything for a hot meal. Lamb stew. Warm bread. The Snake-Girl. Sthenno's arms around him. Medusa's fierce hugs. In this remote place, even the dead seemed as near as the others. But there was the Minotaur. Shyly, Corydon put out a hand, and the Minotaur extended his. They stood like that, only for a moment, then turned to the task of building a snow hut that would shelter them for the night.

They nibbled a harsh crumb of dry bread as they climbed

into it. He wondered if Troy still stood. Suddenly he felt panic-stricken—how long had they been here?

They had to reach Zeus before the survivors set out, while all the gods' attentions were still focused on Troy. Corydon wanted to spring out of the cave and run for the summit now. But he knew that would be madness. Restlessly, he tossed and turned. The Minotaur didn't sleep easily either. He lay still, but his great, dark eyes were open.

Corydon's dreams were a river of burning and running, the screams of women, and the shouts of warriors. The whirlwind djinns entered Troy, summoned by the walls, and somehow turned their fury on the burning town.

Beside him, the Minotaur dreamed and woke and dreamed. Once they woke together.

"Did you see—"

"Yes. A battle of fire."

"Do we see truly?"

"How can we tell? It may be that these dreams are from the coldness all around us." They lay down again.

Outside the snow hut, something about the light had changed.

"Snow light!" cried Corydon, and burrowed out to see the mountainside thickly veiled in heavy curtains of snow. Snowflakes danced as if possessed all around them. Blinding, dazzling, they swirled and jumbled, they confused and bewildered. Corydon looked up to where he knew the summit was, just a few hundred yards away. But he could no longer see it.

"How can this be?" he shouted into the wind. His mouth filled with snow, and his teeth began to ache.

If it had not been for the urgent visions of the night, Corydon would have crawled back into the snow hole. The temperature was clearly dropping and the summit invisible. The Minotaur, shoulders bowed, looked tired. Corydon skidded over to him and seized his hand, trying to tell him how glad he was that he was there beside him.

They set off without further talk.

TWENTY-ONE

THE SNOW AROUND THEM SEEMED TO FORM A MOV-
ing wall, constantly blocking their progress. Corydon felt as if he
were dragging his own dead body. His legs ached, and his hands
were pulses of cold pain. It was as if his monster-strength were
gone.

"It's the mountain," said the Minotaur grimly, reading his
thoughts. "And now the snow. Unnatural. We are as far from ourselves as a hawk from the moon."

At last they were on the final ascent. Suddenly Corydon wondered why he had thought Zeus would be here. It seemed unlikely
that he would stand on a snow slope in a freezing snowstorm. But
still he kept going.

And now they had reached it. The summit of Olympos.

And there was nothing here but rock and snow. Nothingness.
Not even a lichen grew.

His heart plummeted. He closed his eyes. They had done
their utmost, and it was nothing.

But when Corydon opened his eyes again, a pale light was gathering around them. Pale gold, sleek light. And the cold was being displaced by warmth. The stillness was present, dead air, but now it was heavily and expensively scented. He looked down. They no longer stood on snow but on a level floor, pale gold stone, stretching around for hundreds of yards. They were in an enormous palace hall filled with windows and light. Corydon found he could move. Taking the Minotaur's hand, he shuffled forward, his feet still wet and almost frozen. He could smell a strong smell of— was it honey?

"No," said the Minotaur. "Not honey. Ambrosia."

Ambrosia smelled even more dead than the mountainside. Plainly, nature had had nothing to do with it. It smelled false, like . . . Was it sweets on a festival day? No, an older, staler, stronger smell.

He felt suddenly sick. He was hungry, but he would rather die than eat that stuff.

"Quite right," said the Minotaur, reading his thoughts from his disgusted face. "It would make you immortal, though."

"It would make me immortally dead," said Corydon fiercely. "I don't want to stay alive forever. In nature nothing stays alive forever, not even the stones."

"Not true," said a voice from behind him. "I stay alive forever. I eat this every day. And that is why I shall always win. Because I can never change or be destroyed."

They turned. There stood what seemed to be a tall man, impressively robed in gray and purple and white, elegant robes with just a hint here and there of gilding. His long hair was neat, shaded with silver; his beard was immaculate, his face not unlike those of

Hades and Poseidon. Corydon had no doubt that this was Zeus. He reeked of old power, even though he was not displaying it.

"Yes," Corydon said, bowing. "Yes, you speak truly. But you also know how wearying it is to live forever as an Olympian."

To his surprise, something did flicker at once in Zeus's eyes.

"It is true that mine is a burdened life," he said smoothly. "For I must plan and execute the destinies of all who live on earth. Just now I am preparing to blot out a city that troubles me with its cleverness, its energy. Intelligent men put us all at risk. So I shall burn it with everlasting flame."

"Everlasting flame?"

"The fire of men's ambitions, the fire of their greed. I channel all that is worst in them. That is why you are an annoyance. You have interfered in what was fated to happen. The chthonic powers should have vanished from the earth by now. They have been superseded. They were just a phase in the evolution of religion. What should come next is the worship of one god. Me. And yet somehow you, with your little rebellions, have managed to sustain the old gods. And now they have a new champion in your friend Gorgos, who may sustain them for a thousand years."

He sounded both rambling and petulant, old man and toddler.

"Maybe you need to try something different to bring it about," said Corydon fearlessly. "To make people revere you above all others." This might be his chance. The Minotaur was already unrolling his pack. He produced the cloth bundle containing Euryale's statue. Maybe they could do this without Aphrodite.

Just as he thought this, there was a thud, and he looked around to find Aphrodite had materialized behind him.

"You silly boy," she whispered. "Obviously, I'm not the mountain-climbing kind. But I could have persuaded a daimon to bring you here if you had asked me. It's sooo . . . well, chthonic of you to have climbed all this way."

Zeus looked surprised. "What is going on here?" he asked.

"I'm here to talk to you," said Aphrodite, dimpling seductively. Corydon's heart sank. Would Zeus really like this approach? He felt a premonition of disaster.

Zeus looked at her. Aphrodite swayed her hips. "Hello, Aunt," he said very dryly. Corydon's lips twitched, and the Minotaur gave a surprised chuckle. "Now stop it. Go and do some shopping." He waved his hand.

"But I have come to talk to you, darling," she said. "And I want to give you a present. A special one."

"Thank you. No," said Zeus firmly. "Aphrodite, I don't want the present you have in mind. Millions of men would long for it, but I'm not a man. Please, go and bother them."

"But you *could* be a man, Zeus, darling. You could feel the longing and the sweat and the ferocity you haven't felt for years. Centuries."

Zeus smiled. "It sounds charming," he said. "But today I have other plans. I have a city to destroy. And I must also make sure that the draggle-tailed remnant of its people does not escape." His smile was quite empty.

"But, darling," said Aphrodite, her light voice laden with honey, "dearest Zeus, that will not make you happy."

Zeus shrugged. "I have not been happy for millennia. What is happiness? A bubble, a dream that the humans chase. I will not be happy. But I will be free. I will destroy the last of the monsters, the last of those who sought to destroy me. I will not be happy, but I will be safe."

"Safe?" scoffed Aphrodite. "My lord, you are the all-powerful. It is for others to worry about safety. You are about boldness and daring. You are strength itself, though you seem to have forgotten. Let me remind you, love. Let me remind you of the power of living in the moment, of *letting go* of all fear, of the simple pleasures of the body and the earth."

Corydon watched in amazement as Aphrodite's seductive voice seemed to cast a spell on the powerful god.

Zeus murmured something. Then he said it louder. "Perhaps. Perhaps . . . It would make me the opposite of my father. Books. Always books. He cared only for books. The dry whisper of paper. A dry, bookish old stick. Perhaps a red-blooded body—"

"Of course, lord." Aphrodite's voice thrummed. Corydon looked at her and noticed she had somehow begun to shine golden, as if a golden cloud were forming around her. After days of blue-green ice, it was almost shocking. The king of the gods had apparently forgotten Corydon and the Minotaur in his bewitchment. Instead, he stared at Aphrodite. The golden cloud began to envelop him, too.

"Quick!" whispered Corydon. "The statue!" With fingers that still fumbled after days of cold, the Minotaur unrolled the statue that Euryale had made. It looked small and crude, but the Minotaur rolled it dexterously forward, so that it tumbled over and over to Zeus's feet.

"See, lord, what I have for you!" Aphrodite cried. "It does not look like much now. But it was made by a great witch of Thessaly, one of the greatest, many years ago. She foresaw this moment."

Corydon tried to hide his grin. Aphrodite was a good liar. And a storyteller, he suddenly saw, just as he was.

The king of the gods was frowning at the statue, puzzled. "It looks somehow familiar," he said. "Have I seen it in dreams?"

"Doubtless, mighty one," said Aphrodite. "Dreams of your own happiness, of your own ascendance. And it has a magic you may not have recognized."

Zeus frowned. "Show me," he said.

Aphrodite intensified her smile. It made Corydon feel a little sick.

"Mighty lord," she said, "this tiny statue could not be a worthy body for you. But behold!" She waved her arms at the statue. It did not change. Corydon quickly muttered the spell as quietly as he could, hoping his voice would carry to the statue but not draw him to Zeus's attention.

Luckily it worked. The statue quickly bloated to a full-sized man, muscular, with a deep chest, strong arms, and softly tousled curls. The long bronze eyelashes lay on the cheeks. The statue wore an elegant green and white chiton.

Zeus seemed hypnotized. "Well," he said, "if a god must take flesh, this flesh looks perfect."

"And you must indeed take flesh," said Aphrodite, her voice now cooing again, "if you wish to be happy. Your power has not made you happy. And yet no one deserves happiness more than you, great one. Come, remember what it is to be real. Be daring. Be a man."

"Yes. Then men will worship me. And me only. Because I will have chosen—for a time, anyway—to be incarnate, to share their lives. . . . The age of the One True God will dawn. . . ."

Corydon held his breath. He felt that if he made the very slightest sound, Zeus might change his mind.

But Zeus's eyes were bright with eagerness. He stepped toward the statue.

"What do I do?" His voice was that of a little boy, half-scared, half-hopeful.

"You take my hand," said Aphrodite, her voice like honey. "And then you jump. Like a child jumping into a puddle. Jump into the statue."

"Just jump?"

"Just jump."

Zeus took Aphrodite's hand. Corydon saw his knees bend. And he jumped.

Slowly but surely, he began to sink into the statue. Little streamers of golden light ran up those parts of his body nearest the statue; at the same time, the statue itself was changing to a dark gold.

It was working. Sthenno's binding magic was working!

But as Corydon watched, there was a hard black screech. A figure burst out from somewhere behind them. "Zeus! No!" she shrilled.

But it was too late. Zeus was melting into the statue, the statue bleeding into Zeus. There were a few blurred moments, and then Corydon saw a single bronze figure, upright and stalwart.

He looked at the eyes and saw the surprise in them.

"Zeus!" The black-clad goddess pushed Aphrodite out of the way. "Zeus! Can you hear me?"

It was plain that Zeus could hear her, from the way the eyes flickered. But it was also plain that he could do little about it.

"He is trapped!" she moaned. "Help him. Help."

But now her cries died away, and Hera flung back her black hood, seeking someone to blame, as a snake seeks a mouse.

Aphrodite had conveniently vanished, and so she saw only Corydon and the Minotaur and the Minotaur's opened pack.

"So," she said, "you have made of him a creature like yourselves."

"We have given him a body," said Corydon. "His statue will live always at Olympos. The world will come to him. Isn't that what he wants?"

Hera laughed, a sound like wind in the last leaves of autumn. "Perhaps it was, stinking little shepherd boy. Perhaps it was. But it was not what *I* wanted. I wanted to rule the world. I wanted him to rule it. For me. For our children. Forever."

"What children?" Corydon spoke with a sense that his life would soon be over. "Ares? Or Hephaistos, whom you neglect and kick and despise?"

Hera smiled. "My children do disappoint me," she said, looking at him more intently. "Even you, Panfoot."

"What do you mean?"

"I mean you, Corydon. You. You are my son as well as your father's. You have nothing mortal in you, except for his love of things mortal.

"Those funny little dreams you had of Mummy making bread! They used to make me laugh. The woman you lived with as a baby was my shadow. She put you out like a stray cat when I told her to. I saw you'd never be a son I could love. You've never had one second of real love from any mother. Not me. Not your foster mother. No one. You may think you've won. But you can only ever be a loser. All my sons are losers."

The content of her speech took a while to reach Corydon. But suddenly her words seemed to explode in a terrible burst of flame, burning his world, burning his idea of who he was. But there was one small, forlorn post of hope that he clung to. One cool refuge.

"Not true," he said, through lips stiff with pain. "There was always Medusa. She was my true mother. Because only she loved me as a mother."

As Hera opened her mouth to reply, there was a rushing boom as a wall of cloud burst the windows of the gods' palace. A gale crashed in, and Corydon and the Minotaur were caught in its giant fist. As Corydon fought it, he saw Hera latch on to the statue of Zeus. But for him it was too late to hold on to anything. He and the Minotaur were both swept out into the onrushing wall of cloud. Then, like a child dropping a toy it no longer wants, the wind let go of them. They were falling from the summit of Olympos.

In fact, there was no mountain anymore. Zeus's overcontrolled dreamland was dissolving. And the raging storm clouds, released from his control, were bringing it back to wildness.

At first, there was only the feeling of zooming through the air. But as they fell, Corydon was caught in a terrible wave of ice that made his skin feel as if it were being pulled from his body. His mouth was full of warm iron, and he realized he was bleeding— from the nose, the mouth, even the eyes. Then they were encased in the cloud itself. It was like a night when all the stars had been quenched.

Corydon felt something that must have been some ice hit him on the arm. Then a powerful gust took him, and he found himself spinning higher and higher. When it released him, he began the tumbling fall again. Several more ice stones hit him, breaking him. Then another gust, sending him up once more. He could no longer tell where the Minotaur was, and a panicky fear seized him. He was alone. Alone.

TWENTY-TWO

CORYDON WAS SPUN AROUND BY EDDIES OF WIND; bruising ice struck him again and again. He had no thoughts. He survived from second to second. But his heart ached for his aloneness even more than his body ached from the ice.

A finger of warmth touched him. And did he truly hear a voice? "My son, do not fear my wildness. This is intense, but it is as clouds should be. Storms are what we know. We are shepherds."

Corydon felt the warmth steal around his heart. Yes. Yes, he had seen storms. They were running wild because they were like animals who had lost the touch of a master. And that was something he understood.

But terror was still all around. It was the storm clouds' own fears he was picking up. He knew frightened animals can communicate fear to a boy, and it was partly that, but there was also plenty to dread.

Then a blue blade of light split the sky. The sound hit Corydon like an immense wave and sent him tumbling. Which way was down? Which way was up? He knew only the terrible, sickening motion.

Blue waves of light broke the cloud open again. More waves of air rolled him. The motion was like a very rough sea; he was amazed to find himself being violently sick. His whole body ached and shivered and was tossed lightly as a leaf before an autumn gale.

Then there was sudden light.

He had fallen through the bottom of the cloud.

What he saw was angry blue-gray water, storm-tossed as himself. It stretched out foamy fingers to grasp him. Corydon could do nothing to save himself. He plunged on, downward, and hit the sea surface. It felt like slamming into a rock wall. The water was cold with storm surge. And he had no energy to fight this last battle. He let the waves take him.

As he sank slowly into the water, he remembered what the Sphinx had said in the desert. "You *are* the Staff . . . ," she had said.

Medusa had died in saving the Underworld. Now his heart accepted that to save what was left of Troy and the monsters, he must pay a price, and the price was everything.

Dying. He was dying. His mind held the word as his body sagged.

He wished he could see his friends once more. Just once more. But it didn't make him fight the sea.

Dying. This, then, was the end of all things.

As his burning lungs became a red agony, his drifting mind shaped a last fragment of song: "Sea Lord, you are at long last the victor / But I no longer care to win." And he didn't care. His mind fled his body, down a long, dark corridor, a piece of labyrinth that was at last leading to an exit, an exit made of brilliant light and warmth. As he saw it, he smiled as his body convulsed in a last agony. And then it was over, and his mind was free.

The Snake-Girl's body opened after long red struggling. There was a cry from Euryale.

"It's a girl," she said. The infant slithered out, fierce and blood-stained, roaring with fury at being forced from her warm nest. Euryale flopped her onto the Snake-Girl's scaly belly. The Snake-Girl put out an incredulous hand. The baby's roars stilled.

"She's lovely," said the Snake-Girl. The baby was black and thickly furred all over, with a small, squashed face like a monkey. She didn't look like Neoptolemos or like the Snake-Girl either. She looked like a dog-monster of the line of Kerberos.

"Well, she's mine, anyway," said the Snake-Girl. "All mine." Her eyes were fierce.

The other monsters stood around her bed, protecting her. The ship rocked slowly. It was packed to the gunwales with Trojans, boys and girls, men and women. All whom Gorgos had salvaged. In another corner of the hold, a family prayed to the tiny Lar they had brought with them. A girl wove a seaweed garland to the Nereids. The people of Troy had brought their little gods with them into exile. The air was heavy with the escaping daimons, blue as violet petals.

"And she will live in a new land," said Gorgos. "We will build a city greater than Troy there. And we will build it with the ideas of the little gods. And in our city there will be no kings. No

Olympians. There will be a government of the people. By the people. For the people. And it shall never perish from the earth as long as we remember Troy. In this way, all that we loved in Troy will live and cannot be burned."

Sthenno smiled; she had been listening attentively. "Yes, my Gorgoliskos," she murmured. "This shall be. The city shall be called Roma. Men and monsters will err, and the city will not always be as you hope. But it will *be*. Troy will be remembered—though when they remember, they will give you the wrong name, calling you Aeneas, making you a prince of Troy. They will rename all of us. But your city will live. Roma eterna. Its flame will light the world forever." Sthenno paused. "But I still mourn Troy's fall. As the Graeae would say, *'Sunt lacrimae rerum.'*"

"What does that mean?" asked the Snake-Girl. Her baby had dropped a sleepy head on her arm.

Sthenno sighed. "I suppose it could mean something like this: There are matters about which all we can do is cry."

All of them were silent, remembering the last hours in Troy: the burning city, the screams, the ferocity of Neoptolemos as he led the last assault.

It had happened so quickly. They had laughed at the stupid wooden horse, standing dumb in the plain. It was obviously a trap. But the Greeks had managed to make a breach in the walls using their new and terrible catapult, based on an old design the Minotaur had discarded. They had been firing it all day when suddenly one stone had struck a vulnerable spot, and the wall had crumbled. The djinns had risen wailing into the sky. The daimons had fled. The people of Troy knew the moment of doom had come.

And yet the Greeks had not profited as they expected. Neoptolemos had seized the royal palace, certain that riches lay within, and so had missed the departure of the fleet, heavy with Trojan treasure, Trojan ideas, and Trojans.

The monsters had expected some action by the gods, but there had been nothing. The red, smoke-filled sky was silent.

And now, as they sailed farther out from Troy, they began to feel more confident. Sthenno pointed to the west. "Zeus's hour has come. The high gods have fallen," she said. Far off, there was a distant rumble of thunder.

Euryale chuckled joyously. "Zeus, Zeus," she said. "Eternity in a bronze cage. Demand no direr fate. It is you who are the Trojan horse, but for you there will be no escape."

"Men to come will build him a great shrine at Olympia," said Sthenno.

"Misguided fools," said Euryale. "Do they think he still has power?"

"So he does," said Sthenno, surprising them. "It will be a while before men truly see that they are alone with the little gods under free stars."

She looked up. The first stars had prickled into a night-blue sky. "The heavens are free," she said, and gave a great sigh. All of them looked upward. The ships sailed on.

It was the Snake-Girl who broke the silence of remembering.

"But what of the Minotaur?" she said. "What of Corydon?"

"The Minotaur lives, I think," said Sthenno. "We may yet see him again. But someone had to pay the price. The price of saving the world."

"And what is that?"

"What it always is," said the deep voice of a lapis Sphinx. "Life. Only life can buy life."

A single tear drifted down the Snake-Girl's cheek. She brushed it aside. Her heart ached, patient, unsleeping, the immortal heart she would always carry. It would always be empty now, except for her daughter.

"Do not weep, and do not fear," said Sthenno. "He has saved his friends. And he has found his mother. They are the family they were meant to be."

"His mother?" Gorgos looked up.

"Gorgos," said Sthenno, "you and your mother were star-crossed. It was Corydon who was the son of her heart. Now he and Medusa may walk together and make songs for the Lady of Flowers. This is not something to fear or mourn—and Corydon was the one who made it so, remember?"

And for just one moment, all of them saw it. A shepherd boy, alone on a hillside, watching his flock. There came to them the faint sound of pipes playing a tune of glowing joy.

Corydon was home.

GLOSSARY

A note on geography: Our first book, *Corydon and the Island of Monsters,* was set entirely in the world of Greater Greece (Magna Graeca). Greater Greece is the world of Greek colonies. The Greeks themselves thought of Greece not as a place but as wherever people spoke Greek. Atlantis is also part of this world, but it is not geographically within Middle Earth, which is the literal meaning of "Mediterranean." Similarly, Greater Greece included the Greek-speaking colonies of what we'd now call Asia Minor. In the Hellenistic period, which means the time after Alexander the Great, Greater Greece stretched from the borders of northern India through the Middle East and Egypt.

There are really three phases in Greek history: the Archaic period, about which all the myths are written; the age of the city-states; and the Hellenistic period, when Greek civilization was cross-fertilized by Near Eastern culture.

Although all our books are *set* in the Archaic period, the age of heroes and myths, the second book *represents* the era of the polis, while the third book represents the dilemmas of the Hellenistic world, in which Asian and Greek cultures mixed and mingled.

Agamemnon (*ag-ah-MEM-non*) High king of Mycenae and leader of the war on Troy.

Akhilleus (*ah-KILL-ee-us*) The strongest and the fastest and the scariest and the most beautiful of all heroes. Not really liked by the Olympians because he's half god himself.

Amazons (*AM-ah-zonz*) A myth the Greeks made up for themselves (though you will read pseudohistories that claim they were real). In ancient Greece, it was unheard of for women to be involved in politics or war. So the Greeks imagined what a world where women ruled and fought might be like. Amazons can be whatever you want them to be: sturdy hockey girls, dark witches, flower-loving hippies. Ours are none of the above; they are the artistic principle in a fighting society.

Aphrodite (*af-ro-DIE-tee*) The goddess of love. Not the kind of love you have for your little sister or your pet dog (the Greeks had another word for this, *agape,* pronounced *ah-GAH-pay*). No, Aphrodite's love is the kind you have for a boy or girl when you think about them all day, keep their picture in your locker, and maybe treasure some object they once held, like a pen. Crazy, isn't it? Yes, Aphrodite is crazy and she makes people do things they'd never normally do, including betraying their friends or even their countries, spending the whole day staring at a pencil, and writing someone's name a hundred times while playing the same song over and over. It's not harmless. It's the scariest thing on earth, and the most powerful.

Ares (*AIR-eez*) The ugly face of war. Not a marching-band, bright-uniforms, and martial-tunes kind of soldier but a man covered in blood running toward you with a naked sword, his mouth open as if ready to drink your blood. He is one of the only two children of the marriage of Zeus and Hera; the Greeks seem to have thought that power and respectability could only produce trouble as their child.

Athene (*ah-THEE-nee*) One of the twelve Olympians. Extremely powerful goddess who represents cunning (inherited from her mother, Metis—whose name means "cunning") and warrior skills, but also weaving and other useful arts, olive trees, and the city of Athens. Zeus ate her mother and gave birth to her through his forehead. So Athene admires the brainy.

Atlantis (*at-LAN-tis*) A great and proud city that became so proud that the gods destroyed it with a giant wave. The Greeks thought of it as the ultimate cosmopolis, the summit of Greekness. Everyone is a wide-eyed hayseed, rube, and hick when it comes to Atlantis.

chthonic gods (*k-THON-ick*) These are the opposite

of Olympians. Gods that are incarnate, low, and little. They are bound to earth for good and ill. They are powerless beyond it. Or nearly.

Demeter (*DEM-et-er*) Goddess of seed brought to life as plants; without her blessing, nothing can grow. A mother first and last. Worship of her at a place called Eleusis was a secret, so secret that if you told anyone, you could be killed; all we know is that it involved resurrection, just as it does here in our story.

djinn (*jin*) This isn't hard to say. Just pretend the *d* isn't there. Now you can see it's really nearly the same word as "genie." Djinns go back in legends for thousands of years before Islam. Djinns are made of smokeless fire. They live in places humans don't, including the Empty Quarter of Arabia, so called because it's sandy and you can't grow anything there. But the air is full of djinns, and they make weather, especially sandstorms. Hence Bin Khamal is an Arabian monster. The Greeks liked hearing stories about monsters from outside Greece.

eidolon (*eye-DOE-lon*) A double or copy of a person or creature. Helena became an eidolon at Troy; the real Helena went to Egypt and learned magic and had a great, free time.

Euryale (*yoo-ree-AH-lay*) One of the two immortal Gorgons.

Hades (*HAY-deez*) Zeus's brother, but much sadder. King of the Underworld.

Hektor (*HEK-tor*) The greatest Trojan warrior. Very brave, but also a bit of a hero at heart—inclined to show off and rush ahead without thinking, which is how he meets his fate.

Helena (*HEL-eh-na*) "The face that launched a thousand ships," wrote Christopher Marlowe about Helena. Helena was beautiful beyond the dreams of mortals. She was the daughter of a queen and Zeus disguised as a swan, and she hatched out of an egg; maybe that story tells us that she was graceful, as swans are. Because she was so beautiful, all the heroes started fighting over who was to marry her, though none of them seem to have spent much time getting to know her. Finally, all of them had to promise to defend the right of whoever won her, to stop them all from fighting forever. Menelaus was the lucky guy, but he is very unremarkable; picture someone really, really beautiful married to someone dull and worthy. Finally, Paris (aka Sikandar in our story) was given her (whether or not he liked the idea) by Aphrodite in exchange for letting her win the contest between the goddesses over who was the most beautiful. So all the heroes had to go to Troy to get her back, but it was really just a big excuse for the war, which was all about money and the fact that Zeus didn't like the free-spirited Trojans.

Hephaistos (*hef-EYE-stos*) Zeus and Hera's other legitimate son (brother to Ares) and the only monster among the Olympians. He is a smith god. In ancient legend, smiths were always linked with death; they were blackened with the soot of their work. But they were also magical because they could make metal obey them in shining streams and heavy folds. Both these things and his association with earth give him a partially chthonic identity. Hephaistos loves his mother, Hera, but she is ashamed of him.

Hera (*HEAR-ah*) The wife of Zeus. The ultimate Desperate Housewife, Hera is an angry woman whose husband constantly strays. She adores him, but she also hates him. She longs for him to love her again. A mother to whom her children mean nothing, her husband everything. The opposite of Demeter, but she sometimes pretends to *be* Demeter to trick those who long for a mother of their own.

Herakles (and his bow) (*HAIR-a-clees*) Sometimes spelled the Latin way as Hercules. Akhilleus was the greatest Greek hero. Herakles was just the biggest. A big, dumb lummox of a man. He was the Spartan hero, and it shows; he doesn't sound the type to read many books without pictures in them. But he was hugely strong and quite cunning and killed zillions of monsters, so his bow became an important trophy for both sides.

Hermes (*HER-meez*) Cunning Olympian, patron of thieves. Runs errands for the Olympians, though he loathes that job.

Homer (*HOE-mur*) The greatest storyteller and the greatest poet in history. Our inspiration. Stories say he was blind. He made up his songs in his head. He uses comedy and sadness alongside each other, which is one reason that we do, too.

Hydra (*HIGH-dra*) A beast with many heads; every time one is cut off, two more grow in its place.

Kronos (*CROW-nos*) Father of Zeus. Zeus is supposed

to have deposed him in order to take over the world. Represents time.

Lamia (*LAY-me-ah*) Snaky monster below the waist, beautiful woman above.

Medusa (*me-DOO-sa*) The third Gorgon and the only mortal among them. Medusa was transformed into a snaky-haired monster after violating Athene's temple.

Memnon Beautiful and powerful king of Ethiopia, from the Greek viewpoint another exotic type who gets caught up in the war at Troy.

Minotaur (*MY-noh-tor*) Son of Queen Pasiphae and a bull; hence a terrible embarrassment to his mother.

mormoluke (*mor-mo-loo-KAY*) Mormo-demon. Greek children used to play a game in which one of them dabbed black ash on his face and jumped at other children; the scary faces were mormo faces. Greek demons can often be recognized because there's something wrong with one of their legs.

Nemean lion (*neh-MEE-an*) A monster from the Labors of Herakles. The lion's skin is so tough that it can only be pierced by a Nemean lion claw.

Odysseus (*oh-DEE-see-us*) The cleverest of all the heroes and especially admired by Athene.

Olympians (*oh-LIMP-ee-anz*) Olympos is the highest mountain in Greece, where the earth touches the sky. So "Olympians" means "sky gods." High gods. Gods who look down on everyone else.

Pan (*rhymes with "ban"*) Goat-legged god of wild nature, shepherds, pipe playing, wild hillsides, and being alone.

His name is the origin of the word "panic" because he can make people either very afraid (especially in lonely places) or very brave. One of the chthonic deities. Usually opposed to the Olympians.

Persephone (*per-SEF-oh-nee*) The Lady of Flowers. Daughter of Zeus and the goddess Demeter. Abducted by her uncle, Hades, and taken to the Land of the Many. Before her abduction, there were no seasons and flowers bloomed all year round.

Perseus (*PER-see-us*) A really famous hero. Son of Zeus and the mortal woman Danaë. When he cut off Medusa's head, both the golden man Khrysaor and the winged horse Pegasos were born of her blood.

Philoktetes (*PHIL-ock-TEET-ees*) The guy who got Herakles' bow. His foot was wounded by an arrow, and the wound was so stinky and made him cry so much that the Greeks dumped him on the island of Lemnos. Later they had to go there to retrieve the bow. He's the subject of a deeply sad play by Sophocles.

Poseidon (*poe-SIGH-don*) God of the sea. A great one among the Olympians but with some paradoxes. He is also attached to his domain like a chthonic god and hence not usually inclined to look down on humans and monsters from too great a height. He has some of the relentlessness of the sea, of a wave that will keep rolling shoreward. His sons have this unstoppability, too: Gorgos and the Minotaur.

Selene (*se-LEE-nee*) Goddess of the full moon. (Artemis is the waxing moon, and Hecate is the waning and dark moon.) Pan lures Selene's frail light into the darkness of his forests. Their love partly explains why the Selene Amazons are drawn to Corydon.

Sphinx (*SFINKS; rhymes with "stinks"*) The Sphinx is originally Egyptian; there's a huge carving of her by the Great Pyramids. She's half lion and half bird, which means she combines the desert's fierce wildness with the bird's soul magic.

Sthenno (*STHEN-oh*) Looks impossible to say, but it's quite easy if you try. One of the two immortal Gorgons.

Titans (*TIE-tenz*) A race of giants who combined earth and sky in their bodies; they were the children of Ouranos (heaven) and Gaia (earth) and they ruled earth before they gave birth to the gods who became the Olympians. Their other children were buried in the earth and became the parents of the chthonic gods and the monsters.

Troy Really Troios, so if Troy is your name you could respell it. . . . For the Greeks Troy was a city that was really beautiful and enviable but that was also their opposite: a bit decadent, not properly disciplined, given to luxury and excess. The Greeks actually saw Troy the way some people might now see America: rich, enviable, but immoral.

Vreckan (*VREH-ken*) Named from Corryvreckan, a naturally occurring whirlpool near Scapa Flow. In our myth, Vreckan is the Titan of the North Atlantic, an incarnation of its terrifying power, darkness, and cold.

Zeus (*ZOOS*) King of the Olympian gods, or in modern terms, president, gang leader, king, emperor, pope, prime minister, all rolled into one. Likes nymphs and parties.

Doesn't like monsters or being disobeyed. Rules the world. Intolerant: believes everyone must be like himself. For Zeus, difference is uncool and also wrong. Corrupted by endless power and flattery; bored by being a spoiled tyrant, but can't quite let go.

RESOURCES

Wilfred Thesiger, *Arabian Sands*.

———. *The Marsh Arabs*.

Saint Augustine, *Confessions*.

The Outlaw Josey Wales, film, Clint Eastwood.

For a Few Dollars More, film, Sergio Leone.

The Good, the Bad, and the Ugly, film, Sergio Leone.

The Book of the Thousand Nights and a Night, Richard
Francis Burton's translation.

Butch Cassidy and the Sundance Kid, screenplay by William
Goldman.

The Collected Poems of C. P. Cavafy.

Virgil, *Aeneid*.

Quintus Smyrnaeus, continuation of Homer's *Iliad*
(source for Penthesilea and Memnon).

Ovid, *Fasti*.

Leonardo da Vinci, drawings book.

Joe Simpson, *Touching the Void*.

Gavin Pretor-Pinney, *The Cloudspotter's Guide*.
Ennio Morricone scores for *A Fistful of Dollars*, *For a Few Dollars More*, and *The Good, the Bad, and the Ugly*.
Gladiator, film, Ridley Scott.

ABOUT THE AUTHORS

Tobias Druitt is a pen name for the mother-and-son writing team of Diane Purkiss and Michael Dowling.

Diane Purkiss earned a Doctor of Philosophy degree from Merton College, Oxford University, and is currently on the faculty of Keble College at Oxford. Her key academic interests are classical literature, children's literature, and Renaissance literature.

Michael Dowling attends the prestigious Abingdon School, where he holds the Abbot de Blosneville Scholarship, which is almost though not quite as ancient as Corydon. He is studying ancient Greek, among many other subjects.